"You have my sincere [thanks for all that]
you have done. I am i[ndebted to you.]"

"Oh, I did nothing, sir."

"I am sure you did something, Brida," he drawled. "Or at least your healer did."

"Yes, well, I am happy that you seem a lot better."

"As am I." He sighed deeply, looking around the small yet comfortably appointed chamber. "And by the by, I am surprised that you did not feel it unseemly and improper to have me convalesce here—even if I were incapacitated at the time. I wonder at the villagers of Kinnerton being so enlightened and understanding about such an arrangement with a man unrelated to you."

"Ah, there might be a perfect rationale for that."

"And that is?"

She gulped a few times before answering him.

"Well, in truth they… They believed us to be married." She mumbled so quietly that Tom wondered whether he had heard her correctly.

"Did you just proclaim us to be married?"

She grimaced as though she had swallowed something deeply unpleasant and nodded.

"Allow me to understand this, mistress." His lips curved at the corners. "Because I fail to understand why you did not correct them."

"No. I did not."

"I see." He smirked. "How very interesting."

Author Note

The early thirteenth century was a time when religious superstition was prevalent in Europe and around the world. This was also true within feudal England, Wales, Scotland and Ireland—each with their own regional belief system that initially stemmed from paganism but amalgamated in time with early Christian ideology. In part, these highly held convictions provided answers and explanations to everything that happened to an individual, within the confines of their community and society at large. And yet these beliefs, which might seem irrational to us now, could be exploited for nefarious gains, as they often were.

This was the case for my heroine, Brida O'Conaill (Brighid Ni Diarmuid), after her family in Ireland was believed to be cursed, foretold by a local prophesy. As a result, her life choices became limited to either entering a convent or remaining unwed and ultimately being alone.

The hero Thomas Lovent's past is similarly bound in tragedy. Yet his experience as a knight and an agent of the Crown during the turbulent reign of King Henry III makes him far more pragmatic and cynical, as he knows that too often a particular circumstance and weakness could easily be used for profit, to gain advantage. Can he convince Brida, a woman he reluctantly admires, of this while attempting to clear his name as well as uncover a plot against the Crown?

I hope you enjoy Thomas and Brida's story!

MELISSA OLIVER

The Knight's Convenient Alliance

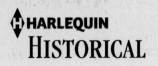

HARLEQUIN®
HISTORICAL™

ISBN-13: 978-1-335-40753-5

The Knight's Convenient Alliance

Copyright © 2021 by Maryam Oliver

This edition published by arrangement with Harlequin Books S.A.

For questions and comments about the quality of this book, please contact us at CustomerService@Harlequin.com.

Harlequin Enterprises ULC
22 Adelaide St. West, 41st Floor
Toronto, Ontario M5H 4E3, Canada
www.Harlequin.com

Printed in U.S.A.

Melissa Oliver is from southwest London, UK, where she writes historical romance novels. She lives with her lovely husband and three daughters, who share her passion for decrepit old castles, grand palaces and all things historical. She won the Joan Hessayon Award for new writers from the Romantic Novelists' Association in 2020 for her first book, *The Rebel Heiress and the Knight*. When she's not writing, she loves to travel for inspiration, paint, and visit museums and art galleries. If you want to find out more, follow Melissa on Twitter @melissaoauthor or Facebook @melissaoliverauthor.

Books by Melissa Oliver

Harlequin Historical

Notorious Knights

The Rebel Heiress and the Knight
Her Banished Knight's Redemption
The Return of Her Lost Knight
The Knight's Convenient Alliance

Visit the Author Profile page
at Harlequin.com.

To my own gorgeous green-eyed boy.

Prologue

Summer 1221—Kinnerton Castle,
on the borders of Wales

Brida O'Conaill stepped outside the great hall of Kinnerton Castle and into the night sky. The air was warm and pleasant, much like the merriment of the wedding festivities inside. She tilted her head back, closed her eyes and took a deep breath, wanting somehow to inhale some of the wonderment from this night. It was a perfect eventide, after what had been a perfectly lovely wedding. A union between two people who could not be more perfect for one another. Yet Brida could not help the feeling of desolation and despair that had grown throughout the day, almost choking her now.

Saint's above, what was wrong with her?

She was glad that her friend, Gwenllian ferch Hywel, had finally found happiness with her long-lost love, Sir Ralph de Kinnerton, after many years apart. Indeed, she wished them both well, only… Only Brida wished that she, too, could one day have the opportunity to live her life in a manner that she chose. But that could

never happen—not for Brida. Her life could never include marriage, children and a family. It was not possible. Not after what had happened many years ago to
her own family in Ireland. The terrible prophecy that
had been cast back then still held true and Brida had
no other choice but to resign herself to a life of solitude and contemplation. Which she had done in good
faith since that fateful day when her kinsmen had all
but been annihilated. And she had sworn an oath to remain unwed and childless before her grieving mother
had entered the convent.

Yet on nights like this, filled with hope and possibility, Brida bitterly understood what she was missing and
what her life would always be confined to. But enough.
She gave a snort of irritation at her errant thoughts.
She, Brida O'Conaill, was a sensible woman—stead-
fast and practical. A useful companion and friend to
Gwenllian, even though everything would change now
that her friend had obligations as a married woman and
chatelaine of Kinnerton Castle.

She dispelled the wistfulness that had somehow
taken hold and smiled faintly at a couple of inebriated
men who spilled out of the great hall, singing bawdy
ditties about covetous women they had met on their
travels. They staggered towards the gatehouse, brushing past the flower garlands that she had painstakingly
decorated with the help of the women folk throughout
the inner bailey of the castle.

Red and blue campion flowers, native to the bride's
homeland of Wales, alongside clusters of pink and pur-
ple bell-heather, tied together with sage and vervain cut
from the Marcher Borders, adorned the archways and
doorway around the inner bailey. Honeysuckle was en-

twined around every pole and column, infusing a sweet, heady fragrance in the air, especially at this late hour of the night. She inhaled, filling her chest once more, and sighed.

'I was wondering where you had gone, Mistress Brida,' a low, male voice drawled. A voice that managed to set Brida's teeth on edge. 'And here you are outside, in what appears to be a contemplative mood.'

She did not even bother to turn and face him— *Sir Thomas Lovent.* The tall, handsome and powerful knight who managed to make her stomach flip over itself with an equal measure of excitement and irritation, ever since she'd become aquatinted with him only a few weeks ago.

She had met Thomas Lovent at the knights' tournament, where her friend, Gwen, had been reunited with a man she had believed to be dead for many years: Sir Ralph de Kinnerton—the man she had once been betrothed to and had once loved. And although their path back to each had not been smooth and had been marred by tragedy, adversity and heartache, Brida and Sir Thomas had formed an alliance of sorts to help their two friends find a way back to one another again. And with the wonderful giddy success of Ralph and Gwen's union came the stark reality of Brida's own situation.

Now the infuriating man had come outside to do nothing other than vex her, which he seemed to take great pleasure in. It was always the same with him. Thomas Lovent just could not help but exasperate her.

'My mood is really of no concern to you, Sir Thomas.' She hoped that the tone in her voice would make him retreat back into the hall. But that would be far too hopeful. He was as persistent as ever in forcing his company where it was most unwanted.

'That, mistress, is quite untrue.' The man moved forward, stepping in front of her and giving her a sardonic smile. A smile that made her bristle with annoyance. 'You see, I would not be serving my friend well if one of the guests at his wedding feast was revelling in being alone outside.'

'I am doing no such thing,' she retorted. 'I found I was in need of air.' As well as time needed to ponder on the future. Her future. However dull and staid that might be.

'Well then, I can stay and keep you company.'

She straightened her spine. 'I would rather you did not, Sir Thomas.'

'Brida, Brida, Brida.' He smiled shaking his head. 'You and I both know that you would rather I accompany you. Walk with you, converse with you. Even pull you out of your current pensive malaise.'

Of all the presumptuous, conceited assertions. Not that they were untrue. How had this man managed to gauge her moods so well? It was certainly disconcerting that he did so effortlessly. No wonder Thomas Lovent was as popular with women as he was. He could read and understand people so well. And he knew it. The confidence he exuded was frankly staggering as well as infuriating.

'Please do not trouble yourself. I need no such assistance, as I am neither dispirited nor suffering from any malaise.'

'Well, that is a blessing,' He chuckled softly. 'Yet, I think I would stay out here on this glorious midsummer's eve, if you don't mind.'

'Do as you must choose, sir. You always do.' She started to move away, ambling along the periphery of the inner bailey as he followed to keep up with her.

'I must, since I'm also obliged to see to your safety, Mistress Brida—alone here in the middle of the night.'

'My thanks, but that is really not necessary. I can see to that myself.'

He raised a brow and smiled slowly. 'I am sure you can, mistress, but allow me a little gallantry.'

'Is that what you are attempting, Sir Thomas?'

'Yes, and also the vain belief that I can somehow coax a smile from you.'

Her lips twitched despite herself. 'Ah, and do you believe yourself up to that challenge?'

'Now what kind of a man would I be if I did not at least endeavour to try?'

She stopped walking abruptly and turned to face him. 'A less than gallant one?'

Brida felt her mood shift a little for the first time that evening as she took in his appearance. He was wearing a fine linen tunic the same colour as his eyes, reminding her of the rolling hills from her homeland, after a rainstorm. A soft leather gambeson was worn over the top and a pair of dark brown braies encased his well-defined muscular legs—not that she was looking *that* closely. He was tall and powerful with an insouciant easy manner, leaning against a stone wall with his arms crossed over his chest, meeting her questioning gaze. Ever since she had first met Thomas Lovent a few weeks ago, he would always try to make any mood lighter, injecting it with his own brand of humour.

'Precisely. You can appreciate my predicament, mistress. I can only hope to remedy the situation.'

She shook her head and pressed her lips together firmly.

'Ah, there, I can see the beginnings of a small one forming on your lips.' She couldn't help but broaden her smile at that. Really, the man was a consummate flirt.

'I'm gratified that worked as well as it did.' He waved his hand. 'And, no, there's no need to thank me.'

'Naturally, you believe that I should.'

'Naturally.' He grinned. His tousled dark blond hair flopped over his eyes that glittered with so much mischief. 'I have often been commended for my insight. Not to mention my irresistible company and charm. Which I believe can be rather infectious.'

'I would think nothing less of someone who held such exulted views of themselves,' she retorted wryly.

'Indeed, mistress. You can always rely on me to attend to you.'

'With your infectious company?'

'And not forgetting my irresistible charm.' He winked. 'It's mere piffle, I know, but something I have often been told.'

'I am assured that you must have been, Sir Thomas, by someone sadly lacking and with little sense. But I find that I have no need of your charms—infectious or otherwise.'

'You are as ever the font of graciousness, mistress.' He chuckled. 'Cease or you shall put me to the blush.'

She rolled her eyes. 'And you, as ever, are provoking among many other things, sir.'

'Ah, Brida, I expect nothing less than your sharp tongue.' He leant forward and raised a brow. 'But you know I am only teasing you.'

This was exactly the manner in which the man managed to befuddle her. One moment she would be exasperated by his swagger and nonsense. The next, Brida would find herself in knots, as awareness and embarrassment would suddenly trickle down her spine.

Thankfully, he seemed unaware of her discomfort.

'So, would you like to convey the reasons for your solitude on this auspicious night?'

And just as quickly he managed to heighten her discomfort a little more. 'Not really, Sir Thomas.'

'Very well then, let's talk of the weather instead and how unpredictable it has been of late.'

'I suppose it has.' She exhaled, glad for the change in conversation. 'We were not sure whether to extend the decorations outside the hall, for fear that the summer rain might drench through everything.'

'I can believe it. One never knows from morn to dusk how it will turn out with the staggering range of elements in a single day. But it turned out well in the end.'

'Yes,' she muttered. 'It did.'

They continued to stroll side by side before Sir Thomas broke the silence.

'I do understand, Brida,' he murmured.

'Understand what, sir?'

He stopped and sighed deeply. 'You may not confide in me, but allow me to say that I do comprehend the need for reflection at moments like this,' he said softly. 'When one is witness to a union as eagerly and happily anticipated as that of our two friends, then it does compel one to consider one's own future with a measure of uncertainty and doubt.'

She gulped, knowing the honesty in his words. She lifted her head and watched him as he stared out in the distance and wondered where this sudden pensiveness had come from. How mercurial the man was, his moods changing within a heartbeat.

'I suppose there must be some truth in that.'

He did not respond, which made Brida curious whether the man was talking about her reflections or his own. Indeed, had Thomas Lovent also pondered on his own future with misgivings and uncertainty as she had? The startling change in him suggested that he had. How strange. Yet this more serious side to the man intrigued her more than it ever should. He sighed again as he looked down at her.

'But come, enough of these solemn musings.'

She nodded, wanting him to tease and smile again. To fall back on the usual discourse between them. Somehow that felt safer. 'We can always return to a discussion about the weather.'

'Indeed. I can mention how warm and temperate this evening has become after such an unpromising start.'

Brida felt a little relieved that once again the mood had shifted. 'And I can add that many things are sadly unpromising. Not to mention disappointing.'

'Ah, but not this beatific night. Not with the pearlescent moon dazzling us with its brilliance.'

'You surprise me. And what of the stars?'

'Those, too.'

A faint smile played on her lips. 'You missed your calling, sir, to scribe fanciful odes and ballads to unexpectant maids.'

'True, if only I could find one at this late hour.'

'If only.' She felt her cheeks getting warm. 'Your talent for the ridiculous could surpass a fool's, Sir Thomas.'

He shook his head. 'You wound me, mistress.'

'Oh, unintentionally, I assure you, sir. I greatly admire your talent for the absurd.'

'And don't forget my infectious charm.'

'As if I ever could.'

Brida startled herself, realising what she had just said. She snapped her head up to see a slow smile spreading on his lips. The air stilled between them as they stared at one another for a moment. Oh, Lord, but did the man have to be so ridiculously attractive? And tempting just by his very closeness and warmth. She watched, fascinated, as the glimmer of amusement in his eyes was suddenly replaced by something else. An unexpectant flicker of desire, so potent that it made her breath catch in her throat.

Brida felt flustered as a frisson of anticipation went through her. She dropped her gaze to the slight curve of his mouth. And before she knew what she was doing she stood up on her toes and pressed her lips to his, none too gently.

Oh, Lord, mayhap she had had too much wine at the feast.

Thomas Lovent's response was one of surprise. Shock, even, that Brida had done something so uncharacteristic. So very brazen. Yet it was strangely satisfying to know that she had somehow unsettled him. And for a moment he froze, too stunned to even move, but suddenly, as if he had roused from a dream, he returned her kiss, covering her mouth with ardour, wrapping his huge arms around her and pulling her close. Too close. Far too close. She had never been pressed against anyone in such a manner. Slammed against the hardness of his body.

It was heady, intoxicating and all consuming. As

was this kiss, brimming with so much longing that it made her knees almost buckle beneath her. He slanted his lips over her, running his tongue over the seam, daring them to open. Which they did. Oh, but could she ever believe that a kiss could be this…this wonderful? This delicious? And with Thomas Lovent of all men.

After all, this was a man whom Brida had not known that long. A man with whom she had been thrown together because of their mutual friends. And he was a man who Brida had vehemently resisted and vehemently believed to be a reprobate, albeit a charming one at that. In fact, she had only spoken to him a handful of times prior to this evening and never about anything meaningful, only light, flippant musings. With the exception that she had never acted in such a manner. Indeed, she had never behaved like this with anyone and it was most *un*like her.

The truth was that Thomas Lovent was more than merely handsome. More than merely possessing of charm. And his kiss was just as deadly and infectious. Against her better judgement she was kissing him with just as much fervour and passion, tasting and devouring him. Oh, God! He was a man she should not have anywhere near her. He was a temptation that she could not risk and reminded her of everything she could never have. It could never end well. Thomas Lovent was far too dangerous for a woman like her, who really should know better.

She pulled away suddenly, stumbling as she took a few steps back.

'Don't,' she muttered gasping for breath. She wiped her mouth as he tried to reach for her again. 'That was a mistake.'

'Brida?' His low, quiet voice reverberated through her, making her shiver.

'I cannot.' She stepped back, shaking her head in disbelief. 'I cannot believe I did that.'

Something in his manner changed. She must have mistaken the flash of hurt in his eyes.

'Come now, it was only a kiss.'

Why was she not surprised to hear that? He was no doubt a man who kissed any woman anywhere, with *this* one being nothing out of the ordinary for him. 'Mayhap to you, but not to me, sir.'

'I believe you forget that you started it, Brida.'

'And naturally you were obliged to kiss me back.'

'Naturally, but come, I think you are making far too much of it.'

'How careless of me.'

He would think that her reaction was excessive. Yet how could the infuriating man know that the longing she felt was something that she could never have? That this connection must always, always be resisted?

'It should never have happened,' she whispered. 'Not with you. Not with someone like you.'

'Someone like me?' He stiffened. 'What is that supposed to mean?'

'Someone who believes his life to be the sum of his charming façade. Who moves from place to place, taking what he wants, with no concern, no constancy, no connection and no care in the world.'

The colour seemed to have seeped from Thomas Lovent's face, his eyes turning steely and cold.

'Is that so?' he said in a quiet, deadly tone.

Oh, Lord, what had she done? Brida realised too late that she had hurled her frustrations in the wrong direction. She had insulted Thomas Lovent and, much as the man infuriated her, he did not deserve it.

He spoke again, his words dripping with disdain and indignation. 'How fortuitous for me to be informed of my prodigious failings.'

Brida knew that she should not have spoken as she had. She should not blame Thomas Lovent for her own behaviour. The fault lay with her, not with him. She should say something, but the necessary words seemed to have stuck in her throat every time she opened and closed her mouth. There was nothing for it. She would apologise on the morrow and blame it on the wine, the moon and the blasted stars. But not tonight. If Brida tried again to explain, she might actually burst out crying. Instead, she turned on her heel and walked away.

Yet Brida O'Conaill never had the chance to make amends since the man left Kinnerton at dawn the following morning and never returned.

Chapter One

London—1224, three years later

Thomas Lovent walked along the narrow, cobbled bridge that led to the South Gate—a stone tower gatehouse that allowed access on to Thorney Island. He always favoured this quiet path over the more direct route of the West Gate to Westminster Abbey and preferred to meander his way around the mill that serviced the island, providing him with ample time to gather his thoughts before he met his liege lord, Hubert de Burgh, Chief Justiciar of England.

But not this night. It was not only that de Burgh as well as King Henry were meeting Llewelyn of Wales, Prince of Gwynedd near the border of England and Wales itself. There was something else that troubled him about the events of this eve that had led him back to Westminster, yet he could not discern what that could be. And for a man who had to use his instinct, intuition and quick judgement when necessary to serve his lord, this did not bode well. It made him restless. Hell, it made him feel uneasy.

It was the serving wench in the tavern by Westcheap, with the dark raven hair, creamy complexion and stormy blue eyes who had him in knots. She had reminded him of a woman he had vowed to forget—Brida O'Conaill. A woman whose derisive words to this day had cut deeper than he could comprehend. Tom had never understood why her scorn had affected him in the manner it had, but it was one of many reasons that he had not ventured back to that part of the country and had only seen his friend, Ralph de Kinnerton, at Court. The less he thought of Brida O'Conaill the better.

God's blood, but what a fool he had made of himself over three summers ago. Tom could recall even after all this time how he had enjoyed sparring and getting a rise out of the woman who was a close companion of Lady Gwenllian de Kinnerton, wife to Ralph. There had been something about Brida O'Conaill that compelled him to be intentionally provoking, during the short time he had spent in her company.

Mayhap it had been her stiff, haughty, condescending manner or the imperious way she looked down her nose at him, but either way, he had enjoyed teasing and confounding her. Then everything had shifted and changed when she had kissed him. When all of his senses had come alive, even if it had been short lived. The woman had spurned him in such a manner that Tom could never truly forget, despite banishing the memory of her from his mind.

He could still recall her cutting words, telling him only after a short acquaintance that she believed him to be *someone who believes his life to be the sum of his charming façade.*

The irony of that was not lost on Tom, as that was

precisely the persona he presented to the world. He always had, since it served him so well for people he met to assume that he was nothing more than a handsome idle rogue with nothing to recommend him other than his brawn, his skill with the sword and his witty tongue. That had always been his intention and also the reason why he went on to be so effective in serving his lord as an agent of the Crown, working on assignments that needed his quick wits, perceptiveness and unflappable manner with just enough ruthlessness when required.

Yet on that long-ago night, said from Brida's lips after he had only just kissed her, it had left a palpable bitter taste. One that he had wanted to wipe clean away and pretend had never happened. Yet a voice whispered that some of what she had said might have inadvertently been true despite how hard he had tried to change and make something of himself. He feared it might never be quite enough to atone for his past mistakes.

It was of no consequence—*she* was of no consequence. All that mattered to him was the covert work he did for the Crown and the silver he accrued to improve his situation in life, as well as the only woman who held his constancy—his poor, beleaguered sister Joan. *This* was his sole purpose: to make enough coin so that he could eventually make life a little easier for both of them after everything they had gone through.

To that end, Tom hoped that he could one day secure a place, a manor or even a small fiefdom, for them to live. Anywhere they could call home. And he would look after Joan properly, as her situation worsened day by day. As God was his witness, he would not fail her again.

Not like before, when he had felt the weight of guilt

hung around his neck, like a chain pulling him further into an abyss. All because he had not been there to prevent the destruction of a fire that claimed his whole family bar his young sister. Never again would he be so damned deficient. So damned idle. He would keep Joan safe and not allow anything to harm her with the hope that one day he might somehow redeem himself.

Tom pulled his mind back to the present and his mission on this night. He made a short cut through the orchard, pulling his cloak a little closer around his head as the breeze from the river whipped the coarse material up around him. He opened the gate and stepped on to a pathway that brought him a little closer to his clandestine rendezvous and exhaled as he peered around. His anonymity tonight was of utmost importance since the man he was supposed to meet had insisted on his ability to be inconspicuous. But why the informant should choose somewhere so open and at the very heart of governance was still somewhat perplexing.

Mayhap the sanctity of Westminster Abbey would provide a certain amount of protection for him. And the man had wanted assurances as well as coin for what he had discovered and would soon divulge. Which meant that he was possibly someone who worked or held high office somewhere in the vicinity. The whole arrangement was equally intriguing and alarming.

Tom could not shake off the feeling that something did not feel right here. He felt rattled and it was more than just mistaking someone who bore a passing resemblance to a termagant woman he would rather forget.

Hell, Tom did not even know who it was he was actually meeting. But he would soon find out and gain the information he sought about a possible seditious plot against the Crown. If he were to uncover anything as important as that, then it might finally go some way to validate his worth to Hubert de Burgh, who was beginning to have misgivings about him.

Although Tom had done well by being commended to de Burgh by his one-time mentor, William Geraint, he could not help but feel that his position was still somehow tenuous. That he still had much to prove to his lord, who seemed increasingly troubled with the unravelling conspiracies against him and the young King as well.

Tom looked in both directions before he moved stealthily around the corner and along another cobbled pathway, which eventually led him to the south cloister of the Abbey. Dark shadows were cast by the moon, as the light dappled against the high wooden arches and beams of the ornate cloister. His footfall was the only sound that reverberated in the silence. But there was something wrong here—it was too quiet, too still and there was no one here. He kept walking slower, his hand clutching the hilt of his dagger tightly, looking in every direction, enveloped in the eerie darkness.

'Who goes there?'

He felt apprehensive with a deep sense of foreboding about this strange assignment that had landed at his feet. He had been singled out with the only apparent reason being that this unknown envoy who was luring him to this meeting place, could only place his trust in Tom. But it was looking more and more unlikely to be the case.

Was he wrong or did this whole appointment have the appearance of an elaborate trap? It was as though Tom was about to step into something far bigger, something outside the realms of his understanding. But to what end? That was one reason he hadn't turned and walked away. He was wary, suspicious, but above all intrigued, and wanted to get to the bottom of what this assignment was all about.

'Is anyone there?'

Tom expelled the frigid air from his lungs and felt his pulse quicken with an increasing sense of trepidation. He drew out one of the torched flames from the metal sconces on the wall, darting his eyes in every direction, trying in vain to see if he could distinguish anything out of the ordinary. But again, nothing. No one was here.

Suddenly he heard it—a faint footfall, halting in the distance, then moving expediently in the opposite direction. Tom gave chase and scrambled to follow hastily in the wake of the retreating footsteps. He turned around the corner of the south cloister, heading east, and snapped his head left and right, trying to make out where the shadowy figure had got to. Tom pursued the man, even though every instinct was screaming at him to be cautious.

'Halt!' Tom blurted. 'What is the meaning of this?'

The man stopped and looked over his shoulder. The deep hood of his green cloak concealing his head.

'Sir Thomas Lovent?' the voice mumbled from afar.

'Who wants to know?'

'Come, follow me. But do not get too close. Not until I can be assured of my safety.'

'Very well, but tell me who you are, sir.'

'Not here.'

The man turned and continued along the long narrow path with Tom on his heels. The stranger then pushed open a creaky wooden door and disappeared behind the archway that led to a stone staircase to the undercroft, his cloak flapping behind him. Tom followed, entering the low-vaulted Pyx Chamber and beyond that the royal treasury. But Tom wondered whether this had been a mistake. The room was plunged in darkness except for the flame that Tom carried.

'Where are you? Show yourself.'

He jerked the flame in every direction, trying to inject some light into the chamber, but again the man had seemingly faded into the shadows. Tom spun around in the room that housed vestments in its large curved chests on one side and tall rows of long chests separating the room that housed important state treaties and foreign policy documents, trying to ascertain where the man was hiding in the room.

'Who are you?' he muttered into the darkness. 'Explain the meaning of this cat-and-mouse game?'

There was no response, except an eerie silence. Not that Tom had any expectation of one, but had hoped that there might be a mistake or a small sound alerting him to the man's whereabouts. But nothing.

Hell, but this assignment was beginning to look more and more like it was a trap with deception at play. He needed to find out what all of this involved tonight and, more importantly, *whom* it did.

Suddenly, without any warning, someone hurled themselves into Tom, winding him, making him drop the flame torch. He was then punched hard in the face as he tried to shield himself behind his outstretched hands. Tom's head was still ringing as he regained his composure and whipped his dagger out in a frenzy, hoping that the weapon might afford some measure of defence against the unknown assailant.

It did not have the desired effect. He was kicked in the stomach with such violence that he doubled over, with the next whack on his back making him fall on to the tiled floor. He coughed and groped around in the dark, trying to find his bearings, before he heard the man's footsteps retreating and the door closing behind him.

Tom groaned and clutched his stomach, dragging himself along the floor to pick up the flame.

What in god's name was that about? He had been lured to the underbelly of Westminster Abbey for a clandestine meeting that never materialised so that he could be kicked and beaten. Why? Was this some sort of warning? To whom, Hubert de Burgh?

Tom pushed himself up, but as he moved to step away, his feet caught on something soft, yet unyielding. He waved the torch back down and gasped—there on the floor was a body slumped on the floor, in a pool of blood oozing from a cut somewhere on his body.

Hell's teeth.

Tom lowered himself on his knee and turned the body around gently. The man was alive, but only just. He made a choking sound, trying to fight for breath and say something at the same time.

Tom quickly got into action, locating the wound in the man's chest, and cut some fabric from his tunic to press against the opening, trying to curtail the seeping blood. Lord, what a mess. The man tried to speak again and made a muffled wheezing sound.

'Steady now, do not make yourself more agitated then necessary.' Tom held the man's head and tried to give him a sip from his flagon.

'Thomas Lovent?' the man rasped quietly.

'Yes, at your service. I assume I was supposed to meet you tonight?'

The man nodded and flicked his eyes close briefly. 'My coin purse,' he mumbled. 'Take it... It is in the furthest vault.'

Tom dashed to retrieve the leather purse from the only open vault, which seemed a little out of place flung in a vessel storing rolls of documents.

He knelt beside the man again, whose breathing had become even more laboured than just a moment before.

'Take...it to Hubert de Burgh.' His eyes widened imploringly, grabbing Tom's tunic. 'Please,' he begged as Tom nodded, unable to comprehend everything that was unfolding on this strange night.

'There's a plot. A traitor.' The man gasped for air.

'What plot? Who? Who is the traitor?' Tom said as the man spluttered and gurgled blood before taking his last breath. Too late. Tom closed the man's eyes, made the sign of the cross before getting to his feet and tying the purse to the inside of his sword belt.

What a damn awful mess and, by the sound of footsteps—many footsteps—getting closer, it was about to become far worse. He moved quickly to the side of the wooden door and waited as two or more men burst through. Tom bided his time, then ran out of the chamber, moving through the undercroft and back up the stairs to the cloisters. The men must have taken in the situation in the chamber and decided that Tom was the culprit because it wasn't long before they were chasing after him.

'Stop!' one of them bellowed, but Tom kept running as fast as he could carry himself. It was unlikely with so much of the man's blood on him that anyone would believe him to be innocent. Besides, he could not trust anyone with this—not the Abbey's clerks, officers or even the men who shared the same official secret work that he carried out. That was how it was organised—each agent of the Crown worked alone and answered to only one master, one lord.

He had to get to de Burgh and quickly. Yet the man was in Wales and still would be for the next sennight or so, if somehow Tom managed to extricate himself from this precarious situation and make the necessary journey to reach him.

He ran down the empty cloister, going north and crossing out into the quad garden, but it was no use. The men trailing him were gaining on him and fast. The only possible way for Tom to escape their clutches was to head into the Abbey itself.

'Stop… Thief… Cutthroat… Assassin!'

Tom ran through the nave and up to the newly laid foundation for the Lady's Chapel and jumped into the pit. He tried to catch his breath as he wondered how the hell he was going to get out of this dangerous predicament. He needed to think quickly, but, judging by the voices that were getting closer, he might not be quick enough.

He scrambled around on his hands and knees, hiding between two huge boulders of uncarved stone with an abandoned wooden scaffold casting a criss-cross of shadows from above. He could feel his heart hammering in his chest as the sound of footsteps echoing surrounded him. Lord, what a damnable coil he had walked into. How in heaven's name was he to leave this place unscathed?

Tom pulled the hood of his cape over his head tighter,

curling himself into something resembling a ball, which was not an easy feat given that he was a big man. He waited and waited as he tried to modify his breathing in the darkness. But then someone seemed to be getting close, flashing their flaming torch around haphazardly.

Hell's teeth!

He needed to be ready for anything. Tom's fingers flexed around the hilt of his dagger, knowing that this would be it, whether it was to fight or somehow manage to scramble away. It was coming. But nothing happened. In truth, the footsteps seemed to retreat and the whole area was once again plunged into darkness, save the thin glimmer of moonlight streaking through.

Thank God! It was time to leave.

Tom lifted himself out of the pit and made his way from one corner to a pillar before he made his way to the nave. He exhaled and stepped out of the Abbey, only to have two of the men who had been following him try to grapple him to the ground. Tom punched one in the face and managed to kick the other in the stomach, winding him before he could apprehend him. He fled across West Gate, flicking his head over his shoulder briefly.

Damn.

He had seemingly alerted more men, since half a dozen were now clamouring to give chase to him. He ran down Tothill Street and through the back streets and narrow cobbled paths, circling back until he was by the quayside on the Thames. Breathing a sigh of relief, he hid under an archway before hopping on to a passing skiff and praying that he had managed to lose those men. He would continue until London Bridge, where he would claim his horse from the watchman of the Chapel of St Thomas Becket, who worked for him from time to time.

After that Tom needed to act expediently. With the events of the night still whirling around in his head, he needed to act fast. One thing was certain. Tom needed to leave London tonight, make his way to Wales and get the dead man's message to Hubert de Burgh.

Chapter Two

Brida O'Conaill rolled her eyes and grimaced as she watched the man approach her in the small village of Kinnerton where she has made her home for the past three years. She had never intended to reside for long in this part of the country, but at the insistence of her friend and chatelaine of Kinnerton Castle, Lady Gwenllian, she had decided to stay and settle here, after all. And Brida was happy that she had. Dwelling in this beautiful lush part of England, so close to the Welsh border, had brought a measure of contentment and peace that she had never expected or contemplated.

She led a life that was of her choosing, living not in the castle as Gwen had proposed, but in a small pretty abode in the village itself. To many it might seem odd that Brida had declined living in the splendour and luxury of the castle, but not to her. It meant that there was somewhere that was intrinsically hers, allowing her the freedom to do as she pleased, even though much of her time was actually taken up in the bower chambers with Gwen in the castle keep anyway.

It was the one place, however small, that she could

have arranged in any way she wanted and enjoy her own solitude when the occasion arose. In truth, it was somewhere she could unwind around her own personal possessions and be herself. More importantly, it was her home.

There was, however, one slight problem to this modest yet agreeable existence: the fact that she had been forced to lie to the inhabitants of Kinnerton that she was married with a husband who was apparently on a pilgrimage, in the Holy Land, or mayhap it was in some lord's mesne. The story seemed to change throughout the past three years as to why her 'husband' had never come back to Kinnerton to live with his wife, yet she somehow had managed to get away with her misleading deception.

She had even taken Gwen, and by extension her husband, Ralph, Lord of Kinnerton, into her confidence and asked them not to betray her little secret. And not only had they acquiesced to her wishes, but avowed the existence of her make-believe husband. Her scheme had mainly worked...until these past few months.

In truth, Brida had been left alone by Kinnerton's menfolk and curious villagers wanting to establish why a young, seemingly hale woman was living on her own despite the apparent mysterious husband who never materialised. After all, this went against the natural order of things, married or not. So naturally, she had to keep embellishing her little lie more and more to the point where she could not keep track of everything she had said. But as long as it prevented the bothersome unwanted curiosity into her life and her status, then it was worth the trouble.

Having a false husband gave her assurances and

peace of mind that facilitated the fact that she would never take a *real* one. It was the only way that she could forestall any man from showing a possible interest, getting close to her, or tempting her with a life that could never be hers. Such attachments could *never*, ever happen. Not if Brida wanted to make certain that the past could never repeat itself again. For that, she had to ensure that the prophecy remained unbroken, and unchallenged, in the hope that it would never cause destruction or heartache again.

God, but she could not bear more than she already had.

Yet recently, her situation was becoming more and more untenable, as her 'marriage' was being openly discussed with many bent on giving her advice regarding her unfortunate position surrounding her missing husband. Many believed that she should enquire to his whereabouts and find out one way or another whether the man still *lived,* of all things…

The concern shown to her well-being might be comforting. After all, when had anyone, and strangers at that, ever shown an interest in her welfare apart from Gwen and her husband? And although it was somehow reassuring that there was somewhere in the world where people actually cared about what happened to her, Brida could not deny that this was all becoming quite difficult. On the one hand she felt guilty continually lying to these good people and on the other…

'Good evening to you, Mistress Brida.' The young Kinnerton hearth knight dipped his head. 'And what are you doing out of doors so late?'

There was this—the attention from the young men in the village who treated Brida as though she were a maid and not a married woman or, worse, a married woman whom they could solicit.

'Nothing that you need to concern yourself with, sir. But if you must know, I have just come from the castle.' She gave him a bland smile and continued on her way. 'With Lord and Lady de Kinnerton away, there has been much to do.'

'Yes, with far more workload for us all.' He followed her. 'But let me at least help you with the provisions you are carrying.' he said eagerly.

She sighed. 'My thanks, but that will not be necessary. You should see to your duties, instead.'

'Allow me.' The man persisted, taking the load from Brida and walking alongside her as they meandered back to Brida's humble timber dwelling.

While the man chatted about himself, extolling his own virtues, Brida realised that it had not been prudent of her to allow him to accompany her. It might be construed as an invitation that she somehow sought his attention, which of course she had not. She hoped that he realised that and, if not, she would have to resort to once again expressing her undying love for her 'husband' and explain that she was not the sort of woman to have dalliances with other men, however long she might have been without the attentions of her beloved. God, but this sort of situation inevitably always happened to her, without her intention.

It was at this inopportune moment that the heavens decided to open, with a sudden downpouring of rain that managed to drench Brida to the skin in the short distance that it took to get back along the path that led back home. It had become far too dark, with an increased difficulty in seeing anything beyond her nose.

'Shall we seek shelter beneath the tree, mistress?' he cried.

'I think not, we are almost there.' She raised her voice over the incessant sound of the torrential rain. 'But you are welcome to return to the bailey and have my thanks for giving me your aid thus far.'

'No need, I shall see you to your door.'

The tone of his voice made Brida grind her teeth together, but she inclined her head instead. 'Thank you, sir.'

They finally approached the entrance of her small house, but something seemed awry. For one thing, quite a few people were waiting outside her home in the pouring rain and they seemed to be waiting for her. All excessively strange and very much out of the ordinary.

'Oh, thank goodness you are here, Mistress Brida.' One of the villagers seemed visibly relieved to see her.

'Is anything amiss?'

'The most marvellous news, thanks be to God.' The older woman spoke with such animated fervour that she looked as though she might burst with excitement. 'Your husband has finally returned.'

Brida felt the blood drain from her face. 'My *what*?' she whispered.

'Yes, he's here inside and, from the looks of things, much in need of your care and attention.'

A husband? But that was not possible.

This had to be a grave, erroneous mistake or some ill-begotten jest.

It had to be. There was no husband.

Brida rubbed her clammy brow, took a deep breath and rushed past the group of intrigued onlookers. She burst through her door and then came to an abrupt stop.

What on earth was she doing? There was, by all account, a stranger in her home, claiming to be her husband, and here she was, rushing to meet him? Brida should turn and run in the opposite direction.

But, no, she stiffened her back and pushed forward, taking one step at a time, with the villagers following behind her as she peered around the corner. Pulling back the bed curtain, she gasped as her eyes widened in shock. This was no mistake, lord help her. There, asleep on her bed, was *Thomas Lovent*.

Brida blinked several times, staring at the man whom she had not laid eyes on for more than three years. What on earth was he doing *here* of all places?

As if sensing her question, the older woman spoke again. 'He had been looking for Lord de Kinnerton, but once he realised that he was away with his lady, he asked for you, so I brought him here. He's not looking too well, I'm afraid, mistress.'

'I see.' But, no, she did not. Not in any conceivable way did she comprehend any of this. Especially why this man, whom she had not seen for many years, was now here in Kinnerton. In her home. On her bed.

The older woman scratched her head. 'I believe he might be injured and I have sent for the healer. I hope I have done as you would have wished?'

Brida nodded without taking her eyes off the man lying unconscious on her pallet bed. 'Of course, and you have my thanks, Enid,' she said, touching the old woman's sleeve.

'But is it not wonderful, Mistress Brida?'

'Wonderful?' she repeated in a daze, unable to take her eyes off the man who was lying on her bed, eyes closed and incongruous to the excitement he had caused all around him.

'Yes.' The old woman swatted her arm. 'You have your husband, and might I add such a handsome, virile man, back home where he belongs, with you.'

Brida felt the rush of warmth flood her face.

'Now mind you keep him and not let him fly away again.'

Thomas Lovent's eyes fluttered open. 'Mistress Brida?' His voice was barely a whisper.

'Yes, I am here,' she muttered, still in shock about the odd turn of events this evening.

'Thirsty…' The man raised himself up on his elbow and swayed. 'So very parched,' he croaked as Brida moved to the wooden coffer and poured ale from a jug before returning and pressing it into his hands.

'Here, take it.'

'Thank you. Tell me something,' Thomas Lovent mumbled softly between taking a sip.

'Yes, what is it?'

'Did you miss me?' he whispered before closing his eyes and collapsing back on to her pallet bed.

There were many matters on Brida's mind, least of all the very unconscious man on her bed. Thomas Lovent had been in that slumberous state for much of the night and the following day. The old healer, Cerwen, visited and tended to a nasty chest wound inflicted by some sharp weaponry. She bled him, stitched up the wound and packed it with a foul-smelling unguent that helped prevent it from festering. But even this failed to awaken the man from his deep, yet fretful sleep.

So Brida waited for him to come around, while occasionally placing a cool damp cloth to his brow in the vain hope of bringing down a raging fever that had taken hold.

'Did you miss me?'

She had thought about those words that Thomas Lovent had uttered in his usual sardonic, flippant manner—even as he was lying there barely conscious, feverish and no doubt suffering with discomfort and pain.

The truth, if she cared to examine it, was that she *had* missed the man—or rather what she remembered of him from that fleeting encounter three summers ago, even though the handsome devil aggravated her so much she could happily throttle him at times.

It was what had led to that ill-advised kiss in the witching hour of Gwen and Ralph's wedding, which Brida still found disconcerting after all these years. She had clumsily kissed him, without fully understanding or accepting why she had done so. The recollection of that excruciatingly embarrassing night was not one she was particularly proud of. She had lived that moment so many times, berating herself over her unpardonable rudeness.

And, if she were honest, her brazen behaviour was a moment that had scared her because she had momentarily lost control and allowed herself to experience something illicit and forbidden. Something she could never have, as the prophecy surrounding her family had sealed her fate to be one that could only include solitude and piety.

Knowing that she would never experience anything remotely like the passions her friend and countless other women enjoyed in the sanctity of marriage, it could have been that she grabbed the moment, when she could. Much to her shame.

To make matters worse, Brida had blamed Thomas Lovent at the time. Even now, she cringed, just thinking about what she had said to the poor man and without getting the opportunity to rectify the situation by apologising for her part. Thomas Lovent had left Kinnerton without notice or even a farewell and had kept away all these years. Lord only knew what had brought him back now.

Yet for that one brief glorious interlude in midsummer three years ago she had felt an affinity despite herself—a kindred connection with the man lying unconscious on her bed, even though it could never be. Yes, it had terrified her and now the man was once again back in Kinnerton, however fleetingly.

'Don't die,' she whispered repeatedly as though it were a prayer. 'Please don't die.'

By the following morning, Thomas Lovent's fever finally broke. He stirred, thrashing his head from side to side before opening his eyes and pleading for a drink. Brida made him sip a warming broth from a bowl that she brought to his lips, accompanied by some cool restorative water that she had carried from the stream earlier. She watched him as he fell into a deep sleep once again. But this time he appeared far more comfortable and at peace, his breathing deep and measured.

Thank the heavens.

For the first time in the past couple of days, Brida felt a huge burden of weight dropping off her shoulders, knowing that by the time Thomas Lovent woke up and felt like his old self, it would be replaced by another, widely different set of troubles. She had reconciled herself to the events from the past while he had been abed fighting the bad humours in his body, knowing that the man was still due an apology—which she owed him. But then afterwards, he could not leave Kinnerton fast enough for Brida's liking. In every conceivable way, it would be far better that he did.

Yet there was one unforeseen problem that she could never have anticipated. And that was the general belief that they were married. She would have to think about that later, as her main concern was getting the man back on his feet after such a terrible ordeal and getting him to leave here as expediently as possible. Yet how to make Thomas Lovent hold his tongue about the assumption that he was her husband? God, but the prospect of having to explain the situation and request that he remain silent about this predicament she now found herself in made her exceedingly flustered and embarrassed.

That evening he did wake, frowning and blinking several times before opening his eyes.

'Mistress Brida?' Tom muttered quietly, turning his head.

She ambled towards the side of the bed. 'Yes, I am still here, Sir Thomas.'

'Ah, so I did not conjure you up in a dream?'

'No…' she sighed '…you did not.'

She watched as a deep furrow appeared on his brow in apparent confusion before he looked up and met her eyes.

'I am gladdened to hear that, but may I ask, what the hell are you doing here?'

She smiled faintly at that. 'This is my humble dwelling in Kinnerton, Sir Thomas.'

'Apologies. Mayhap I should express that differently by asking what the hell *am I* doing here?'

Brida had managed to treat unwanted male attentions with a firm but friendly discouragement. But the memory of this man had somehow etched himself in her head from a time before, when he had addled her senses. And now the villagers of Kinnerton believed him to be her long lost husband come back to her.

Oh, Lord.

'I am afraid I cannot answer that, as I do not know.'

Chapter Three

Tom rubbed his brow, trying to recollect the dangerous events of the last few days, and bit back a groan as his memory of not just the past few days, but weeks, tumbled back into his head. He had scurried out of Westminster Abbey and eventually out of London as expediently as he could muster, making sure that he had assured his sister's safety and removed her from the lodgings he had acquired in London to somewhere far away, where no one would find her.

With personal matters thus arranged, Tom had ridden as fast as possible to get to Wales, but the assailants from London had trailed him and so he had been forced to make a slight deviation from his course to cover his movements. But annoyingly, he had not avoided a skirmish, which resulted in the wound that he had sustained. He had managed to lose the men who were bent on apprehending him and made his way to Kinnerton in the hope that he might gain immediate support and assistance from Ralph de Kinnerton. However, that seemed futile now as his friend was evidently away with his lady at the behest of the Earl of Chester to be in attendance at Llewelyn of Wales's court.

It seemed imperative for Tom to get back on his feet and complete this mission, which, if he was honest, he would be glad to see the back of. It had brought nothing but perilous danger and complication that he could do without. Not that he understood what any of it even meant.

He looked up and noticed the strange manner in which Brida O'Conaill was watching him and he exhaled, running his hands through his hair awkwardly. He had not expected to see this woman again and had made a concerted effort to avoid her altogether. Yet here he was, rousing from *her* bed after suffering from an injury caused by men who were still no doubt in pursuit of him. The fact that she had attended to him while he had a fever was surprising in itself, but that she should do so in her own home was even more perplexing. However, he had no time to ponder on such musings. Tom had to be away forthwith.

'I must thank you for your ministrations, but I must leave Kinnerton as soon as may be.'

'Oh, but you have only just got over your fever. You must build up your strength before moving on, sir.'

'That is a kind offer, but unfortunately I have to, Mistress Brida. Urgent duties call.'

It was nevertheless true that he still felt weak. But Tom had to leave. He had to get to Wales and deliver the message that the dead informant had given him to pass on to Hubert de Burgh, even if he still felt physically unable to.

'What can be so important that you cannot take a day

or two to recover? You could do without a setback and are in need of a little more rest, Sir Thomas.'

'True, but I do not have the luxury of time.'

He pulled the coverlet off, noticing that he was wearing very little clothing, and pulled it back again, snapping his head around. 'It appears that I am without my clothing, mistress. Can I ask why that may be?'

'Er, well…you were feverish, sir.' A rose-pink hue crept up her neck and bloomed across her cheeks, which Tom somehow found strangely endearing—something Brida O'Conaill could never be described as. 'The healer, you understand, explained that you must be divested of all your clothing, which had to be complied with.'

'Did it now? How very reassuring.'

He took a little pleasure in causing her some discomfort as she was forced to disclose the reasons for his dishabille. Reasons he had instantly realised but had remained silent about, preferring instead to watch her with his arms crossed as she flushed with further embarrassment. And she had continued to stutter and speak. 'But you should know, Sir Thomas, that I did not remove your…your…' She waved her hand about.

He decided to help her out. 'My clothing?'

'Yes,' she whispered, looking away.

'Pity.' He smiled faintly, despite his recent troubles and impending difficulties. 'I was sure I could recall your fair hands tending to me.'

'As I said, that was the healer.' She turned to move away. 'And they were laundered and dried as well.'

'My thanks. You seem to have thought of everything.'

'I tried my best,' she said tightly. 'Now, is there anything else I can fetch you?'

'No, mistress, and you have my sincere gratitude for everything you have done. I am in your debt.'

'Oh, I did nothing, sir.'

'I am sure you did something, Brida,' he drawled. 'Or at least your healer did.'

'Yes, well, I am happy that you seem a lot better.'

'As am I.' He sighed deeply, looking around the small yet comfortably appointed chamber. 'And by the by, I am surprised that you did not feel it unseemly and improper to have me convalesce here—even if I were incapacitated at the time. I wonder at the villagers at Kinnerton being so enlightened and understanding about such an arrangement with a man unrelated to you.'

'Ah, there might be a perfect rationale for that.'

'And that is?'

She gulped a few times before answering him.

'Well, in truth they…they believed us to be married.' She mumbled so quietly that Tom wondered whether he had heard her correctly.

'Did you just proclaim us to be "married"?'

She grimaced as though she had swallowed something deeply unpleasant and nodded.

'Allow me to understand this, mistress…' his lips curved at the corners '…because I fail to understand why you did not correct them.'

'No. I did not.'

'I see.' He smirked. 'How very interesting.'

'Not really, Sir Thomas. In the confusion and aftermath of your arrival here, with everyone worried about you, I must have forgotten to clarify the situation.'

'And were you?' He raised a brow. 'Worried about me?'

She frowned as if not understanding him. 'Of course, sir. How could I or anyone else fail to be?'

'You may find this hard to believe, mistress but there are many who would be glad of my demise.' He sighed. 'Again, I must offer my heartfelt gratitude. Now, would you mind passing my clothing, if you please.'

'Yes, of course, sir. I shall leave you in peace while you dress.'

'That will not be necessary. You may turn around if you want to hide your maidenly blushes or stay as you are if you wish to fill your eyes with my glorious nudity.'

She turned her back as Tom knew she would.

'I see that you must be better since you can engage in your usual unashamed provoking manner. Oh, but how I have missed that.' She tossed this over her shoulder sardonically as she picked up the jug and mug on the coffer.

'Have you indeed? I suppose such redoubtable charm and good humour may be in short supply in Kinnerton?'

'Quite,' she muttered tersely. 'I am not sure how I coped without it.'

Tom could see that his teasing was once again causing her to try to hold on to that formidable tongue of hers. He really should not goad the woman—especially since he truly was indebted to her for giving him shelter and attending to his feverish wound, but old habits rose to the surface. Her forthright manner somehow always managed to get under his skin. He couldn't help it, or rather chose not to.

In truth, he had always enjoyed sparring with Brida O'Conaill in the brief time he had known her, except that one night in Kinnerton beneath the stars when things between them became too candid, too bewildering and too heated. Then just as quickly it descended into bitterness and regret that had been hard to understand or erase. He knew he had been just as much to blame three years ago as she had, yet he could never forget how her words had affected him so deeply.

It was best that the whole sorry episode had been consigned to the far reaches of his mind, but it still puzzled him why it had happened in the first place. It might have been the ale or wine or the occasion of Ralph and Gwen's wedding that made them behave so out of character, but Tom had been resolved to forget all about this fiery woman and her glittering blue eyes.

'Peace.' He held out his hands. 'I am only teasing you, Mistress Brida, and in truth, I am happy to see you so well settled in Kinnerton. Although I am surprised that you stayed here. I believed you were meant for the convent.'

'My plans changed, sir.'

'Did they indeed? Well, either way, I would hate to think that on my account your good deeds would somehow be frowned upon once anyone in this village realises the truth—that we are not married. Mayhap you could say that there was a maid, or washer woman, present the whole time.' Tom stood up after finishing dressing. 'You may turn around now.'

But just as she did, his legs felt as though they couldn't hold him up. He wobbled as Brida rushed forward to lend him her support.

She helped him back in the bed. 'I did try to convince you that you were not ready to leave.'

'And here I thought you were attempting to hang on

to my scintillating company.' He gave her a small impish smile, trying to feign a light-hearted tone when in
truth he felt tired. So excessively tired.

'Of course.' She returned his smile, seemingly playing along. 'Stay and rest a while—that is, until you feel
more like yourself than you currently do.'

'Thank you, Brida, and I must say at this moment
you're being quite wifely with your strict edicts.'

She shook her head and sighed. 'You really are incorrigible, Sir Thomas. Now get some rest.'

The following morning, Tom stirred as the old healer,
Cerwen, returned to prod, poke and linger a little too
long with the patient on Brida's bed, who was finally
opening his eyes after a long sleep.

'Well, Mistress Brida, I must say that this fine strapping man here will be back on his feet in no time at all,'
the healer said, as her wrinkled hands patted him absently on the cheek. 'And thank the heavens he's awake.
Tell me, how do you fare, Sir Thomas? Brida and I have
seen to your wound with fresh, clean bandaging.'

'My thanks,' he mumbled. 'To you both. I'm feeling much better.'

'Good, good. That is what I like to hear, but then
with someone so…' the old healer looked him over
'…fit and hale, I did believe that you would.'

Brida threw Sir Thomas an amused look as he raised
a brow at the healer's forwardness. 'Er, I am much
obliged to you, Mistress Healer.'

'"Mistress Healer", indeed! Call me Cerwen.'

'It would be my pleasure, Cerwen.' He gave the old
woman his most devastating smile. 'And I'm Tom.'

Was it Brida's imagination or had the curmudgeonly old woman just giggled? 'Where are my manners. Can I offer you some repast? You must be famished.'

The old healer turned to her and rubbed her stomach. 'Thank you, now that you mention it, that would be most welcome. And I think Tom could do with some of the pottage, judging from that delicious smell.'

Brida went behind the curtained counter and dished some into three wooden bowls and served two before returning for her own. 'Yes, it should be tasty, as it is freshly made and from the castle kitchen.'

The old woman slurped hers ravenously before nodding at Sir Thomas. 'Good, the sustenance has given you some colour.'

'Again, my thanks to you, Cerwen, I owe you a great deal.'

'Oh, I am glad to have been of some help, but you know Brida was always at your side.'

'Is that so?'

Brida turned away, embarrassed at this disclosure.

'Not surprising really, Tom, after so long apart. Although, one might wonder at it—your wife here was very attentive.'

Brida snapped her head around to find Sir Thomas's bemused eyes fixed on hers. 'I am certain you are right. My *wife* is evidently a ministering treasure with many commendable traits.'

'Oh, it really was nothing.' She gave him an imploring look not to expose her and reveal the fact that they were not actually married.

'"Nothing", she says.' The old woman waved her hand, vigorously, admonishing her. 'You may have been

on your own for some time now, Brida, but there's no
need to be all maidenly.'

'No need at all,' Sir Thomas chimed in, raising his
brows and crossing his arms over his chest, clearly enjoying himself. 'Especially since the Brida I knew was
never one to be so bashful and maidenly.'

God, the man was utterly shameless.

'You leave her be, young man. We're all very fond
of your lovely wife, here in Kinnerton.' The old woman
smiled at her before turning back to the man sat in her
bed. 'And mind you hang on to her properly this time.'

'Never fear. I'll endeavour to do many things *properly* this time.'

'Is it not getting late, Cerwen?' Brida's voice rose
up a notch or two as she felt the heat colour her cheeks
at the exchange and desiring an end to this mortifying
conversation. Oh, Lord, make it all stop.

'You are a tease, Tom.' The old woman chuckled.

He shrugged, grinning as he dragged his fingers
through his dark golden hair. 'I can but try when one is
in the presence of such lovely ladies, Cerwen.'

'Oh, stop or you shall put us both to the blush.' The
old woman swatted his arm playfully.

'Ah, the truth is, Cerwen, that Brida and I are not actually…' His eyes caught hers as she gave him a pleading look.

*'Don't do it. Please don't tell her that we are not
married…'*

'That you and Brida are not actually…?' The old
woman repeated his words, waiting for an answer.

He tilted his head to the side and smiled slowly at
Brida before flicking his gaze back to the old woman.
'We are not actually long married. I had to leave in

haste more than three sad years ago, after making our sacred vows.'

'Oh, I never knew that. How is it that I never knew that, Brida? And Lord, what a shame,' the woman gasped as she covered her mouth with her hand.

'Indeed, Cerwen. My lovely, maidenly wife and I had but just a few precious hours before my departure.'

The old woman shook her head in sympathy. 'And I assume your hasty departure was due to your duties for your liege lord that Brida told us about?'

'Just so.'

The old woman's forehead furrowed with deep creased lines as if she were deeply contemplating. She then lifted her head. 'Then I know just what we need this eventide. A celebration of your nuptials.'

What?

Brida suddenly felt a little faint. 'No, no, Cerwen. I am sure that will not be necessary. After all, Sir Thomas, as in *Tom,* my avowed husband—' whom she would gladly throttle, presently '—is still weak from his ordeal.'

'Nonsense, my attentive, maidenly wife. I think it an excellent plan.'

The old woman rose and clapped her hands together. 'Then I shall go and see to the preparation. And, no, Brida. Stay here and reacquaint yourself with your husband. Everything will be in hand. Kinnerton village will give you both a proper welcome.' She cackled excitedly before leaving through the arched door.

Brida stared after the old woman in disbelief. What in heaven's name had just occurred here? They were to attend a makeshift celebration for an imagined marriage?

'I know exactly what you are thinking, Mistress Brida.' He nodded. 'And really there is no need to thank me.'

To Thomas Lovent?

Brida turned around slowly to face the man. 'You believe that I should thank you?'

He shrugged. 'Why, yes, but consider, it was the least I could do after all of your attentiveness when I burst through your door and collapsed all feverish and wounded on your bed.'

She closed her eyes and let out a shaky breath. 'What are we to do?'

'It seems to me that you have two options, mistress. Either attend a celebration given in our honour as a married couple. Although I must say that I'm still per-plexed why you would have chosen to lie to the good people of Kinnerton about being married.'

'Never mind about that,' she said, rubbing her fore-head. 'What is the other option?'

'Only that you inform them of the truth.'

Dear Lord.

No, that she could not do. How could she ever hold her head up in this village again if they were to find out that not only was this man not her husband, but that she was not actually married at all? And she never would be and had lied to them all this time. God, she could never explain the reasons why she must remain unwed. Alone. For the remainder of her life. On account of what had happened to her family in Ireland. On account of the dreadful curse and the prophecy. On account of it all being her fault.

She gulped uncomfortably. 'In that case then, I believe that if you are feeling well enough, Sir Thomas, we have a celebration to attend.'

He smiled slowly. 'Oh, I am certain I feel well enough for that, *wife*.'

Chapter Four

That evening's festivities were a riotous affair where makeshift trestle tables had been dragged out in the middle of the square by the villagers, arranged in a squared horseshoe shape and covered with their own materials, creating a pretty patchwork effect of different-coloured cloth. The tables groaned with piles of food and ale that had been supplied by the villagers themselves, which humbled Brida to her core. These wonderful people never failed to amaze her with their generosity and kindness. Something that now gave her pangs of remorse and guilt because of the lie she had concocted. But it could not be helped.

Thomas Lovent's arrival in Kinnerton, albeit injured and with a soaring fever, had somehow given flesh and bones to her make-believe husband. And although unexpected, she gladly took this inadvertent gift, knowing it would give her the affirmation she so badly sought. And once this evening was over and the man left Kinnerton, her life would hopefully resume its peaceful sedate pace, with the added benefit of being finally accepted as a married woman and finally left alone. And the sooner Thomas Lovent left, the better. Yet why did Brida feel so uneasy and apprehensive about this evening? Mayhap it was the fact that it was all so public, making her feel so exposed. Nevertheless, she had no choice other than to see the evening through.

She was sat with Tom, in the middle of the assembled group, with her seemingly popular *husband* charming the villagers of Kinnerton in his usual entertaining way. It was incredible to believe that the man had only lately got over his ordeal, yet here he was, having the most marvellous time and being exceedingly merry with everyone around him.

He had regaled and spun so many stories about his adventures that even Brida had almost been diverted by him. That was, until she reminded herself that it was all nonsense. Sir Thomas Lovent, the loquacious, witty knight, loved nothing better than to amuse and captivate an audience with his particular brand of droll nonsense. She shook her head absently as he finished the last of his tales with such an animated flourish that many who had congregated around them burst into spontaneous applause.

As the villagers dispersed, he leaned over to her and drew her sheer linen veil across one shoulder.

'Come along now, Mistress Brida,' he muttered quietly in her ear. 'At least you could pretend as though you are having a merry time.'

'Do I really need to, when you are *merry* enough for the both of us?'

He caught her hand in his and caressed her fingers. 'Ah, but someone needs to. You look as though you have summoned the blacksmith to extract a rotting tooth.'

'Must you jest about everything?'

'That is not what I am doing, my maidenly, attentive wife.' The way the man looked into her eyes just then made little butterflies unfurl inside her stomach. She tore her eyes away and shuffled along the bench, reminding herself that he was play acting for the benefit of the villagers. 'And let us not forget that this was a scheme that *you* devised, Brida. One which I subsequently agreed to.'

'You have my eternal thanks.'

'It is the least I can do after all your attentive ministration.' He inclined his head, giving her a knowing smile. 'And I am just doing as you bid me to do. To be your doting husband.'

'Indeed, I know that this is for appearances' sake, Sir Thomas.' She tried to pull her hand free, but he held it firm in his. 'But mayhap you are taking this all a little too far?'

'Oh, not nearly enough.' He kissed the sensitive skin of her wrist. 'Lest we forget that these good people believe that you and I are married.'

'I am aware, Sir Thomas.'

'And have been apart for the last three years.'

Brida did not like the direction that this discourse was going in. 'So what of it?'

'Truly, I am all agog.' He turned her hand around slowly and brushed his lips along the fleshy palm. 'As it seems that it was most fortuitous that I arrived in Kinnerton when I did. Even in that sorry state.'

'I cannot know what you are trying to convey.'

'Can you not?' he gave her a wicked smile. 'All of this does rather beg the pertinent question I have been asking myself, ever since I was declared to be your long-lost husband, which, by the by, I am very flattered to be.'

'I am sure you are.' She managed to pull her hand free. 'But dare I ask what this pertinent question might be?'

'Why have you lied to these people for all this time, Brida? With, I am quite certain, Ralph and Gwen's blessing?' He studied his fingernails before he flicked his penetrating gaze back to her. 'This, tonight, the pretence of a marriage between us, was not as I initially believed a way to explain my inopportune arrival here and subsequent convalescence at your abode. Although that was exceedingly unwise, I could nevertheless appreciate it. After all, you and I are not related and it would have been wholly improper that I was alone with you, even in the state I was in. So, yes, for that I can understand the need for a little deception.'

'I am glad to hear it.'

'What I cannot understand is why you have been lying to the good people of Kinnerton for such a long time.' He raised a brow. 'Care to explain, *wife*?'

'Not especially, my incredibly irritating and infuriating *husband*.'

He chuckled softly as he tore off a bit of bread and starting chewing. 'You know, Brida, it is as though we truly are an old married couple, the way you berate me.'

'Mayhap it is the effect you somehow always have on me.'

'A thousand apologies, mistress. I had not meant to be so vexatious.'

'Really?' She snatched the bread from his fingers and also took a bite. 'You surprise me.'

He chucked softly. 'Come now, you must know that you can confide in me,' he whispered, conspiratorially.

'How clumsy of me. I had no notion of this being a confessional.'

'Why not? You can always allow yourself to believe that it is.'

God, but was the man always so perceptive?

'I would rather not.'

'Suit yourself.' He shook the crumbs off his hands before reaching for his mug. 'But I give you fair warning, Mistress Brida, I shall find out your secrets.'

She shrugged hoping that she emanated a nonchalant air. 'You make it sound far more interesting than it actually is, Sir Thomas. Besides, if you tell me yours than I might consider disclosing mine.'

'And what, pray, is this secret of mine that you wish to discover?'

'Ah, let me see.' She tapped her chin. 'What happened to you prior to your arrival in Kinnerton? Who injured you and, finally, who was it that you were running away from?'

A flash of something akin to uneasiness flared in his eyes before it was masked over by his usual levity.

'So, you believe that I was being pursued by some dastardly villains, bent on ambushing a brave, gallant and, may I add, heroic knight of the realm.'

Or mayhap she had imagined it. 'I know how you enjoy your own gallantry, but I somehow thought it might have more to do with a poor cuckolded husband giving chase to you.'

His low laughter rumbled through her, making her respond with a smile as well. It was rather a nice laugh, she conceded. 'Well, do I have the right of it?'

'No.' He took a sip of ale and wiped his lips with the back of his hand. 'But you have a vivid imagination, mistress. I'll allow you that.'

'Either way, sir, I will eventually uncover your secrets. I will seek and I will somehow find. So, with that I give *you* fair warning.

Thomas Lovent frowned briefly before the lines on his forehead smoothed and he gave her a slow languid smile. 'Has anyone ever mentioned what a real treasure you are, mistress?'

'No. I believe you must be the first.'

'Ah, that warms me to the soles of my feet, my attentive, treasure of a wife.'

'Cease or I shall expire with uncontained pleasure and happiness,' she retorted sardonically.

'Well, I can always attempt to show you other ways to give you pleasure.'

Brida knew that he was only trying to get a rise out of her, but, Lord, the man was outrageously shameless. He had to be to resort to such base lewdness.

'Oh, I rather doubt that, Sir Thomas.' Oh, dear... she regretted the words as soon as she said them, especially after the heated look he threw at her, knowing that what she had uttered was untrue and, worse than that, he knew it, too.

'Is that a challenge, Brida?' he drawled. 'We can always test that theory.'

Was it her imagination or was he was referring to that night? That one foolish and ill-advised night, three summers ago, when she had lost control of her senses and initiated *that* heated kiss. When she had desperately wanted to taste pleasure for herself and not with just anyone, but with Thomas Lovent, who might have infuriated her, but also made her feel things she really had no right to. Ever since that night, she had tried to forget it had ever happened and been careful not to repeat that sorry episode.

'I believe you forget yourself, sir.' She shifted uncomfortably.

'Do I? How very remiss of me.'

'Indeed,' she muttered with a touch of asperity. 'If you recall, it is the pleasure of your company after being away for such a long time, as well as your recent ordeal upon arrival here, that is the reason for this celebration, my frankly ridiculous *husband.*

'How can I forget, Brida?' He smirked. 'But you know that was not what I meant.' His eyes sparkled with amusement.

'What I know, Sir Thomas, is that you and I are *only* acting as husband and wife. No more than that,' she hissed under her breath.

'Then we had better put on more of a performance for these good people, my sweet treasure of a wife.'

'Tell me again when you intend to leave Kinnerton?'

'Never say that you will pine for me, oh, wondrous wife?'

'As much as that blacksmith summoned to extract a rotting tooth, my, oh, so odious husband.'

He cut an apple and offered one half to Brida before taking a noisy bite into it. 'Ah, then it is a good thing that I shall be leaving on the morrow.'

She bit into her half and nodded. 'It certainly is, sir.'

'And on that, I had better take my role more seriously, wife.' He pinched her chin before he stood and raised his voice. 'I would like to address you, the good folk of Kinnerton.'

Tom looked around the small noisy square and tapped his mug against the table and waited until the din quietened gradually, as he caught everyone's attention. He held his hand out to Brida, who thankfully took it and rose to stand beside him, giving him a dubious, uncertain look. He winked at her before turning around and cleared his throat before speaking.

'I would like to thank you all for this wonderful evening, and for making me feel welcome among you. But, more importantly, for allowing my fair wife, Brida to reside with you here in Kinnerton. You have all shown her friendship, support and love in my absence.' He raised his mug and slipped an arm around her waist, pulling her a little closer. 'So, I propose a toast...to my lovely, sweet Brida.'

Tom bit back a smile as he felt her stiffen at his touch. So incongruous with the warmth of her body that he could feel through the many layers of clothing that she wore, where his fingers wrapped around the small curve of her waist. It was then that an unexpected jolt of pleasure shot through him and which he naturally ignored. It would be a very unwise thing to acknowledge.

The assembled group of villagers raised their mugs and echoed, '...to Brida.'

The woman in turn smiled blandly at the villagers and flushed before nodding her gratitude.

Tom spun back around. 'And to you...people of Kinnerton.' He raised his mug and took a swig before making one last declaration. 'Now let's get drunk.' Which naturally brought on the biggest cheer of the night.

The evening wore on, well past the witching hour. The revelry became more raucous with inhibitions being thrown to the wind as the villagers did indeed follow Tom's advice and became very jolly after consuming barrels of ale and crisp local cider. Music hung in the sweet sultry air, accompanied by achingly tender ballads and boisterous country jigs and dances.

Through this Tom kept his head, alert to everything around him. He once again questioned his foolish decision to stay that evening and attend this ridiculous celebration, knowing it would have been far wiser to have left earlier. It was imperative for him to complete this damnable mission and get whatever message the dead informer had left to Hubert de Burgh. It had only been earlier that day, when Tom had had his first opportunity to properly examine the contents of the leather purse the man had entrusted to him.

Not that he could glean much from a scrap of parchment with a ciphered message on it, a gold ring with a strange, unfamiliar insignia and a couple of expensive whalebone chess pieces. Much as he hated to admit it, he had wondered whether the man had been another operative working for de Burgh. After all, his liege lord rarely had any of his men meet one another. Yet the man who had lain dying in his arms had sought Tom out. Again, he wondered why. The whole thing was far more perplexing than he had ever imagined and the sooner he left Kinnerton to make his way to Llewelyn's court, the better.

Yet he could not but help feel obliged to help Brida O'Conaill with this scheme of maintaining their faux marriage, even if he had felt uncomfortable about doing so. He understood too well the way of the world, knowing that it had not been prudent for a sensible, proud woman like Brida to take him into her home and attend him herself, even if he was grateful that she did. After all, if the people here knew that they were not married and had no familial connection at all, it would not bode well for her at all. She would lose all respect and her standing in this village, even if she were a close friend of Gwen, Lady Kinnerton, and be cast as a woman of the night.

Yet it had transpired that Brida had been using the guise of a married woman far longer than Tom had initially believed to be purely accidental. In fact, she had, from what he had learned, disclosed much about a husband who had until his arrival been absent as well as seemingly non-existent.

Why?

It intrigued him more than he could explain to comprehend the reasons why she had been lying to the villagers of Kinnerton for all these years. Would they not have eventually found out? Or what of the possibility that she might have met someone whom she actually wanted to marry, but couldn't because of this rather elaborate falsehood? Tom should certainly not take any interest in or be in any way curious about Brida O'Conaill. The woman was nothing but troublesome and God knew he had troubles enough presently, but there was something about her, something intangible that did indeed intrigue him. It was the same three years ago when they had met under a very different circumstance.

They had both aided their two friends in their own way at the tournament three years ago to rekindle a lost love in the hope that they would find each other again. And they had. Gwen and Ralph had overcome their differences and found a way back to each other, in the process throwing Tom and Brida into each other's company, much to the woman's unbridled annoyance and obvious disapproval of *him*. Which was frankly unjust and exceedingly irksome.

And it had been this that he had never understood—Brida O'Conaill's hostility towards him. He might not be the most self-effacing man, since he knew perfectly well the effect he had on women, young and old, but he had never done anything to cause this woman's censure. Yet it had been there from the first time he set eyes on her. It spurred Tom to being even more flippant and more provoking around her. He knew he should not do it, but he just could not help it. The more frustrated and irritable she became, the more he teased her.

He darted his gaze around the square until it collided with hers. Brida O'Conaill was a strikingly beautiful woman, with glittering blue eyes, full lips, long dark hair and a lush body that he really should not dwell on. But the woman would be far more attractive if she wasn't such a tempestuous termagant. Yet Tom had to admit that he did quite like that about her. Her quick wit and that fiery temper were admittedly diverting, if one was careful not to get singed now and again.

'Ah, behold, there goes my adorable wife.' Brida was surrounded by a small group, who parted to make way for Tom as he ambled towards them and stopped to stand beside her.

'Husband,' she muttered absently. 'I trust you are well.'

'Indeed. This has been a most pleasant evening, has it not?' He lifted her fingers to his lips. 'But I believe it is time for bed.'

He noticed her inhaling sharply while the group gathered around them cheered and made suggestive comments. She pursed her lips and gave him a look dripping with annoyance.

That might have been an ill-advised statement to make in front of these people, but at least it would beg him leave of these continued celebrations. He must leave on the morrow as he had delayed long enough. Then again, he wouldn't mind taking Brida to bed just so that he could wipe the look of disdain from her face. Really, though, did the woman not realise that he was trying to make their deception more convincing?

'Yes, take your wife to bed this instant, Tom. It has been so long, do you think you know the way?' The old healer, Cerwen, chuckled as the others howled with laughter.

Brida, however, did not share in the amusement. In fact, her cheeks flooded with colour.

'We should give them a proper bedding ceremony.'

'*What?*' Brida's eyes widened in horror. 'That will be not be necessary.'

'What a wonderful idea!' another villager said, as if they totally misheard her. 'And very necessary.'

The time had come to put an end to the nonsense. 'I think not,' Tom muttered in a low steely voice. And before anyone uttered another thing, he swooped Brida up into his arms and walked back towards her home. 'And I swear, Cerwen, if you pinch my bottom one more time, I will have no choice but to give you what for.'

'Promises, promises,' Cerwen cried from somewhere behind them.

'You old minx!' He shook his head and took long strides away from the square.

'What do you think you are doing?' Brida hissed, once they were out of earshot.

'I believe that it was quite evident, my maidenly treasure.' He winked down at her, noting her scowl before continuing. 'And very soon, I shall carry you over the threshold, honouring customs of old.'

'How very quaint, but really you can put me down now, Sir Thomas.'

'Patience, Brida. Besides, I would have thought that you would have appreciated this for appearances' sake.

'I promise you that I don't.'

'Ah, so you would have preferred that half of this infernal village parade us back to your home and watch some damn bedding ritual?' When she didn't respond, he added, 'No, I did not think so.'

'But this is most humiliating and let's not forget that you have only just resumed your health. I doubt you have the necessary strength to carry me all the way back.'

'Very true, my graciously considerate wife, especially as carrying you in this manner is not at all gratifying. Not to mention my poor deflated strength.'

'Humblest of apologies. I was not aware that I should provide you with such gratification,' she said, rolling her eyes. 'But then, I had no notion that I was to be carried in your arms.'

'No need to thank me, wife. I aim to please.'

'Of course you do. With your fabled charms and gallantry?'

'Just so, the very same.' He chuckled. 'And it would have served me far better had I hauled you over my shoulder and carried you over my back like a hemp sack filled with heavy grain.'

'Why, Sir Thomas, how did you know that I love nothing better than being compared to grain?'

He winked at her. 'I am far more perceptive than you give me credit for.'

'Naturally, but I thank the saints you desisted from hauling me anywhere. Otherwise, I would have had no choice other than resorting to biting you on your person, which would really have been most unbecoming.'

'Indeed, and God only knows what these people would have thought had they witnessed such an unbecoming spectacle.'

'I am convinced it would have strengthened their conviction of our marriage even further.'

He chuckled as he kicked opened the wooden door of Brida's abode and walked in. 'You really are a treasure to behold, mistress.'

'Thank you,' Brida said in a prim voice. 'Now, you may put me down now if you please.'

'Gladly,' he said as he dumped her unceremoniously. 'Apologies, I had not meant to drop you in such a manner, but then again my limited strength has all but dwindled.'

'True, it had become sadly evident.'

He towered over her and crossed his arms. 'A thousand pardons. How terribly unseemly.' He grinned. 'We knights are known for our diminished strength.'

She got back to her feet and raised an eyebrow, before rushing off to the furthest corner of the chamber and grabbing a handful of bedding blankets and returning to stand in front of him.

'I thank you for a marvellous performance this evening, Sir Thomas. It was most entertaining being married to you for the duration.' She handed over the soft woollen blankets. 'Here take these and sleep wherever you wish as long as it is not in my bed.'

'As if I would, mistress.'

She gave him a look as though she did not quite believe him. 'I am glad, sir, as I am claiming my bed now, if you please.'

'I would not dream of denying you the luxury of your own bed. Especially since you forsook it to me when I was recovering.'

'Precisely, Sir Thomas. I bid you goodnight.' She inclined her head.

'However, should you be in need of a warm body to lie next to, I would like to return your kindness by offering up myself to you.'

'That will not be necessary, sir.' She gasped in outrage, giving him an imperious look before closing the bed curtain tightly.

He chuckled lightly as he lay down the blankets to fashion a makeshift bed on the floor before lying down on it and staring at the wooden ceiling.

'Brida?' he muttered quietly, wondering whether she would respond.

'Yes.'

'I hope you realise that I was only teasing you there.'

'Of course, Sir Thomas. It is what you enjoy most,' was the rejoinder that echoed in the darkness.

'Very true.' He smiled languidly as he tucked his hands underneath his head, pondering on the woman abed behind that thick bed curtain. His mind wandered where it really shouldn't, as he mused on the bedclothing she would be wearing and how her long dark hair would tumble down her back, now that she had it unpinned and unveiled. The very thought of it made his blood rush to his groin. God, but these were indecent and unseemly reflections about a woman who had helped him when he had most needed it. He closed his eyes and swallowed uncomfortably.

'And just remember, I shall be away on the morrow, so you do not have to dispense any further concern regarding my health or well-being. Not to mention my sadly deflated strength.'

'Well, that is a relief.'

'Quite so.' He smiled to himself. 'Well, goodnight, my proud, maidenly wife. Try not to dream of me.'

'I shall endeavour not to, my annoyingly confounding husband.'

Chapter Five

Brida's eyes fluttered opened as she caught a yawn in her outstretched hand. Blinking, she remembered that Thomas Lovent had spent the night in her home and in the same room, but this time without the impediment of being unconscious or grappling with fever. She gulped, recalling being carried back from the square in his huge arms and her rather ridiculous notion that he somehow lacked strength as he did so. Which was as far from the truth as possible, since he had carried her as though she weighed nothing at all, despite his protestations to the contrary. No wonder that the man could so easily laugh at himself. Yet there were few people—even fewer men—whom Brida could recall being able to see themselves, and the world around them, with such mirth and humour.

Was there nothing that he was serious about? Nothing that ever worried or caused him concern? Did he really have no care in the world? She rather doubted that the infuriating man had, and yet... Yet, Thomas Lovent *had* arrived in Kinnerton with a flesh wound, which he was strangely reticent to discuss or explain the manner in which he had acquired it. Instead, he had skillfully averted attention away with more of his usual droll nonsense, which did make her a little inquisitive about him, as questions swirled around her head.

Not that Brida should even remotely be interested in Thomas Lovent, in any conceivable way. But in truth, she really did not know much about him in any case and had met him only a handful of times three years ago, and then again when he barged into her life just a couple of days ago. In both circumstances, their interaction had always been the same. The same witty, humorous façade.

Yet, there had been a fleeting moment three years ago under the moonlight—a moment so rarefied that she had wondered whether she had imagined it—when he had let his mask slip and there in its stead was a man who was pensive, wistful, if not a little brooding.

Brida sighed, threw off the coverlet and dragged her legs over the bed, then jumped as her feet touched the coldness of the floor. She took a deep breath and ignored the anticipation bubbling in her stomach before pulling back the heavy bed curtain. Her eyes flicked around, observing the empty room, and she felt a sudden disappointment. She frowned. Thomas Lovent had already left and once again before she had risen.

Well, it did not matter. Why should it? Everything had been determined and smoothed over the night before and at least on this occasion the man had left on good terms with her. Not that it signified, of course.

Brida walked to her wooden coffer and completed her morning ablutions with a large bowl of clean water infused with rose petals that she always left for the following morn. She quickly changed her clothing and combed and dressed her long dark hair before rubbing her forehead. Just then the brass handle of the wooden door turned and in walked Thomas. She spun around and blinked, meeting his gaze.

'Good morrow, mistress. I come bearing provisions before I depart. There are warm wheaten rolls of bread and…' His eyes narrowed. 'Is everything well, Brida?'

'No—I mean, yes, of course, sir.' She shifted from one foot to another. 'Why shouldn't it be?'

He raised his brows. 'Why indeed? Here, take these and we can break our fast together.'

'My thanks,' She turned to calm her errant senses by attempting to be useful. She fetched some plates and lay them on her small table in the corner of the chamber. Her fingers brushed against his as he passed her the basket of food. 'I thought you had left.'

'Ah, now I believe I can understand your look of anguish.' He smirked, shaking his head. 'I could not leave without bidding farewell to you.'

'You did once before.' She flushed, knowing that she had not meant to disclose that. God, her hastiness and her terrible habit of speaking before thinking—it would one day be her undoing, as her mother had once chided when she was a little girl.

'Did I?' He smiled, a flicker of amusement in his green eyes. 'How remiss of me.'

The man knew perfectly well the time she was alluding to. Yet if she were to apologise for the hurtful words she had uttered on the eve of Ralph and Gwen's wedding after their kiss, this was her opportunity.

'Yes, but in truth, Sir Thomas, there is something I have wished to say to you about that regrettable night, three years ago.' She rubbed her fingers together, before she looked up and met his eyes. 'I had wanted to apologise for the dreadful things I said to you that eventide, all this time, but never had the chance to. It was unpardonable behaviour.'

'Please, mistress…' he waved his hand dismissively '…think nothing of it. I have had worse insults hurled in my direction. Besides, it was a long while ago and I have given it little thought myself.'

And since then, he had not returned to this part of the country. 'In any case, I am glad that I have now had the chance to remedy that and offer my apologies. Will you take them?'

His brows furrowed in the middle as he pinned her with his intense gaze. An emotion that she could not quite fathom flashed in his eyes before he blinked and whatever had been there dispersed and faded.

'Yes, Brida. I will,' he muttered. 'And in return, I would like to thank you for what you did for me here these past few days. I am not sure what would have happened had I not received your ministrations.'

She shrugged. 'It seemed that you proved useful in the end as everyone in Kinnerton now believes you to be my husband, which works rather well for me.'

'I am glad to have been of use,' he said softly, the glimmer of amusement fading, replaced by something Brida did not want to acknowledge.

'Good.' She held out her hand, wanting to diffuse the tension. 'We can part as friends?'

He looked at her outstretched hand for a moment before clasping it tentatively. 'We can.'

The chamber descended into silence as they tore away their gaze and looked with surprise at their entwined hands. The very air stilled as the tension in the room heightened. Slowly, very slowly, he pulled her gently by her hand until they were close. So much closer than before. She stared straight ahead at his taut chest muscles as they rose and fell and willed herself not to look up at him. It would be too much. She might see something in his face that she did not want to know was there. Brida took a step back and pulled away, her hands falling by her side now.

'Well, I am glad for that, Sir Thomas.' She swallowed, pasting a bland smile. 'And all the time you spent here we managed somehow not to kill each other.'

'Quite so. Although I am sure it was a close thing at times, mistress.'

Brida looked up to find that he seemed just as keen to forget the strange interlude moments ago, as if nothing had passed between them. Thank goodness. It was quite a relief to recommence as before. Besides, the man would soon be gone and would no longer need any consideration.

'Can I tempt you with a roll?' He leant against her table and offered her the soft warm roll of bread that he'd drizzled with honey. 'And do not worry, mistress. Your secret is quite safe with me.'

'My secret?' She raised a brow. 'And I suppose that you believe you have uncovered that?'

'Come, you can admit it, Brida. You can admit that you would miss me once I leave here.' He winked at her, taking a bite from his roll.

For once, Brida felt grateful for his flippant levity. It gave her a little time to gather her senses, while easing them back into their usual sparring. Something they both knew how to navigate well.

'Oh, yes,' she said taking a bite of the roll that he'd

offered to her. 'I shall miss you as much as a plague of frogs, flies, locusts or any other type of pestilence.'

'Why, Brida—' he smirked before clasping his chest '—I did not know you cared.'

'I don't.'

'By and by, I was also referring to another secret, or should I say an unforeseen talent, that I never would have presumed about you.' He nodded at her lute perched against the wall in the furthest corner of the chamber, hidden away from prying eyes. An area no one usually ever noticed.

'That is really nothing of interest. The instrument belonged to my father.' Brida hoped this short explanation would suffice and bring about an end to the conversation. But then again this was Thomas Lovent before her. A man who was good at probing and enquiring into matters that did not concern him.

'On the contrary, it is extremely interesting. And exquisite, I may add.' He tilted his head as he watched her. 'So, you do not play?'

'I do…or rather I did a long time ago, back home in Éire.'

Brida felt a little uneasy disclosing something personal and intimate about herself, not that this was much anyway. Yet, she still managed to feel a little exposed and uncomfortable. In truth, she never liked talking about herself or about her past to anyone, preferring to forget everything that had happened a lifetime ago.

'I must confess that it would have been a pleasure to have heard you play, mistress,' he drawled. 'Even if you have not played for many a year.'

'I no longer play.' She poured ale into two mugs and pressed one into his hand.

'Thank you.' He took a sip before continuing. 'That is a great shame and something I never knew about you.'

'There are many things you do not know about me and, quite frankly, some are best kept hidden, Sir Thomas.'

'Is that's so?'

Before Brida could respond, Cerwen burst in through the front door, trying to catch her breath as she attempted to speak. 'Quick, you must be away.'

'What is it?' Brida jolted forward. 'What is the matter, Cerwen?'

'There are men come to Kinnerton looking for you, Tom.' She rubbed her forehead and shook her head. 'And they do not look very friendly.'

All at once Thomas Lovent sprang into action, with every look of amusement and humour wiped away and replaced by something far more serious and alert.

'It is too late for me to leave now. I cannot give them the opportunity to hunt me down, as they did before.' He prowled around the room as the two women looked on. 'Cerwen, go back to your home and behave in the manner you usually do. Brida, I would advise the same to you. You must both act as naturally as possible. Let us pray that no one will say anything about my convalescence here for the last few days. I would not like to bring danger to any of you.'

'You have not, although, I hope no one will mention your name, your connection here and your recent arrival.' Brida frowned.

'No one in the village shall, but I cannot say the same for anyone in the castle itself. I'd best leave.' The older woman swung on her heel and turned to leave as Brida gave Thomas a knowing look.

'I think it best you hide, just in case these men come looking here.'

'Yes.' His brows furrowed in the middle before he looked up and gave her a faint smile. 'After all, I do have a lot of practice hiding from errant, cuckolded husbands.'

She glared at him as he moved around the room with an agility of a cat, settling on a hiding place. Only Thomas Lovent would feel it appropriate to jest at a time like this.

Tom exhaled slowly, trying to keep his breathing even as he hid beneath Brida's bed. Waiting. It had been ill advised and extremely risky remaining here in Kinnerton and, in his desire to help Brida O'Conaill in return for the care she had given him when he was first here, he had inadvertently made things far worse. God's breath, but look where his efforts had led—bringing peril to her very door.

He suddenly heard it. The muffled voices from somewhere outside getting closer. A gust of cold air blew in, making the rushes on the floor rustle and scatter as the front door was swung open and two, mayhap three men stepped inside. All Tom could see, as he peered from under the small confined space when he slowly lifted the bed curtain a fraction, were the booted feet of these men. Their low, hard voices reverberated around the chamber as they questioned Brida.

Hell's teeth, what a tangle this situation had become.

And in many more ways than one. He had believed that he'd lost these blasted men who had trailed him from London. Yet here they inevitably were, like a persistent rash that he could not quite shift. Tom had hoped that once they had struck and wounded him with a dagger, they would have turned back, believing that they had achieved what they had set out to do. But then again, without his rotting corpse lying in a ditch somewhere they would have kept searching. He had always known that there was a strong possibility of these men continuing to look for him, but had ignored it. Damn. He'd foolishly believed that he had more time.

Yet all he had achieved was to misjudge the situation, bringing nothing but danger. Again. This time by dragging an innocent woman into the fray as well. A woman who he had almost lost his head over and taken in his arms only moments ago. And all because she had apologised to him about what had happened three years ago, when she had kissed and then slighted him. A woman who, he had discovered, owned a beautifully crafted and incredibly rare instrument that by her own admission she used to play. Oh, yes, she was indeed a woman who intrigued him far more than she should.

What the hell was wrong with him? Why did he always manage to misstep around Brida O'Conaill?

'So, mistress, you say that you do not know Thomas Lovent very well,' one of the men asked.

'No, I do not. I met him three years ago at Lord and Lady de Kinnerton's wedding.'

'And yet you by all accounts tended to this man when he came here wounded and with fever?'

'I did, sir. As I said, I knew him to be a friend of Ralph, Lord de Kinnerton, and as such gave him the aid and respect that would be expected for a man of his station.'

'I see. Then can you explain why many here believe

Thomas Lovent—a wanted criminal, a murderer, no less—to be your husband?'

Tom heard her gasp. 'I… I had no knowledge of him being so, sir. No one in Kinnerton had, otherwise we would have notified the authorities immediately.'

'You have not answered why the people in this village believe you to be married to this man?'

'It must have been an assumption they made, possibly because he convalesced here. Besides, Thomas and I had an understanding of sort.'

What in God's name was she saying?

'Oh, what kind of understanding?' The man's voice softened a little.

'The usual sort, sir,' she said with a slight huskiness. 'But the man is a liar, a cheat, who treats me with disrespect after everything I have done for him. We argued as we always do, before I told him to leave.'

'What? Lovent has gone?'

'I am afraid so. He left before sunrise and I have no knowledge where he might be heading.'

How easily the lies slipped from her lips and how grateful he was that they did.

'You had better be telling the truth, mistress.' The man spat. 'Because if I discover you are lying, woman…'

'By all means search my home, sir, if you do not believe me.'

God's teeth, what was she doing? Inviting more trouble?

Tom held his breath for a moment before he heard the man say, 'No need, I am sorry to have troubled you, mistress. We shall leave you in peace.'

But just as the men moved to the door, the main

leader spun around again, seemingly to confront Brida again.

'Wait!' He strode back with purpose. 'There's a setting for two here. Two mugs. Two plates of food. Two of everything. Would you care to explain, mistress?'

Tom became alert to their every move as he sensed the men crowding around Brida. He filched his dagger from his belt and crawled closer, assessing what he might need to do to get the woman out of this dangerous predicament of his damn making. Just when he was ready to spring into action the healer, Cerwen, opened the door and walked inside. And then must have stopped abruptly.

'I'm sorry, Brida. I did not know that you had company.'

'No, Cerwen, come in. We can break our fast in just a moment. These men are here to find out about Thomas Lovent and his whereabouts.'

'Who knows where that dreadful rascal has gone, but if he shows his face in Kinnerton again God only knows what I might do to him.'

'Not unless I get to him first,' Brida said in that imperious voice that she used from time to time.

Tom felt a surge of gratitude towards these women who were risking far more than they should for *him*.

'He stole some valuables from me.'

Ah, but mayhap they were pushing it a little far now.

'From me, too,' the older woman added dramatically, her voice becoming more woeful and tragically lamentable. 'And the only precious item I have left of my late mother as well.'

They were definitely taking it too far now.

'Never fear, mistress, we shall find the scoundrel,'

one of the men muttered. 'Shall we leave these women to their peace, Sergeant?'

'Yes,' the main interrogator responded. 'But only after we search this woman's house.'

God's breath! Time to act.

Brida's heart felt as though it were firmly lodged in her mouth as she watched these men, loyal to the Bishop of London, search through her personal belongings. What on earth had Thomas Lovent done? And why had she not questioned him more thoroughly about the way in which he had arrived in Kinnerton? By all accounts he had apparently absconded justice, was now charged with murder and had even plotted against the Crown. Yet here she was, actively aiding the man and dragging the old healer along with her into God knew where.

In truth, however, Brida did not believe a word of it. Thomas Lovent might be many things, but she didn't for one moment believe that he could be responsible for any of the things he was accused of. She might have known the man for the scant few times she had met him, but there was more to him then she had first perceived. He was far more mysterious than she had envisioned. But a conspirator? A murderer? No, that was not possible. She did not know how, but that much she did believe of him.

But what could she do? These men would eventually look beneath the bed and what then? Surely they would discover him there and would also realise that she and Cerwen had lied to them. Then what? Brida felt as though she were losing her grasp on the situation around her and walking into a strange unknown world filled with intrigue and deception. This was all becoming far too dangerous and risky for her. And where it might lead, Brida did not know, which made her feel very uneasy and apprehensive.

'What is in that chest, mistress?' one of the men asked.

'A few items of my personal possessions.' She shrugged, hoping that she exuded an air of nonchalance. 'That is all.'

'If that is the case, then why is it locked?'

'For that very reason, sir,' she retorted. 'But I can open it, if you wish to inspect its contents.'

'I do. So, if you please, unlock it, mistress.'

Brida's fingers shook as she grappled with the lock, while glancing from the corner of her eye at one of the men. He had moved to the side of the bed and was checking the pallet by pushing down on it.

'Hurry along, woman, we haven't got all day.'

'I apologise, sir, for I have the wrong key. Here it is,' she mumbled, keeping an eye on the man surveying the pallet. 'Ah, here, it's open. Please, you are welcome to look,' she said as she darted a look at the other man who had now knelt on his knee and was looking beneath the bed.

Oh, Mary, mother of God!

Brida's breath caught in her throat as she closed her eyes, knowing that they had failed. Thomas Lovent would soon be found under her bed. Her heart was pounding so quickly in her chest that she felt she might actually swoon.

She dared not think what these men would do to him. And with Lord Kinnerton away, Thomas had no one who would stand by him, in his hour of need.

'Sir, you might want to see this.' The man nodded at

his superior, who gave him an irritable glance before crouching on the floor. He drew his sword out of its scabbard before thrusting it under the bed haphazardly. But nothing happened and not a sound came from under the bed. The man then rose and brushed his hands on his cape before addressing Brida.

'It seems, mistress, that you have a problem.'

'Yes?' She could barely breathe as the man narrowed his eyes at her.

'Your pallet is broken, mistress. The woven rushes are strewn everywhere.'

They were not, however. Not before Thomas Lovent had hidden there.

She had to think quickly, in the hope that they would cease searching there. 'Yes, I know. It is something I have been meaning to repair.'

'Make sure that you do. It cannot be easy sleeping on something so uncomfortable.'

'You are quite right, sir. It is most uncomfortable in its current state.'

The man made a single nod. 'We have importuned you long enough. Thank you for being so accommodating.'

'I am glad to be of help, sir,' she said, pasting a polite smile on her face. 'And I hope you catch Thomas Lovent soon.'

'Believe me, we shall, mistress. We will look everywhere for that criminal. He cannot have got very far.'

Chapter Six

They had all waited, not trusting themselves to speak until they heard the footsteps of Bishop of London's men become more and more faint and distant. Until then Brida felt as though she had been holding her breath with trepidation, rubbing her clammy hands together in a silent prayer. She was confused as to why those men had not discovered Thomas Lovent hiding under her bed, but decided to pause before investigating further. After staring at the door for a moment longer, she quickly snapped her head around and dropped to her knees to peer beneath the bed.

'You may come out from under there, Thomas.'

'Ah, thank God. At long last,' a faint mumbled voice came. 'It's exceedingly difficult to breathe in here.'

She blinked, unable to see anything apart from the mass of loosened rushes from the bed. 'Where are you? I cannot make you out.'

Suddenly, without notice, there was a big thud as Thomas Lovent fell from somewhere inside the pallet.

Oh, thank the heavens.

Brida could not help but admire his ingenuity at cutting away the mattress made from woven rushes and then hiding within, while loose rushes scattered on the floor, giving the impression of a faulty bed.

'You cut my bed up,' she said as he got to his feet, brushing dust and loose strands of rushes off his person.

'I promise I shall get you a new bed, once I get out of this mess.'

'Once you both get out of this mess,' Cerwen muttered as she shook her head. 'Listen to me, Brida, as there is very little time, but you must make haste and leave with Tom.'

Brida flushed as she shook her head. 'I cannot do that.'

'You must. If those men suspect you in any way and learn that you have misled and lied to them, then you face imminent danger. And with no one here who could protect you?'

'But I am needed here,' she whispered, not wanting to take in the severity of the situation.

'No, you are not.' Cerwen started to collect a few provisions from the table. 'You must make haste and pack a few essentials, dear. What if anyone blabbers about the celebrations last night, or that Tom is indeed your husband, despite what you just said to those men?'

But he is not really my husband! Brida wanted to scream at her. Oh, God, what a tangle she had caught herself in.

'I am afraid Cerwen is right, Brida,' Thomas Lovent said with a sudden urgency. 'You cannot stay as it is not safe. I can take you with me as far as Wales. And once there you may return with Lord and Lady Kinnerton.'

She turned to the older woman. 'What about you, Cerwen? You might be in just as much danger as me.'

'Never you mind about me. I have my own ways to protect myself. You, on the other hand, are a young woman, Brida, and have always drawn attention to yourself without ever meaning to, even being married and everything. But with Lord de Kinnerton away, you would have no protection if you remain here.'

Brida wanted to resist this, knowing it would not be prudent to be in close company with this man, but what other choices did she have? She knew that what has been said was true and that it was imperative for her to follow their advice.

She closed her eyes in resignation. 'Very well,' she muttered on a sigh. 'I shall come with you.'

'Good, now listen, both of you.' Cerwen frowned, the lines on her forehead deep and troubled. 'Get yourselves to the woods, near the woodman's cottage, Brida, by the narrowest part of the stream there.'

'I know where you mean.'

'I have managed to get two horses for your journey, which should be tethered somewhere there. But make haste, they shall be waiting. You must leave as soon as may be.'

Brida frowned at how quickly everything was happening. 'How could you know what to do at such short notice?'

'The moment those men stepped into this village your safety was in doubt. And knowing that the only way to ensure it would be for you to leave with Tom, I made these hasty plans on your behalf.'

'And we're beholden to you, Cerwen. You have my thanks.' Thomas clasped the older woman's hand and pressed a quick kiss on the back of it. 'How can I ever repay you for all that you have done?'

'It's nothing.' The old woman squeezed his hands in hers. 'But look after her, Tom.'

He made a single nod. 'With my life.'

Dusk had descended before they finally scurried out of Brida's home, having packed a few items for the relatively short journey to Carreghofa Castle on the Welsh border, where the English and Welsh courts had convened. They left the village, not through the square where they might stand out and arouse suspicion, but through deserted paths that were seldom used, concealed under the guise of an ordinary man travelling with a young servant. They had taken care to hide every vestige of Thomas Lovent being a knight, so that he might appear to be a little more inconspicuous. Hiding behind walls and around corners, they darted from one place to the next until they eventually scrambled out along the path that led to the nearby woods. They made their way in the direction that Cerwen had given, taking care that they had not been followed.

'Hurry, this way to the woodman's cottage,' she muttered, breaking the long silence that had existed ever since they had left the sanctity of her home. Which, thanks to Thomas Lovent and her own stupidity, was no longer her safe haven. Not that travelling with the man was any safer for more reasons than one, but Brida had limited choices presently and travelling to meet Gwen and Ralph had been the best they could come up with, at such short notice.

She felt him stilling her by the elbow. 'Allow me to say how sorry I am to have you embroiled in my troubles, Brida. It was never my intention for this to happen.'

'I know, but it might have been useful had you explained that you were a wanted man. All this might have been avoidable and you could have left as soon as you regained your strength.'

'Yes. I should have.' She noticed his jaw was clenched tightly and his eyes were without his usual spark of humour. 'I became complacent and believed that I had lost those men. In truth, I believed I had more time than I actually had.'

Brida had never seen Thomas speak with forthright honesty. It almost made her wonder so much more about him and whether she even knew this man at all.

'Never mind, sir. We'd better make haste, in case those men realise that you have only recently left Kinnerton and catch us up.'

It was quiet and thankfully no one had ventured to this part of the woods.

She pulled down a branch and pushed through as the path narrowed with the lush coppices and thickets on either side and Thomas following behind her.

This opened out to a running stream and there, on the other side, were two young horses tethered to a tree, with Cerwen's grandson waiting beside them. Her old friend had surpassed herself in the aid she had given them so that they could gain safe passage out of Kinnerton.

Once more Brida questioned the decision she had made in leaving with Thomas Lovent and felt a ripple of nervous tension run down her body. She hoped it was purely down to nerves, otherwise she might find herself in more trouble than she had bargained for.

'Here, give me your hand, Brida.' Thomas held out his hand, in an attempt to give her aid across the slippery stepping stones.

'I can manage, thank you,' she said as she tentatively stepped out on to the stones.

'Are you angry with me, mistress?' The corner of his mouth twitched a little as it curved, making her want to push him into the stream.

'Can you honestly blame me?'

His half-smile faded as he shook his head. 'No. You have every right to be. And if it makes you feel better, I am furious with myself for being so careless. Please believe me when I say that I do not usually behave in such a capricious, reckless manner.'

'Rest easy, sir. We all make mistakes.'

'True, and I have been making far too many recently.' He followed her from behind as they crossed the stream. 'I must also thank you for not exposing me back there. I hope that you might have faith that I am innocent of the charges I am accused of?'

'I do.' She sighed as she jumped off the other end. 'You may be reprehensible in so, so many ways, Sir Thomas, but a murderer? Plotting against the Crown? No, that I cannot believe.'

'I'm glad to have your support, at least.' He nodded in gratitude. 'And do you not think that we should drop formalities now? We are man and wife after all.'

'How could I forget?' A faint smile played on her lips.

He helped her mount the smaller palfrey, sending a rush of heat where his large hands had flexed around her waist. She looked away, hoping he hadn't noticed as he saw to his own mount. 'Indeed. So please call me Thomas or, better still, Tom.'

'Very well, *Tom,* on one condition.' She turned her

head back around to meet his perceptive gaze. 'Tell me, why are you a wanted man?'

Tom grabbed the reins and proceeded to canter along the path, biting back a groan. He knew this would happen. He knew that someone as intelligent and inquisitive as Brida O'Conaill would eventually want to know far more about what she had witnessed earlier to understand the predicament they had now found themselves in. It was bad enough that he had heedlessly involved the woman into this unmitigated mess with the subsequent guilt that followed. But it also questioned the wisdom of his decision that she accompany him to Wales. Yet Tom was adamant that this was the only way to ensure Brida's safety. After all, she had deceived the men on his trail, who could have at any moment returned to interrogate her further—and not so nicely—had she stayed.

He needed to entrust her to the care and protection of Ralph de Kinnerton and his wife, then he would be able to acquit himself of her responsibility. Something which he had not wanted. And that was what made this all so damn difficult for him. The thought of having the responsibility for another's welfare and care, least of all *this* woman, foisted on him made him uneasy and apprehensive.

Indeed, it terrified him, should he fail as he had done in the past, when his honour and duty were put to the test, leaving only devastation, tragedy and heartache in its wake. God, he could remember it still, on that sickening day when he had arrived too late to find the charred, burnt remains of his family manor home. His younger sister, Joan, the sole survivor of the raging fire that had claimed everyone and everything, including his parents, their retainers and the rest of his younger siblings. And all because Tom had not been there to stop his father in one of his drunk stupors, who had not been aware of what he had unwittingly unleashed. His stomach churned in a knotted coil just recollecting that harrowing time, over ten years ago.

He blinked away the memories, turning his head instead to study his companion on this journey. Brida wanted to know something of why he was being pursued. But could he trust her enough to tell her the truth about the nature of his work? He found it difficult revealing anything of consequence regarding himself at the best of times, but this was a different matter altogether. It might be prudent for her to know a little of his life, now that they were forced to spend more time than either of them would have liked on this short journey. And much as he liked Brida O'Conaill, finding her intriguing and immeasurably alluring, he would have preferred that they had not been foisted on one another. It was not something either of them had wanted and he was a man used to being alone in any case.

'Are you going to explain any of what happened back there in Kinnerton?' she tried asking again.

'It is not that interesting, Brida,' he said with a sigh.

'I rather doubt that. I am sure the reason why those men followed you all the way to Kinnerton is as gripping as I imagine it to be. Tell me…if you can.'

'The truth is…' he exhaled through his teeth '…that I witnessed a murder in the undercroft of Westminster Abbey. And since the man bled to death in my arms, with no one else in the vicinity, I became the main, or rather the *only*, suspect to have committed the crime.'

That and the fact that Tom had not waited to explain himself and had fled, knowing that he could not trust anyone.

'That's dreadful,' she muttered softly. 'The poor man. Did you know who he was?'

'No, I'm afraid I did not get a chance to make his acquaintance.'

'But why would you happen to be there? Why were you in the undercroft of Westminster Abbey in the first place?'

There was nothing like getting straight to the heart of the matter.

'It is a good question. Let us say that I was there to meet someone, but in reality I had actually been lured there under false pretences.' He gave his rein a quick flick, making his horse speed up a little. They rode side by side as the narrow path through the woods opened out to wide craggy hills and valleys beyond. He hoped that this would somehow be the end of this conversation as it was making him feel a little uneasy.

She turned her head and narrowed her gaze. 'And so, when you were caught in the undercroft of the Abbey, you ran?'

'Yes, or rather I rode—hard and fast.'

'All the way here to Kinnerton?'

'Indeed.'

'From London?'

He gave her an exasperated sigh as he scratched his head, wondering how much he could readily explain and how much he needed to hold back further. 'Ralph is my oldest friend, Brida, and, to own the truth, I needed his counsel.'

'And there was no one else who might have provided

you with the necessary counsel as well offer a place where you might easily conceal yourself? Somewhere closer to London mayhap?'

Damn, but the woman was perceptive.

'Tom?'

As well as emphatic in her incessant probing.

'Apart from Lords Tallany and de Clancey—Hugh de Villiers and Will Geraint—Ralph is the only man I could trust with this.' Especially since Kinnerton was on the Marcher lands, Ralph was also strategically the closest to where Tom needed to go—Llewelyn's Court in Wales. But Brida O'Conaill did not need to know this.

'So, you were saying that these men followed you from London?'

'Yes.'

'To charge you with a murder that you did not commit?'

'Precisely.'

'And in a passing skirmish, they managed to wound you?'

'There.' His jaw clenched. 'You now know everything that occurred.'

'Do I?' She threw a suspicious glance in his direction. 'Because I must say that there seems to be far more that you are not disclosing about this than you actually are.'

'Come, now. That is ridiculous, Brida. It's your imagination running away from you here.'

'I am sure it's not.'

'What happened in there was simply a misapprehension.' He dragged his hand across his jaw. 'I was simply at the wrong place at the wrong time.'

'I see. You were somehow lured by some unknown assailant into the undercroft of the Abbey.'

He snapped his head in her direction. 'Yes.'

'May I ask why were you lured there in the first place?'

'You may, Brida but I might be inclined not to answer.'

She looked at him from the corner of her eye, seemingly waiting for his explanation. He did not offer one, not that he could anyway, but by God she was single-minded.

'Well, one thing is for certain. You are far more mysterious than I could ever have given you credit for, Tom.'

'What a fanciful notion.' He glanced around in every direction, making sure that no one was following them before frowning at her. 'And I'm really not sure to what you refer.'

'Do you not? With all your secrecy, I wonder whether I had ever known you at all.'

Well now, how to answer. On the one hand there was the other, more ruthless side of his personality, which was essential in the work he did for the Crown and not something he could easily reveal.

But then there was the more private, serious, contemplative side of his character that Tom hid behind the jovial façade, which was not something he particularly wanted to share with anyone. Especially as it would force him into the darkness that shrouded his past. Where the constant reminder of his failures to his family—the obligation he owed them—would always be there, mocking him. Oh, yes, his mistakes, followed swiftly by the bitter regrets, hung around his neck, almost choking him. He did everything he could to forget it all. And with the dangerous work that consumed all of his time, he usually succeeded in never having to face his past. With the exception of his sister and her near blindness being the only reminder of that damn awful time.

He looked up and noticed that Brida was frowning, watching him intently, and forced himself to smile at her.

'Of course we know one another.' He winked. 'But I would prefer if we ceased this topic of conversation.'

'Very well. But I know that there is far more than what you have disclosed regarding what happened.' For once he did not want to respond. And Brida could no doubt sense the change in him from his stiff demeanour. The teasing smile vanished from her face as she pushed ahead through the dense wood. She spoke again. This time far more softly. 'I hope that you will come to trust and confide in me, Tom. You may find it somehow beneficial. Indeed, I have been told that I am a good listener.'

He inhaled the crisp cool air before responding. 'I am sure you are, Brida, and if there is anything that I ever need to divulge, I shall keep you in mind.'

'I am glad to hear it.'

'Come, let's be away from here. There is a storm brewing and I would rather we weren't caught in it.'

Chapter Seven

The gathering storm did eventually come, breaking through the expanse of ominous grey, with its rumbling bluster and gleam of light flashing across the caliginous sky. In its wake came the deluge of relentless rain and wind, making visibility incredibly difficult. In fact, it was impossible to continue riding.

'What are we to do?' Brida cried over the clamouring din of the elements.

'We cannot continue in this. The ground has turned to sludge and it's too slippery to risk these animals. Not to mention risking ourselves,' Tom shouted, gripping the reins tightly in the vain hope that it might calm the skittish horse. 'We will have to find shelter and soon.'

'I know somewhere nearby where we might be able to do that.' She pointed above the hilly terrain in the distance. 'There are cavernous areas up there that we use on occasion for feast days.'

'I'm not sure, Brida. It's precarious attempting to ride up that hill in this weather,' he bellowed, barely able to see her in the downpour. The ferocity of the rain was blistering his skin.

'It's the only place I can think of.'

He looked around in the hope that there might be a better solution that would present itself, but there wasn't. Not that he could see anything in this bleak torrent.

'Very well, but we'll climb the hill and lead the horses on foot.'

'Yes. Good idea.'

They dismounted and gradually made their way up the slippery, craggy hill. God, but every step was arduous. Pulling the reins of animals that didn't want to budge and were becoming increasingly anxious was demanding in these harsh conditions. He glanced at Brida to ascertain that she was not being overwhelmed by her palfrey, but naturally she coped admirably under the circumstances. She was soothing her horse and seemed to be as assured as always, without the need for any help. But he decided to offer it anyway.

'Let me have the reins to your horse, Brida.'

'My thanks, but I can manage,' she ground out, just as Tom somehow knew she would.

He wondered, not for the first time, whether she always had to just *manage*. Whether there had ever been that person whom she could rely on and allow to take on some of life's heavy burden. Or was it that Brida O'Conaill did not need anyone to take care of her or hadn't had to care for anyone other than herself? After all, she had remained unmarried, seemingly down to the choices she had made. Even if she had insisted on their preposterous fake marriage as a way to give credence to a fabricated story she had no doubt woven. Nevertheless, Tom could not help but be intrigued by her—and her solitary existence. Not all that dissimilar to his, if he were honest. Yet there was something about the woman that had piqued his interest. Something about her that he could only marvel at. Whether it was her determination, her quick intelligence or her witty, caustic rejoinders, Brida was bound in some sort of mystery, which he would happily unravel.

'Very well, but let me know if you need any help or assistance.'

She nodded her thanks as he turned back and continued trudging up the hill.

Their jumpy horses panted and skidded a few times, needing to be calmed and soothed before they made their way to the wide cliffside and into the mouth of the vast cave. They entered the dark, dank hollow and found a jagged slab of rock to tether the horses. Relief flooded his senses, grateful that they had managed to reach this forbidding cleft. The cave might be cool and damp, but it nevertheless provided the shelter they needed for the night.

He turned and blinked several times as he stared at Brida standing before him. Even though it was dark and he could hardly make her out, Tom could still somehow see her. She was soaked from head to toe, the male garments she wore clinging to every curve of her luscious body. Her hair was dripping wet with droplets of water hanging from the ends and hitting the ground intermittently. God, but even in this dimmed light, she was lovely.

'You are cold.'

'I am,' she muttered, beginning to shiver, her teeth chattering.

What an asinine observation to make. Naturally she was cold and wet. As was he, yet he could feel the highly inappropriate rush of blood coursing through his veins, with every part of his body hardening and attuned to her very nearness. He suddenly wanted to capture the scent of her, to touch and feel the silky-smooth softness of her skin against his own.

He licked his dry lips and cursed. What the hell was wrong with him? Was he so dissolute that he would have such base, licentious thoughts about this woman at a time like this? But then again, the interaction between them was beginning to shift and change. He did not like it. Not one bit.

The longer he spent in Brida O'Conaill's company, the more he liked her and the more invested he became in *her*. Only earlier she had invited him to confide in her—a nonsensical notion and not something he could readily do. Tom had never wanted or needed to get close to a woman before. And he certainly did not need to disclose the sad truth about his past or the important covert work he was now involved in.

This had all been his fault. If he had never barged back into her life, if he had not been wounded and made to convalesce at that damnable village, if he had not pretended to be her husband, if he hadn't been so damn careless. If…

If only they would fall back into their usual rapport with his flippant teasing and her withering scolds. The familiarity and easiness of it would be more desirable, as well as being a hell of a lot safer. It would be far better for his peace of mind. He would welcome that over any form of attachment. No, that he would never invite.

'Come.' He frowned, annoyed with himself. 'You must get out of those wet clothes.'

'*What?*' She watched him with shock, her jaw seemingly dropping. 'I cannot do that,' she hissed. 'Everything I have is wet.'

Meaning that she had nothing else to wear. Ah, not the predicament he had envisaged.

'You must, Brida. You are soaked through.'

'As are you, Tom.'

'This is no time for you to be coy,' he muttered, trying to hang on to his patience. 'You need to get out of those wet clothes and dry them as soon as may be.' He unbuttoned his gambeson and shrugged his arms out of it as Brida stared in horror at him.

'What in heaven's name are you doing?'

'Precisely what I advised you to do.' He pulled his sodden tunic over his head and threw it down. 'I'm getting out of these wet clothes.'

'But…but you cannot undress,' she fairly squealed. 'It is not seemly.'

'I am sorry to shock those maidenly sensibilities of yours, but it's either this or the possibility of sickness and fever. And I for one have had my fair share of that recently, Brida.'

'Surely we can try to ignite a fire to warm our bones and to dry out our wet clothing, without the need to remove them?'

He shook his head. 'We have to act more expediently than that. I shall see about some drier clothing, but you must peel away all the sodden ones you're wearing.'

Noticing her reticence, he could not help but smile.

'Come now, it's nothing you haven't seen before.' He winked at her, his mouth twitching at the corners. This was what he had been missing. This was what was familiar to him about his interplay with Brida and he was in no mind to change it. 'Don't pretend that you did not sneak a look under that coverlet of yours, after you had divested me of all my clothing when I lay at death's door in Kinnerton.'

He watched in rapt fascination as her colour no doubt heightened. She spun around, with her back to him.

'I certainly did not.' Her voice was clipped with indignation. 'And you know perfectly well that Cerwen did...all that was necessary. I had no part in any of *that*.'

'Either way, spare your blushes. My nakedness is not something that should readily shock you.' He pulled a clean and thankfully dry tunic from one of the saddlebags and dangled it over her head. 'Here, you can wear this. You can move further into the cave, around that corner for some privacy, and remove your wet clothes. Do it now, if you please, as this is also very necessary.'

He pulled another drier tunic out of his saddlebag for himself and quickly put this on and found a pair of hose that had a couple of wet patches, but was otherwise dry. His next task was to make a fire using the essential kindling he had brought with them. Although how he was supposed to accomplish the task when everything was mostly wet was another matter. At least it gave him something to do rather than ponder on the soon-to-be scantily clad female he happened to be travelling with. As much as Brida intrigued, fascinated and, God above, attracted him, it was imperative to keep things between them the same as always. Personable, friendly with a little teasing now and then. But nothing more.

Brida let out a shaky breath as she moved further into the hollow darkness of the cave, feeling the rough jagged edges of the cave with the tips of her fingers and began to do as Tom had bid her. After ensuring that she would be unseen, she began removing all of the wet garments that had pasted themselves to her person. She pulled the tunic he had given her—*his tunic*—over her head, and shivered as she pushed her arms through each long sleeve.

The garment was much too long and far too big for her, and slid over her damp, cold body, stopping above her knees, but at least it offered a little warmth. She picked up her wet clothing and retraced her steps, making her way to Tom, who was busying himself with making a fire.

At the sound of her footsteps, he turned his head and gave her a faint smile. But he seemed guarded, a little on edge, his countenance rigid and serious. It was as almost as if this man was different to the one she believed she knew. But then this had been a very trying day and night. He was no doubt as weary as she was.

'Come, Brida, and sit here.' He beckoned. 'I should have the fire going in a moment.'

'Thank you. I see you have made a good start already.' She perched down on the cold uneven ground, tucking her bare legs beneath her and tugging at the hem of the tunic, conscious of her lack of clothing.

'We should hopefully get some warmth in our bodies, soon enough,' he muttered, without glancing in her direction.

She nodded before dropping her chin to rest on her raised knees, feeling decidedly awkward. It was absurd to be this aware of Thomas Lovent—after all, the man had only recently spent three days and nights at her home in Kinnerton. But never quite like this. And never did Brida feel so exposed and a little vulnerable—alone with him in a cave, in the middle of nowhere, with scant clothing on, feeling cold, wet and dejected with the rain thrashing outside. Not that she did not trust herself with Tom. He was someone who had honour and integrity coursing through his veins, yet she had not imagined the heated look in his eyes when they had first stepped inside the cave, to be quickly masked over. A look that she had felt to her very toes.

'You are quiet, Brida.'

'As are you.'

'I suppose this was not the most ideal way to commence a journey such as this.'

'Yet, considering our hasty departure, it was the best we could have hoped for.'

'Except for the damn weather.'

She smiled. 'Except that.'

He ambled towards the horses, gliding his hand down their muzzles to settle them before retrieving a few supplies from his saddlebag.

'We should eat,' he said as he passed a few packages that had been wrapped in many layers of linen. 'It's all a little soggy, I'm afraid.'

'No matter. I'm famished.' She unwrapped the parcels containing rounds of cheese, bread, slices of ham and a couple of apples and offered Tom a plate.

He took a bite of food as he splashed some ale from his flagon into two wooden mugs and handed her one. She nodded her gratitude as they continued to eat and drink in silence. After finishing, Tom brushed the last crumbs off his fingers before breaking the silence.

'Thank you again. For trusting me and believing in my innocence.'

'As I said earlier, you may be many, many unscrupulous things, Tom, but I could never believe any of the charges levelled at you.' She threw back her ale, enjoying the warmth it provided. 'That is, unless I have been extremely misled somehow and now find myself alone with a murderer. May I have some more ale?'

He poured some more into her mug and lifted his head. 'That would be unfortunate. But lucky for you, I am just a wanted man in a godforsaken cave near the Welsh border.'

'Yes.' She raised a brow, not quite able to decide whether this was a blessing or not, as it was still *this* man she was stuck with. A man who made her feel many things she really shouldn't. 'How are we going to cross the border without alerting attention?'

'Are you suggesting that our quickly assembled disguise might somehow be lacking?' he asked wryly.

She tried again. 'You must have thought of the predicament we might face?'

'I have and the solution might be in concealment.' He yawned and stretched his arms out over his head. 'But do not worry, Brida. Once an opportunity presents itself, we shall seize it.'

'Do you not think that might be a little reckless, not to mention being somewhat impulsive?'

He laughed. 'No, some of my best laid plans are the ones that happen spontaneously.'

'But surely that cannot be a reliable method to plan and scheme.' She wrapped her arms around her knees. 'It would be like stabbing in the dark.'

'Not quite. The truth is that you can never control the elements around you or predict the outcome in any given situation because circumstances can change quite unexpectedly. Instead, you must attempt to be prepared and weigh each possibility. Above all, you must rely on skill and fortitude, and trust your instincts.'

'Spoken like a seasoned soldier.'

'Exactly. We can, as you put it, plan and scheme down to the smallest detail, but even the best-laid plans must be adaptable to change.'

'And I suppose your rationale has been successful of late?' She knew she was being intentionally provoking, but probing Tom at this time might gain answers to myriad questions swirling around her head.

'No, not of late. But I'm alive when others would gladly have my corpse on a spike.'

'They have my sympathy.'

'Naturally.' He grinned, winking at her. 'Haven't you heard that I am an unscrupulous rogue?'

'Indeed.' She was glad their discourse had somehow returned to what she was accustomed to. It made her feel a little relieved 'But you must have some idea who might be the real culprit of the murder at Westminster Abbey?'

Brida wondered whether he intended to mollify her with some nonsense and change the topic of conversation or would actually dignify her question with an answer. Eventually he spoke.

'I have a few suspicions, but admittedly not enough. The whole incident was particularly odd and confounding.'

'Have you ever examined whether you were deliberately targeted?' She was once again baffled by his evasiveness regarding being a wanted man. There was much that he seemed to be holding back.

'So that I can be the one to blame?'

'Yes, precisely.' She nodded. 'Which begs the question of whether you just happened on that unfortunate incident. An innocent caught in a web of artifice and duplicity. Or...' She paused momentarily, flicking a brief glance in his direction.

'Or...what, perchance?'

'That you were somehow part of this elaborate contrivance, without ever meaning to be.'

'What a fertile imagination you have.'

She shrugged. 'After all, you did just concede to taking a stab in the dark.'

'You said that, not I.' He frowned. 'And especially not that particular night in the Pyx Chamber of Westminster Abbey.'

'I am sorry.' She made a face. 'That was badly done of me. And I did not mean to imply that you were involved in the poor man's demise.'

'No, because, thanks be to saints, you believe in my innocence.'

'Of course.' She nodded. 'But can you not tell me what you were doing there that night?'

'Brida, Brida, Brida,' he muttered shaking his head. 'I never took you to be *this* relentless.'

'I can be quite determined when I want to be. And you must admit that the whole incident that you describe seems so...so outlandish. Not to mention vexing and extremely perplexing. You said yourself that it was odd and confounding.'

'Just so.' A corner of his mouth lifted slightly.

'Well? Are you going to tell me or would you prefer that I guess what you were doing there that night?'

And just as quickly, his amusement vanished.

'I believe I have already explained that.' He gave her a look that brooked no further discussion regarding how

he'd come to be a wanted man. But something inside her
had become emboldened. It might be the ale or the fact
that they were alone here in this cold and dark cave that
she could not help but enquire a little more.

'Yes, you disclosed that you were *lured there under
false pretences*.' She raised a brow. 'Could you not tell
me why you were lured there and who it was you were
meeting?'

He did not respond.

'I see that you cannot,' she muttered, tapping her
chin. 'In that case, would you mind if I hazard a guess?'

'I'd rather you did not.' His voice held a steeliness
that seemed so unlike him. Yet Brida still did not heed
the warning.

'Let me see, now—you're a seasoned warrior, a man
who now works primarily on his own, a man who trusts
only a handful of men and lives in mystery.' She was
beginning to enjoy her powers of observation, but heavens, had he...had Thomas Lovent just growled at her?
She snapped her head up as their eyes clashed over the
crackling and spitting fire. Oh, dear, she might be enjoying her musings, but he certainly was not.

'Enough,' he muttered quietly, his eyes hard and void
of any of his usual warmth.

Brida did not comprehend his reaction. Again, it
amazed her how unlike the Thomas Lovent she knew
he was behaving. It was as though the mask that he hid
behind had slipped a little. And mayhap it was this—
the very fact that she had guessed somewhere close to
the truth.

She knew that for some reason it was difficult for
him to discuss this, but she did not want to be the cause
of his discomfort. Before she knew what she was about

to do, she reached over and placed her hand on his shoulder. And everything around her stilled. Her breath caught as this ordinary, yet friendly touch somehow evoked a strange unfettered ripple through her whole body that made her shiver. Beneath her fingers she could feel the hard, corded, sinewy muscles of his powerful shoulders tense suddenly.

She quickly removed her hand, as though her skin had been burned. She swallowed uncomfortably, looking away. How mortifying. Had she not just moments ago peered at Thomas Lovent in a state of dishabille and tried to dismiss the image of him in all his glory, clad in only his skintight hose, from her mind? Indeed, she had. It was futile to have such scandalous recollections regarding this man and she should refrain from touching him again in the future—friendly or otherwise.

She bit her lip and turned her head back to meet his curious gaze. 'I'm sorry, Tom. I just wanted to be of help.'

'It's of no consequence.' He gave her a small smile. 'Mayhap we should get some sleep.'

Chapter Eight

They had resumed their journey at dawn and ridden down the valley and through woods, rather than staying on the main paths, in silence and after only a few short hours of slumber. Not that Tom had had much sleep, having stayed awake to keep watch most of the night. He had reluctantly switched places with Brida briefly, but had returned to do what he was tasked to do—protect them both and ensure that no one had followed them to the caves.

This was nothing new. Having been on many campaigns, he was used to surviving on only a scant few hours of rest, but for some unknown reason he was tired and bone weary following yesterday's travails. And it had mainly to do with the woman he was travelling with. Her blithe words and sentiments, however well meaning, somehow managed to nettle him.

In fact, her incessant need to understand the reasons why he was a wanted man was aggravating. Indeed, it would be grave for Brida to learn more about him: that, as an agent of the Crown, he was actually far more ruthless and cunning than anyone would ever credit him for and only showed that side of himself when he absolutely needed to. After all, the guise of being an affable, irreverent tease had always served him well. No one assumed more of him, except those who knew him better.

However, Tom needed to ascertain now whether Brida should also be allowed to join the few he trusted enough to impart the truth without equivocation. He knew full well that it was more about necessity than anything else.

On the one hand, Tom needed to maintain his alias, feeling far safer hiding behind his dissimulation. He preferred not to have to explain himself to anyone, least of all Brida, who was beginning to see through him, stripping him bare with her curiosity. But on the other hand, Tom recognised that the longer they were together in each other's company, as they would be for the next day or so, the woman would start to piece much of what she understood about him together in any case. Besides, he needed to explain his plans to her and show that they were not as impulsive as she believed them to be.

'I just wanted to be of help,' she had uttered the previous night, shocking him into silence. He did not need her or anyone's help, but nevertheless felt gratified, even begrudgingly, that she had offered it. He could not recollect the last time that someone had thought to be of help to him.

'I believe we should stop here by this brook and allow the horses and ourselves a little respite.'

'Thank you. The opportunity to stretch my legs would be most welcome.'

She looked a little relieved, causing a surge of guilt to rush through him. He really should have thought of her comfort earlier. But then he had been in a hurry to put distance between Kinnerton and the men trailing him.

'Tell me sooner next time and we can break the journey when we can.'

'I shall keep it in mind. Although I am sure you are even keener not to tarry after your sojourn in Kinnerton.'

'Yes.'

Tom realised that this was the first time they had actually spoken more than a handful of words since the previous evening in the cave. An evening that was also difficult not just because of his dilemma regarding whether he should tell the woman more about himself, but for a far more disturbing reason. He had felt the full force of desire rushing through his veins when Brida had sat wearing precious little by the fireside. It was unfortunate. It was unwelcome. But above all it was extremely alarming.

Tom enjoyed teasing and even flirting with the woman. But last night had been different—he had wanted her, much to his shame. He had inadvertently drawn her into his troubles and she'd been forced to flee her home, before riding through horrendous conditions, only for him and his damn lust to be ignited. Hell's teeth, it was unwanted. His only excuse was that he was a foolish red-blooded male who had seen far more of her comely, lush body than he should have. He needed to erase the memory as though it had never happened.

He jumped down from his horse, tethering it to a nearby tree, striding over to help her dismount, but she had already done it herself.

He raised his brows. 'I would have helped you, Brida.'

'My thanks.' She gave him a bland smile. 'I know you are famed for your gallantry, Tom, but I find that I am not in need of your help.'

He smiled faintly at her riposte. She would have to make her point patently clear.

'As is your wont. And I must say that if there is one woman in this realm who can really stand on her own two feet, it is you, Brida O'Conaill.' She inclined her head as he continued. 'Even if you do insist on conjuring up pretend husbands now and then.'

She fetched a blanket to lay on the long grass. 'Yes, it seems you know all about pretending and dissembling, Thomas Lovent.'

'And what, may I ask, are you suggesting?'

'Oh, nothing of consequence.' She fetched more bundles and lay them on the blanket. 'Shall we break our fast?'

'Yes.' He bit into a small, tart apple. His eyes fixed on to her. By God, she was canny, as well as impudent. And once again that inconvenient spark of desire.

Damn and blast.

'Can you tell me something, Tom?' The woman continued to eat without once meeting his gaze. 'Do I have some unfortunate spot of dirt on my face? For that could be the only reason why you are staring at me in that unbecoming manner.'

He shook his head as the corner of his lip curved. 'You are deliberately trying to provoke me, Brida, but you will not succeed.'

'I'm sure I do not know to what you are referring. Indeed, how very irritable you are this morning.' She gave him a benign look. 'Mayhap you could do with some sleep to pull you out of your current mood?'

He crossed his arms over his chest. 'I am not, nor have I ever been, *irritable,* mistress.'

'Of course not,' she said with a flash of a smile that set his teeth on edge. 'But the offer is there should you need more rest.'

'Thank you, but that is not necessary.'

'In that case, I will come straight to what I wish to discuss with you.'

'By all means do. I wait with bated breath.'

She sat very primly, in the clothes she had worn yesterday, now dry, and laced her hands together, as though in benediction.

'Go on, Brida. I can see that there's something you want to say.'

'There is. I have been thinking about your evasiveness regarding the reasons that brought you to Kinnerton and all that has developed since… well, I have given it a lot of thought and I want to tell you that I accept.'

'Pardon?' He frowned. 'What do you accept?'

'Your proposal, of course. On the night of the celebrations in Kinnerton.'

'Brida, Brida, Brida. You misunderstood.' He grinned. 'If memory serves, we only pretended to be married. I never proposed to you, unless I imbibed far more ale that night than I believed.' He scratched his chin.

'Must you always be so vexing?' Her brows furrowed in the middle. 'You know perfectly well that I refer to the bargain you sought to make with me. You told me that you would explain the reason why you came to Kinnerton wounded, if I would explain the reasons I lied about being married, for all these years.'

Well, this was a surprise. He certainly had not expected this uncommon request and he had to admit to be intrigued as he constantly seemed to be with Brida O'Conaill.

'Ah, but you now know the reasons for those wounds,' he replied softly.

'No.' She shook her head. 'I believe that there have been many inconsistencies with your story. In truth, I would like to know as much as you're willing to tell in exchange for the questions you put to me that night.'

He did not need to think about this. 'Very well, ladies first. Please do explain.'

After all, he had only just acceded the need for clarity in their current predicament anyway. Yet, here he was about to gain more about this woman from her own inquisitive lips. And all for nothing. Not that she was aware of these musings.

'If you wouldn't mind, I would rather that you provided your part first.'

He smiled. 'Ever the negotiator, Brida. The Privy Council should bring your skills to their employ.'

'Thank you.'

'Very well. Since you were so kind to reference that I'm a man famed for my gallantry, I should be happy to comply with your wishes.'

'Again, you have my thanks.'

He ran his fingers through his hair. 'The truth is that much of what you alluded to yesterday was quite staggering in its veracity.'

'And would that be the reason for your discomfort?'

'It would.' He inclined his head. 'What I am about to tell you must remain confidential. Just between us.'

She leant forward, her evocative scent curling around him. 'Of course, you may be assured that I would never betray your secret.'

'Very well.' He exhaled through his teeth before continuing. 'How to begin?' He paused for a moment, taking another swig of ale. 'The truth is that I work in the gathering of information for Hubert de Burgh.'

Tom watched as her jaw visibly slacken. 'I beg your pardon, Tom. Did you just disclose what I believe you did?'

'Well, that is hard to answer. What is it that you believed me to say?'

'This is no time for jesting.' She leant forward and bit her lip. 'But tell me... You...you work for Hubert de Burgh?'

'Indeed, I do.'

'In the position of gaining information?' she said slowly, shaking her head in disbelief. 'But it seems so unbelievable.'

He sighed. 'And yet it is the truth. I have been working for my liege lord since I was last in this part of the kingdom, having gained his notice through Lord de Clancey, William Geraint.' He did not add further that his friend had also once worked in a similar capacity as a disgraced knight in exile and did everything he could to recommend Tom to this exulted yet dangerous office once he married the heiress, Lady Isabel de Clancey.

'I see.' Brida flicked her gaze to his. She was so uncommonly lovely when her face was animated in thought. With her brows furrowed, her bottom lip caught between her teeth and her blue eyes intense with excitement, he almost reached for her there and then.

She smoothed down her cape with graceful hands, the gesture somehow at odds with her guise as a boy. 'I suppose the reasons for meeting the dead man in Westminster Abbey makes a little more sense. I wonder, were you meeting him because he had information you sought?'

Clever, Brida.

'Yes.' He continued watching her piece together everything he had revealed to her. 'But unfortunately, I never got that chance to understand more. And before long I had to leave London in haste, accused of the man's death as well as plotting treason.'

'But that's absurd. You work for the Crown.'

He smiled. 'Not many know of the double life I lead. In fact, many believe that I'm nothing more than *the sum of my charming façade.*'

Tom could not resist reminding her of what she had said to him that night after they had shared a kiss, three years ago. Something that had remained with him, branded into his brain even after all this time. Not that he had been working for de Burgh then. Yet Tom had never truly been without the sort of obligations that Brida O'Conaill had alluded to that long ago night. First and foremost was the care of his sister Joan, which had always been his responsibility and would always remain so.

She dropped her gaze to her hands resting on her lap. 'All this time, I have felt nothing but deep mortification regarding what I said to you that eventide.'

'Think nothing of it, Brida.' Instantly Tom regretted the reminder of that night. 'It was unchivalrous of me to have mentioned it.'

'Nevertheless, I have always felt a great deal of remorse for the way in which I spoke to you.'

'Please…' he waved his hand in the air '…it is all in the past now and is of no consequence, I assure you.

You have already apologised and I am but a fool with yet another example of my ill-timed jests.'

Her lips curved into a small smile that was unlike any that he had ever seen on her face. It was a little shy, if not demure, and made his breath catch in the back of his throat.

'I'm sure I do not know to what you refer.'

'Quite.' He raised a brow and returned her smile before frowning into his mug. This whole conversation was becoming far more intimate than he was comfortable with. He returned to their discussion before it had veered into uncharted waters. Much safer. 'In any case, due to the nature of the furtive work I do, many do not know that I am in the employ of Hubert de Burgh. Nor can I readily divulge that particular information as I have to you.'

'I am honoured.'

He dipped his head. 'So, I did what I had to and left London expediently.'

'But why the need to run from the scene? Why not stay and defend your tarnished name?'

'There could be no opportunity for me to stay and plead my case. Otherwise, I would risk exposing the nature of the operation that de Burgh runs.' He rubbed his chin, wondering whether it had been prudent of him to allow this woman to know all of this about him. Too late now.

'I see, and so you fled to Kinnerton. To meet with Lord de Kinnerton?'

'Precisely, but what I had not bargained for was a festering wound and a maidenly wife.'

She smiled. 'The pretend maidenly sort can be so demanding.'

He chuckled, marvelling at her ability to laugh at herself. 'True, but they are also highly skilled negotiators.'

They descended into a silence. And after the lightness of the moment dissipated, Brida spoke.

'Tell me something.' Her countenance was once again thoughtful. 'Did you not know anything about the man who died in your arms or what his message might have been?'

He grimaced. 'No, I had never met the man before and did not stay long enough to find out who he was. As for the information he had, it pertained to something that was, and still is, shrouded in mystery.'

'Ah, since he was killed before he could pass it on to you?'

Tom deliberated whether to divulge the rest. 'Not exactly. You see, he left me a leather purse containing a curious, cyphered message on a parchment, a couple of whalebone chess pieces and a gold ring with an unfamiliar insignia on it.'

'How very confounding.' She sat in rapt attention, absorbed by his every word. 'And what will you do with it all?'

'Take it to de Burgh who, like King Henry, as well as Ralph, is convening with Llewelyn of Wales, Prince of Gwynedd, at this very moment.'

'At Carreghofa Castle?'

'Indeed, along with the eminent lords from this realm including the Earls of Chester and Hereford as well as Hugh Foliot, the Bishop of Hereford.'

She frowned before shaking her head, as if clearing it. 'So, do you understand the meaning behind it all?'

'Not a whit.' He sighed deeply. 'I have not yet had the chance to decode the cyphered message. But regardless, I hope de Burgh knows what the blasted things relate to.'

She caught her bottom lip between her teeth and frowned again, looking so damn adorable. Tom pondered whether this little quirk only presented itself when Brida was deep in thought. Either way it made her far more endearing than he would ever have believed the fiery woman to be.

'May I ask you something?' She lifted her head. 'Would you be able to show me the contents of the leather purse?'

'Certainly. I have had little opportunity to study the contents myself.'

Tom reached inside his gambeson and untied the purse before handing it to her. She nodded her thanks and took out each item, carefully laying each one on the blanket, before sitting back and staring at the items.

'Well, then,' she muttered, studying each item. 'What have we here?'

'A rather odd assortment, to own the truth.'

'So it seems.' She tapped her chin with her fingers. 'What do you suppose any of this could mean?'

He had an inkling, especially in the case of the ciphered message, and what it might suggest. Tom had not had the time to painstakingly decrypt it, but knew instinctively that it alluded to something precarious with far-reaching implications for de Burgh and even King Henry himself. Indeed, the very fact that this had all transpired now when the English Crown were abroad made it seemingly unusual…and dangerous.

'I can see that you have your suspicions.'

He looked up to find that she was studying him intently. 'Well, firstly we have the king and the knight pieces, which I would surmise refer to King Henry and any number of his lords, including the Earl of Kent— Hubert de Burgh—as there isn't a chess piece that denotes a lord.'

'But missing the bishop and the other pieces?'

'Yes, exactly.' He nodded. 'And then we get to the difficult items.'

'The ring and parchment with the cipher.'

'I have never seen the like of this cipher before. Usually, the method used by scribes is a facility of substitution, where anything can be replaced by one or more characters. Once the pattern is decoded, it all then falls into place and the message is then clearly comprehensible. But this…' he picked up the parchment '…this does not observe the usual practices. Not in the least.'

'How can you tell if, as you explained yourself, you haven't had much of a chance to crack it?'

He smiled brazenly. 'Apart from my obvious brawn and my easy charms ready to extract necessary information, decrypting can be counted as one of my rare talents.'

She raised a brow. 'As is your talent for bluster and swagger. Not to mention your propensity to admire your good self.'

'Someone has to.'

He watched as the corners of her lips twitched before giving way to peels of throaty laughter. Not at all a laugh one would associate with such an exquisitely lovely and graceful woman. But then everything about Brida O'Conaill seemed a contradiction.

She shook her head. 'You really are incorrigible, Tom.'

He winked, grinning at her before nodding at all the contents on the blanket.

'There is one thing that niggles me about all this and that is that I cannot help but think that the timing with all this is not so much fortuitous but rather coincidental.'

'You mean because of the English Court conferring with Llewelyn of Wales's.'

The woman really was exceptionally quick to grasp his meaning.

'Precisely. After all, it is only six years since the Treaty of Worcester was signed between King Henry and Llewelyn. And their peace is as ambivalent as it is uncertain.'

'But Llewelyn is married to the King's half-sister.'

'That does not signify, since neither man trusts the other,' he muttered, returning all the items back in the leather purse.

'And you believe that someone intends to sabotage the fragile peace treaty between the two kingdoms?'

'That…' he shook his head '… I do not know, but it does render the situation precarious, with the need to get to de Burgh as quickly as possible. Already I have tarried far too long.'

She nodded. 'At my behest. I wonder why you stayed longer than necessary in Kinnerton.'

He shrugged. 'I was indebted to you for everything that you did for me. And I always pay my dues, Brida,' he said softly, pinning her with his gaze. She blinked several times before looking away. Ah, it seemed that he affected her just as much as she did him. He coughed, clearing his throat before speaking again. 'Besides, I stupidly believed I had more time than I evidently had.'

'Let's hope that there is still enough time to relay the message contained somewhere within the leather purse.' She paused as though she had suddenly thought of something. 'May I see the ring again?'

'Certainly.' He retrieved the gold ring, dropped it on to her outstretched hand and watched her brows furrow as a look of confusion and puzzlement crossed her face.

'What is it, Brida?'

'I cannot be certain,' she whispered, sinking her teeth into her bottom lip. 'But I think... I believe that I have seen this strange insignia before.'

Chapter Nine

The journey continued through shallow brooks, old deciduous woods teeming with local wildlife, to grassy mounds and misty-topped hills hugging the lush thickets and coppice in the valleys below. God, but even the fragrant air seemed so different here—heavy and dense. It lent an almost magical quality to the ephemeral landscape that verged close to the place where mythical dragons were believed to reside.

Heavens but Brida loved this part of the kingdom. It somehow evoked a whispered time from her long-ago childhood home on the Emerald Isle, making her chest ache. It ached for her family and childhood kin frozen shapeless in a time and place that no longer existed. Where the passage of time somehow rendered the ghosts from her past to fade, but not entirely. Not enough. They still plagued her in her nightmares. They still haunted her and still managed to govern her past, present and future. She pushed the memory away, wanting it gone, knowing that it would not serve to dwell in that dark, bitter place which had brought her nothing but pain and sorrow.

Instead, Brida turned her thoughts to Thomas Lovent's disclosure earlier that day. She was still shocked to learn secrets about the man—so incongruous and conflicting to what she had supposed him to be. In fact, before his calamitous appearance in her life again recently, she had only ever thought the man to be a vain, flippant, handsome charmer. Yet there was far more to Tom than she could ever have believed. So much so that the more she learned about him, the more she wondered whether she had ever known him at all. And not just the work the man did, but also how much danger he, and by association she, was now in.

As well as this, the mystery of the leather purse certainly intrigued her. If only she could recall where she had seen that strange, twisting, two-headed serpent on the insignia of the ring. Brida knew in her bones that she had seen it somewhere before, possibly adorned on someone or something, but could not remember where or whom.

Mayhap she had imagined it, but, no, something about it niggled her. She would think about it later and hoped that her memory of it would return. But, for now, they had a more pressing dilemma. They were teetering along the border, trying to find a suitable place to cross. However, they could not chance it. Not yet.

It would come soon, nevertheless, when they would cross the border, getting a little closer to where they needed to be. And apart from a handful of other travellers on foot or on horseback, they had largely been journeying alone, yet the closer they got to the area where they could cross, the stretch of land that separated one kingdom from another, the more the feeling of trepidation grew.

It afforded them very little comfort to know they were just a day or so away from where they needed to be—Carreghofa Castle in Powys, which clung at the border on the Welsh side and where Llewelyn was holding court. Yet, every time they made an attempt for an opening to cross, they would encounter far more guards than usual.

Naturally the security was of paramount importance as Llewelyn of Wales and King Henry, along with their Courts, were all in attendance. This would be expected for such a conference and was frankly commendable, considering all the ill-begotten blood between the two kingdoms. However, and more importantly for them, it made crossing the border somewhat impossible.

'It is no use.' Tom snapped his head around. 'We cannot gain safe passage through this, without possibly attracting the wrong kind of attention.'

'Do you think the watch patrol here would be looking out for a lone knight? If so, there are two of us and you are also without your usual attire.'

He grimaced, pressing his lips into a thin line. 'Even so, we cannot risk it, Brida. I have very little information at my disposal at this moment, but can only suppose that if the Bishop of London's men came as far as Kinnerton on my trail then they would also have alerted the look-out garrisons along the border.'

She worried her lip. 'What can we do?'

'The only thing we can. We change and adapt our plan, seizing any opportunity that comes our way.'

'And what if it doesn't?'

'We pray.' He must have seen something akin to panic in her face because he quickly added. 'But never fear, Brida. As I told you last night in the cave, an opportunity can always be found if you look very diligently for one.'

'And have you?' She flicked her gaze to his as they cantered side by side. 'Been fortunate to have encountered one?'

He gave her a wolfish smile. 'Fortune has nothing to do with it. And, yes, I believe I have found something that might possibly work. After all, I'm not unscrupulous for nothing.'

'Would you care to share what this is with me?'

He nodded. 'If you look down that valley yonder, you shall see a cortège of wagons, men, women and horses.'

'What about them?'

'I have been following their progress and, like us, they have hung close to the border, slowly making their way north, which suggests that they are in all likelihood venturing to Carreghofa Castle.'

Her brow knitted in confusion. 'Even by following their progress, I cannot see how you could possibly have deduced that.'

'By observing the target.' He flicked his rein, encouraging his horse to go a little quicker. She followed, eager to understand more. 'Consider that this rambling cortège is large, yet it travels north along the border. Why? If it was heading anywhere in England, it would have moved west and on to safer, more certain roads, rather than staying so close to hostile borders. Equally, if it was heading into Wales, then it would have already crossed the border by now, rather than straddling it. So you see, Brida, my summation really does use sense and logic.'

'I'm impressed.' She raised a brow. 'Now if we assume that your talented display of sense and logic really does have merit and that the convoy of wagons down there is travelling to Llewelyn's Court as you predict, then how is it of consequence to us?'

'Ah, well, we must use our resolve and wits and somehow join it—breach it, even.'

She frowned again. 'I am afraid I do not follow. To what end?'

'Right now, there is a rather dangerous possibility that every garrison and patrol watch along the border are being alerted to either one, or mayhap two people with our description, travelling to Carreghofa Castle. However, if we join that cortège, than we have every chance of getting over the border without much ado.'

She smiled slowly. 'I really dislike having to admit this, but that is a genius plan.'

'Ah, but only if it works.'

Daylight dimmed and the sky was bathed with its last vivid rays of burnt ochre streaked with crimson and grey. It cast enough light so that they were able to continue stalking the slow-moving cortège as dusk settled around them. Brida, for one, was heartily relieved when at long last the wagons came to a halt. Her stiff limbs could do with a respite from the long day on horseback. But first they needed to slowly make their way down to the valley.

'Tom?' She threw him a quick glance. 'Tell me, what are we going to do and say that might ingratiate ourselves with these people?'

'Use our natural charms.'

His reply made her instinctively roll her eyes. 'I am being serious.'

He turned his head towards her and made a single

nod. 'As am I, Brida. We must be everything that is friendly, likeable and non-threatening, so that we can be accepted into their group.'

She exhaled, feeling the nervous jitters low in her stomach. 'Well, let's hope we are friendly and likeable enough.'

'And charming,' he added, grinning. 'Don't forget a little charm can go a long way.'

She returned his smile, shaking her head at him. 'Whoever instructed you of that was highly misguided.'

'I assure that I received no such instruction. Besides, I live and breathe by my own rules, making them up as I go.'

'Of course you do.' She chuckled. 'Why that does not surprise me at all?'

'Ah, so you cast me out as being predictable *and* unscrupulous, now? For shame, Brida O'Conaill.'

She ignored the way in which the low timbre of his voice licked down her spine, making the whorls of restless tension in her stomach intensify. No, she could not allow such feelings. She remonstrated with herself, knowing she must be more immune to Thomas Lovent and his teasing manner, than she currently was. Somehow, he was slowly breaching the secure wall she had built around herself, ensuring that she did not form any sort of attachment to anyone. Her resolve seemed to be slipping, eroding away, but she disavowed that notion, knowing that she had to remain strong. And she would do it. She would resist Thomas Lovent and his immeasurable charms.

By the time they made their way down the valley and followed a narrow dirt path hugged by towering trees, and thick, unruly brambles, darkness had descended. This night, however, was far milder and more temperate than the ferocity of the storms from the previous night, which at least was a small mercy.

Tom pulled a thin spindly branch out of the way to allow them further admittance along the path that narrowed and veered in one direction and then the other, before opening up to a clearing. Here three large timber wagons, housed by large swathes of mismatched fabric odds and ends, had come to a stop. It formed a strange sort of temporary fortification with their cattle stabled together on one side and a large inviting central fire, with flames that blazed and licked up the wood kindling. Around the warmth of the fire six or so men and women sat together congenially chatting, drinking and eating.

Crack.

Their horses stepped along the dried fallen twigs and branches, which naturally drew the attention of the small group huddled around the fire. The men stood and marched one by one towards them, looking suddenly suspicious and apprehensive, quite different from the merriment they had been enjoying only moments ago.

'Who may you be, encroaching on this here patch that we've fashioned for ourselves?'

'Peace, friends, peace.' Tom had seamlessly changed his accent to one Brida had not recognised, but one that certainly sounded convincing to her ears. He held out his palm, showing he carried no weaponry in his grasp. 'My wife and I, who be travellin' to Carreghofa Castle, are in need of some friendly hospitality and shelter. See, our tent was destroyed in that torrid storm last night.'

And just like that Brida and Tom were back to being married again.

Oh, Lord...

The man scowled, scratching his head as though he were pondering on Tom's words. 'Carreghofa Castle, you say? Why, that's where we are headin'. And what will you be doin' there, then?'

Tom dismounted and helped Brida do the same. 'Well, seein' as not only the King of England but also Llewelyn, Prince of Gwynedd, are all but parleying in the castle, and how my lovely wife here is talented with a lute, so much so that she sounds just like an angel— a delicate songbird—we're headin' there to offer and provide some song and music to them grand folks with some adjourning entertainment.'

Brida felt as though the blood from her veins had suddenly drained. The earth beneath her feet seemed to have shifted, opening up a chasm of uncertainty, dread and misgiving.

'What are you *doing*?' she hissed quietly, as a mist of panic rose through her.

'Everything I can to ingratiate ourselves with them,' he whispered back, from the side of his mouth, switching to his usual voice. 'I thought that is what we agreed?'

'Yes, but... I can't. I told you before, I don't know how to play the lute—not any longer. Do you not understand?'

'Yes, but I am certain it won't come to you having to actually play anything. It's just a way to gain admittance into this group.'

She let out a big gulp of that breath she had been holding. 'I hope you are right, Tom, because it has been years and I do not... I never play. Not any more.'

'Come now, Brida. No need to worry.' He caught her fingers in his and gave them a reassuring squeeze. 'All will be well. I am sure of it.'

The other man who had spoken before seemed to be about a decade older, with receding hairline, a weak chin and colourful clothing. But his smile gave him an approachable, friendly air, which he did not extend until after he had finished conferring with the rest of his party. He finally glanced in their direction and nodded.

'We seem to be going to the same destination and for similar reasons to you, friend. We're a troupe of minstrels.'

'How fortuitous is this?' Tom threw his arms into the air, dramatically. 'What a chance of fate can this be?' Brida was amazed how easily the lies rolled off his tongue. He turned to her. 'Did you hear that, dearest? We're *all* to be entertaining the courts of England and Wales.'

Ah, this was her cue. 'Wonderful,' she muttered, pasting a smile that did not quite reach her eyes.

Tom quickly stepped in again. 'We have our own supplies that we would gladly share with you if you do not mind endurin' our company?'

'You may join us on this one night. Come…' The man extended his arms out. 'I am Baldwin the Tame and my wife there is Amma. And that is Ulric the Fool, Bertrand the Witless and Roland the Large. With their wives, Agnes, Mildred and Peg.'

Brida was glad that she had dressed in female attire once more, but she somehow still felt lacking compared to these colourful, yet scantily dressed women.

'Pleased to make your acquaintance, friends. I am Thomas the…the…'

'Simple,' she answered, ignoring the dumbfounded look on his face. 'And I am Bridget.'

With the introductions made and pleasantries done, Tom and Brida tethered their horses to a nearby tree before returning to be welcomed around the fire and to join the others.

'Simple?' he said from the side of his mouth. 'So, I am now a predictable unscrupulous simpleton?'

'It was the first thing that I could think of,' she muttered defensively.

'Why, Brida...' he smirked '...you say the nicest things imaginable.'

'I do try.'

'You could have tried *Thomas the Gallant* or *Thomas the Brave* or even *Thomas the Strong*, but instead I get... *Thomas the damn Simple.*'

'I was thinking of my first impressions when I first met you.'

His mouth quirked. 'Cease or you shall put me to the blush.'

'If you recall, it was when you'd swapped places with Lord de Kinnerton to play gallant knight to his oaf squire during the tournament three years ago. Or have you forgotten?'

'Nay, I remember those days with such fondness.'

'Hush.' The corners of her lips twitched. 'Just be thankful that I did not say Thomas the Knave.'

'Indeed.' His chuckle rippled through her. 'That is a small mercy.'

Chapter Ten

The group of men and women whom they had more or less foisted themselves on were affable and altogether agreeable. The mood became light and convivial as the evening wore on, with chatter, laughter and not to mention imbibing of the extra cider they had brought. Tom informed Brida as they also shared the rest of their supplies—dried fruit, nuts, leftover rounds of cheese and dried meats for the evening repast—that this one easy and effortless endeavour always managed to secure the trust and confidence of hapless people he'd just met. After all, most people liked their ale or, in this case, crisp, yet potent, Kinnerton cider.

Gradually, the tight uneasy knot of tension that had gripped Brida's stomach since they had left Kinnerton started to loosen, allowing her to breathe with a little more ease. She felt lighter, somehow, being in this company and not as apprehensive as she had been with the threat of danger from the men intent on finding Thomas Lovent, or the threat of something else, just as dangerous, that she did not wish to identify about her travelling companion.

Her awareness of Tom and her growing ripple of attraction was beginning to become far more difficult to dismiss, even as she pretended that it was baseless and false. She feigned indifference and acknowledged Tom as an acquaintance or, at best, a friend. And only managed to mask her feelings with the same levity and mirth that he hid behind. But it was all a lie.

In truth, Brida could not help but like Thomas Lovent—*a lot*. He infuriated and vexed her, annoyed and exasperated her. But he also challenged and made her laugh with his absurdities and those vivid green eyes that glittered with impish mischief. He was considerate and kind, honourable to a fault, and she itched to touch him. To smooth away his worries and the sadness that sometimes lurked behind his smile when he believed no one was looking. Indeed, there was nothing *simple* about the man, despite her announcement to the contrary earlier.

'Well, now, we seem to have all but finished our meal,' proclaimed the head of this eclectic group of minstrels, Baldwin the Tame. 'So, I suggest we entertain ourselves tonight under the silver moon. A show of our talents to amuse and delight, if you will.'

The others in his group burst into a chorus of whoops and cheers as Brida tried to damp down her concern.

'Sadly, we cannot partake in such delights, as we've grown tired and weary,' Brida exclaimed out of turn, realising her mistake too late, and knowing that she had unwittingly drawn unwanted attention to herself. Oh, but her unruly mouth always managed to get away from her at inopportune times like this.

'My, you seem to let your woman talk for yer there, Thomas,' the man said, his tone churlish.

Tom, to his credit, remained as composed as ever and even had his signature nonchalant grin pasted on his face.

'Well, I'm not called *Simple* for nothing, Baldwin the Tame. My tempestuous woman here does sometimes talk for me, but I find that I likes it. Don't I, petal?' He winked, giving her chin a pinch for good measure, as the other man chortled.

Brida supposed she deserved that. It would not do to set these people against them by offending their sensibilities, when Brida and Tom had gone to great lengths to follow their movements all day and only just secured admittance into their group.

'Indeed, dumpling. Just as I love the temperate way you cajole and lessen my bite.' Oh, God, she had done it again. Brida closed her eyes and groaned inwardly. How in heavens had she managed to sound even more like a shrew than she already had?

'Ah, but, puddin', you have never stung me with your barbs.' He shook his head vigorously from side to side. 'No. Only prickled me with your thorns. Yet I finds it manages to amuse and tickles me more.'

Baldwin the Tame and his cohorts laughed and cheered as Brida looked around in surprise. Did they actually find their sparring amusing? she wondered as she turned to Tom.

'True. I find that my mouth does run away with itself by and by. Though, in my defence, it fills the very pregnant pause you leave, my honeyed loaf, when you are still pondering on what you should say.'

'Mayhap he should be called Thomas the Slow,' Ulric the Fool or Bertrand the Witless or whoever retorted to whoops of laughter.

She smiled. 'I dare say the epithet does rather fit.'

Thomas clasped his chest dramatically. 'Ah, heart of mine, how I love a lashing from that sharp tongue of yours.'

This garnered even more peals of laughter from the men and their women. However, Brida was unsure whether it was their ridiculous witticisms or the fact that the group were now inebriated that was the main cause of this mirth.

'Come on.' The man slapped Tom on the back in a friendly manner. 'Are you sure that this here comedy between yer two isn't what you be entertaining the grand folk at Carreghofa Castle with?'

'You assume right, friend. Our act has a bit of this, a bit of that and quite a bit of anything else we wants to add.'

'I knew it were. No matter how simple you may be, friend, no man wants their womenfolk fierce like a she-wolf.' He wiped a tear from his eye. 'Come, now it be yer turn to watch and hopefully enjoy our performin' a bit o' this and bit o' that.'

'We would love nothing better, eh, petal?'

'Of course,' Brida said absently, her mind elsewhere.

'Well then, a toast.' Baldwin stood beside Tom and managed to throw an arm around his neck even though he was almost a head shorter. 'Here's to our wives and sweethearts. And may they never meet.'

The others all joined in the toast and cheered, raucously. All except for Brida.

She felt as though she had been punched in the gut.

Fierce like a she-wolf?

Was that how she was viewed by acquaintances she either knew or met for the first time? God, how mortifying. The thought that this might be a possibility made her chest squeeze painfully. Was this how Gwen or Ralph, Lord de Kinnerton perceived her to be? That she was some strange oddity, without the usual feminine softness which she had purposely ground out, so that all that remained were her sharp talons? Had she become someone so difficult and brittle that they only just accommodated her?

God, but was this how Thomas Lovent believed her to be? Not that she understood why *his* opinions mattered, only that they somehow did. In any case, Brida knew that Gwen loved her like a sister and valued their friendship, but she was nothing like the gentle, caring, and affectionate Lady de Kinnerton, who was a perfect chatelaine and always put her husband's needs before her own.

Or even these women tied to these men here. The truth was that she had carefully built a wall of ice around herself, around her heart, so that she would never have to feel anything like the harrowing loss of her family. She carefully moulded herself to be impervious to close attachments of the heart, as well as resisting the attentions of men, in reverse. But this was slowly becoming harder and harder to maintain.

'Are you well, Brida?' Tom low's murmur brought her back from her reverie.

She blinked turning her head to meet his gaze. 'Of course, I was just contemplating what the morrow might bring.'

'Mayhap we might find what we are both individually looking for.'

'Do you believe that?' she said softly, her gaze colliding with his.

'If you seek, then you might hopefully grasp whatever it is that you need.'

'Just as I thought. You do design your schemes meticulously after all.'

'Ah, as you may remember, I prefer not to plan in too much detail, with the expectation that everything will fall into place. It rarely does, I am afraid. So, I adapt to change and take anything that might come my way, trusting both my impulse and instinct.'

'Remind me again whether that has always served you well?'

'Not always, no.' He took a swig of ale before addressing her again. 'But we have exhausted this conversation. I would much rather you keep your part of the bargain.'

Confusion knitted her brows. 'What do you mean?'

'Have you forgotten already?' he drawled. 'You were supposed to regale the reasons why you have pretended to be married all this time.'

'I… I.' She snapped her mouth shut and turned to face him. 'Tell me, why are you so curious about this?'

He shrugged. 'If I am to play a role, I want to comprehend, at least, why I am playing it in the first place.'

Baldwin the Tame chose this moment to stand up before the group. He coughed several times before speaking. 'First to entertain us on this auspicious night is Ulric and Mildred singing the ditty, "A dalliance with his delicate flower", accompanied by Roland the Large on the riddle drum.'

They all cheered and clapped as the three gathered in the middle of the group and began their song. *Oh, Lord,* but it had to be a bawdy ballad they would be singing. Ribald stories about the pleasures of the flesh.

'Well?' Tom muttered from the corner of his mouth as he kept his eyes on the performance. 'Are you going to impart your reasons or not?'

'You are as persistent and relentless as a gnat on a cat.'

'A gnat on a cat?' he repeated as he clapped and nodded at the group of minstrels. 'I believe our friends here are beginning to rub off on you. In any case, we had a bargain, did we not?'

'I assure you it's not very interesting.' She paused for a moment before taking in a deep breath. 'The truth is that I was once betrothed.'

'That is most certainly interesting.'

She ignored him as she continued with her sombre explanation. Better to make this as quick and painless as possible. 'Nothing ever came of it because…he, well… he died.' As did every member of her immediate family, with the exception of her mother who blamed Brida for all of the horrific deaths of her kinsmen.

'I warned your father. I warned him that the curse still remained on our house, but he would not listen to me, Brida, and neither did you! Alas, no one did and now look how the depths of hell itself have unleashed death and destruction on all of us for the sins of his past.'

She blinked, taking in the absurdity of this terrible recollection while around her was a loud cacophony of laughter and merriment. The din became more of a dull noise pounding in her ears, as she remembered the oath she had made to herself. Never again would Brida doubt the veracity of the prophecy that foretold her family's damnation. And never again would she tempt the curse that would always remain with her until she breathed her last.

Tom was watching her as slowly his mirth vanished and was replaced by something akin to sympathy and compassion. 'I can see that the the loss of your betrothed has obviously been a difficult burden for you to bear.'

As had all of them. Her father, and all of her family, including her eleven-year-old brother, in the particularly gruesome manner in which they had all been killed... and in front of her very eyes.

'Yes, it has.' She swallowed uncomfortably.

'How long ago did he die?' he asked so gently in the midst of the bawdy din of raucous music and song.

Her head drooped. 'Nearly eight years ago.'

'And you pretend to be married. So that no one might be curious about you or want to ask you uncomfortable questions about your past?'

'Yes,' she whispered. 'Something to that effect.'

'Except someone who is as persistent as a gnat on a cat.' His eyes were filled with remorse, as he slowly shook his head. 'I am so sorry. I could kick myself for being so insensitive. I really had no notion that this might be the reason.'

'Rest easy, Tom. It happened a long time ago.'

'Yet it affects you still.' He covered her hand with his much larger one and squeezed it, but did not see the need to remove it, something which Brida was surprisingly grateful for. She found this small tender gesture somehow heartening as well as comforting and ignored the darts of warning that this intimacy, however chaste, had to be avoided. Not now. Not tonight. Brida felt the need for this contact, this warmth that Tom readily gave through his compassion and concern. Oh, yes, for once, she would gladly take it.

'Yes, it does, but let us not ruin this evening by dwelling on such sorrowful tales. Let us instead listen to theirs.' She nodded to the performance by the fireside.

'I rather doubt you would want to listen to anything these people want to sing.'

She smiled. 'They are rather dreadful, are they not, Thomas the Simple?'

'Call me that once more and I shall find and bring forth a damn cat with a thousand gnats.'

She smiled softly and stared back at the couple in front of her who had duly finished their performance.

'That's better.' Tom had kept his keen eyes fixed on her. 'I would not be the one to cause you misery, Brida. Even in reminding you of your loss. We shall talk no more about it, but know this—if you should ever choose to confide in me, I will be honoured to be at your service.'

She blinked several times surprised by his soft, tender words. 'Thank you,' she murmured.

Hell's teeth.

Tom could kick himself for being the inimitable ass that he was. Of all the asinine, foolish, ill-advised things that he had ever done in his life, this discussion, which had been at his behest, had to rank as one of the worst. He had inadvertently inflicted pain on this woman by insisting that she explain her reasons for her pretence of having a make-believe husband.

If he had only considered the possible explanation, then he might have arrived at the outcome a lot sooner, rather than embarrass them both with his misjudged levity. He should have realised. He should have known that Brida O'Conaill had suffered from heartache. That she *still* suffered from the loss of her betrothed. The very fact that she remained unmarried and vowed to continue to—even going to such elaborate lengths to maintain an alias as a married woman—suggested that her love for this man, whom she had lost, was profound.

It would be the kind of love that would inspire such a misguided devotion for a woman as lovely as Brida to reject the possibility of future happiness. To dedicate herself to a life of loneliness by keeping alive the memory of a man she'd loved and lost. There was something tragic about that. In fact, Tom had always believed that there was something sad about Brida O'Conaill's whole situation.

Yet he could not deny that at least she had lived this—she had known and felt the intimacy and connection of courtly love. Something Tom could never afford or allow himself to experience. But even so, pangs of regret and something else suddenly ran through his veins. Something that chased this with a whispered thread of…jealousy that managed to catch him off guard.

He felt the spark of instant resentment towards the dead man who had captured this beautiful woman's heart so completely. It made no sense since he had no interest in capturing it himself. Oh, he could not deny that he was embarrassingly tempted by Brida and that he wanted her, but it was nothing more than base attraction. And one he was careful not to act on.

'You have nothing to thank me for. We are friends now, after all.'

'And no longer adversaries?'

His lips twitched and he felt relieved that the conversation had moved away from the previous difficult one. 'I was not aware that we were ever *that.*'

Just then the performance was at an end before another couple from this madcap troupe stood to entertain them.

Brida leant over to him. 'Well, you never did return to Kinnerton after Gwen and Ralph got married, so what was I to think?'

His relief was short lived, as once again he felt as though he had been hurled, head first, into deep uncharted waters. Yet, how to answer this directly? On the one hand Tom did not really know his reasons, having told himself for years that he had been too busy with his work for his liege lord to travel to Kinnerton, but in truth he had also wanted to avoid the companion who sat beside him now—Brida O'Conaill. And such he would have remained had his situation not been as dire and dangerous as it had recently become, with the need to seek Ralph de Kinnerton and get to Wales. He remembered well how she had explained that she should not have kissed someone like him three years ago. The memory of it still seethed and burnt inside.

'Someone like me? What is that supposed to mean?'

'Someone who believes his life to be the sum of his charming façade. Who moves from place to place, taking what he wants, with no concern, no constancy, no connection and no care in the world.'

Tom had never truly examined why Brida's words had made him as indignant and unsettled as they had. Was it because she had spoken a truism or that they were, in fact, far from the truth? If he were honest, it had hurt that she had once believed the distorted image that she had of him. And why wouldn't she? It was, after all, an image that he had always cultivated, hiding more of his real self behind the levity and devil-may-care attitude. And it had served him well, especially with his work for the Crown.

Yet, when Brida had found him wanting after a kiss no less, Tom realised just how much he had cared about her opinions. And how much this realisation had scared him. He was not the sort of man who should care about the impressions of a woman like Brida. Or indeed be drawn to her. And although she had apologised for her 'unpardonable behaviour', as she put it, in the cave, the words had embedded themselves in his head for good. In fact, Brida was as much a danger to him now as she was back then and he would do well to remember that.

Chapter Eleven

Tom turned to face Brida. 'No, I did not return.' He drew his fingers through his hair. 'For very many reasons. Firstly, my work with the Crown demanded much of my time. Indeed, the very nature of the work prohibited those close ties that I once enjoyed. I had to maintain an anonymity that would allow me to do the work I did and still do effectively without endangering my friends and family. And this vow held true until this particular assignment which as you know, has gone spectacularly awry.'

'I see.' She sank her teeth into her bottom lip. 'How terribly difficult it must be for you to also bestow these same rigid standards on your own family.'

'I have no family, save my sister.'

'Oh, I am so sorry. I was not aware of your situation.'

'Why would you be?' He shrugged. 'My family perished a long, long time ago.'

'May I ask what happened to them?' she said quietly.

'A fire in my family's manor caught and spread and unmercifully claimed everything and everyone in its wake.'

A gasp escaped from her lips as she covered her mouth with her hand. 'That's awful.'

'Indeed it was, from all accounts. Not that I had been there to witness it myself,' he muttered bitterly.

God's blood!

How in heavens had it come to them discussing the awful misfortune that had befallen his family? A conversation which he *never* had with anyone. Very few knew of the tragedy that surrounded his family's demise or that Tom held himself responsible for it, even though he had been absent when the fire broke out. He had always been riddled with so much guilt that it was akin to having lit the torch himself.

Mayhap that was the reason why Brida's cutting words on that moonlit night three years ago had skewered him so much. They resonated because he knew that somehow Brida O'Conaill had seen him and known what kind of a man he truly was. He had been precisely the sum of what she had believed him to be. A man with *'no concern, no constancy, no connection and no care in the world'*.

He had been all of those things and more. He had only selfishly thought of himself, knowing full well that his father was not only a drunk, but also had a peculiar sickness of the mind. But Tom had turned his back on his familial obligations and responsibilities at the time and chosen the life he wanted for himself as a knight, the consequences of which was the tragedy that later unfolded.

He should have known better. If Tom had remained, then mayhap the fire and the deaths of so many people could have been avoided. Had his mother not begged him to stay and take up the running of the manor and its land holding from his overbearing and obstinate father the last time he had seen her alive? Had she not had that deathly pallor when she had dismissed him as irresponsible and unreliable? Indeed, he thought bitterly, and she had been ashamed of him since he was believed to have no constancy for his family, or his vassals.

'And your sister?'

'Joan is my sole responsibility.' Even to his own ears, his voice sounded strangely aloof and altogether defensive. 'I apologise. I did not mean to be curt, but this is something that I find difficult to discuss.'

'I understand.' It was now Brida's turn to console him, it seemed, by covering his hand with hers. He stared at her long elegant fingers not quite reaching the expanse of his.

He exhaled irritably through his teeth. 'My sister is practically blind—her sight has been fading since she was a small child, Brida.'

'Oh, I am so sorry.' She turned her hand around so that they were palm to palm.

'Do not be. Joan may be young, but bears it all with grace and vivacity and does not allow people's enmity and derision to pull her low.'

Brida's eyes widened. 'She is derided because she is nearly blind?'

He nodded his head. 'Because of her affliction they believe Joan to be cursed. Some even believed at the time that the fire was her fault because of it.' He grimaced as Brida gasped. 'And that is why I am so protective of her. Even at this very moment she is being escorted by someone I trust implicitly, to be taken where no one can ever reach her.'

'It is commendable that you look out for her.' Her

smile was small and tentative. 'And you are lucky to have one another.'

She said this so wistfully that Tom found himself to be curious as to whether she had any living family left. Ralph had once mentioned that she was alone in the world, but he could not risk asking Brida now. Not after what happened earlier. Besides, tonight had been strangely revelatory as it was.

'Thank you,' he said, softly, returning her smile. 'It is strange. You may not be instinctive or impulsive, since you need to carefully contain and manage everything around you, but in many ways you remind me of my sister.'

'Me?' Her eyebrows knitted in bewilderment. 'How so?'

Tom shrugged. 'Not in your looks or mannerisms, but, similarly to Joan, you have indominable spirit. Indeed, I admire your fortitude and your resilience to the challenges you have faced, despite your heartache and loss, Brida.'

He watched her as her eyes unexpectantly welled up. Oh, Lord, he had not meant to upset her. And just when he was about to think of a way to make amends, she grasped his fingers tightly.

'Thank you.' She sniffed in a most unladylike manner. 'That is one of the loveliest things anyone has ever said to me.'

He caught her gaze and held it, mesmerised by the tinge of sadness as well as wistfulness again, fused with an unfettered yearning so intense that it made his breath hitch in the back of his throat.

The burst of applause signalled the end of yet another damn awful performance and Brida dropped her gaze, joining in with the clapping. Baldwin the Incompetent, as Tom had rechristened him, padded over to where they sat and offered a lute to Brida, who blinked in surprise.

'Come now, yer lovely fierce woman here can rise to this occasion. Will you not gratify me—' he swung his arms around dramatically '—and all of us?'

Tom held up his hand as the man jerked the instrument forward towards Brida.

'Yer can do it. You can rise to this challenge,' the odious fool kept on berating, as his group joined in with him pestering Brida, who was looking around with that haunted look in her eyes. What was it about this instrument that petrified her so? He wondered whether it reminded her of another time and place or someone specific. Mayhap her long-dead betrothed, who still kept the damn constancy of her heart.

'That is enough, friend.' Tom said in a quiet steely voice. 'As the lady said earlier, she is tired and weary and is not inclined to perform tonight.'

'Wait…' Brida wrapped her fingers around his arm, turning to meet his baffled, enquiring stare. 'I find that I want to meet this challenge, Tom. For once I want to be more impulsive and not so contained.'

He studied her, noting that she had almost shocked herself with her words.

'You have nothing to prove and you do not need to do anything that might bring forth any anguish and apprehension,' he muttered quietly.

'Thank you.' She offered him the faintest of smiles. 'But I am certain that I should do this—that I should face my fears.'

'Very well,' he said, in her ear. 'If you believe it might bring you comfort, if it can in some way reconcile you to whatever this instrument represents and that it might ease your distress, then do it.'

Brida stared at him for a moment before tentatively reaching out for the instrument. She stood, swallowing down her obvious uneasiness as she padded to the area the others had performed. Her fingers traced the smooth curves of the instrument, as though she were recalling and reminding herself of the feel and shape of it.

He watched in fascination as her fingers flexed and stretched over the strings of their own volition as though recollecting the notes from her memory. And then Brida began to play and all rational thought was lost as the evocative, melodious music wrapped around him, making his chest ache. He was completely enraptured as she thrummed the strings so effortlessly with her long, graceful fingers, pouring every emotion that she had been holding into the mesmerising, yet achingly beautiful music.

He would never have believed this. He would never have believed that the prickly, fiery yet witty and alluring Brida O'Conaill would be able to conjure such breathtakingly stupendous music. It rendered him speechless and made him ponder why she had been reticent about sharing her exceptional talent. Why she had kept her father's lute at her home in Kinnerton, but pretended she did not remember and had forgotten how to play.

God, but she was lovely.

He was transfixed by the emotions playing on her face, her eyes closed tightly in rapt concentration, her lips forming shapes and moving with so much expression as she played, lost in the sheer delight of her performance. Tom had never seen anyone so enthralling, so utterly compelling as Brida looked in this brief yet glorious moment. She wove a tapestry with the melodious music, filled with regret, longing, loss and pain… and it sang to him, touching him so deeply, sending a ripple of surprise and longing through him.

He suddenly realised that this display was more than just about being impulsive—she was letting him see something more. Something that was part of the real Brida O'Conaill—a window to her very soul. And he felt humbled and privileged to have this precious insight. It somehow soothed him.

And then, just as quickly as it had begun, the beguiling music came to an end. For a moment there was a pregnant pause of silence before the others around him began to applaud and cheer. Brida opened her eyes and scanned the area before settling her eyes on him. Their gazes locked and he saw for a moment that breathtaking splendour, as though she had been stripped bare by the music she had just created.

There in the hidden depths of her deep blue eyes glittered a vivacity mixed with a certain vulnerability that made him want to march up to her and haul her into his arms and never let go. But her eyes masked over and she dropped her gaze. The fleeting moment was over far too soon and he wondered if it had been there at all.

Brida stood outside, surveying the landscape before her, wrapping her arms around herself. The moonlight cast a shimmering luminant glow over the dark velvety hills and woodland on the horizon that blended with the stillness of night sky. She breathed the frigid air into her lungs, feeling intoxicated by the magic that had somehow woven around this beatific night, and sighed.

'Ah there you are.' Tom ambled towards her, wrapping a blanket over her shoulders, his fingers lingering over her longer then strictly necessary. His touch made her skin tingle, as heady warmth spread from her shoulders down to her very toes. He cleared his throat, removing his hands before standing beside her looking at the view around them. 'And you shall be glad to know that we have, albeit reluctantly, secured a place to sleep in one of the wagons. You'll be going in with the women, while I am stuck with Bertrand the damn Witless and Ulric the pointless Fool.'

She bit her lip, trying not to laugh, knowing she had the best of it. 'It is better than nothing. At least they welcomed us, where others might not have.'

'Very true, I am rightfully chastened and I shall make my prayer in thanks to our good fortune,' he muttered quietly into the night. 'And also add that it is my sincerest hope that this night will pass without much ado—without any snoring, farting or any other vile bodily functions from my bedfellows.'

This time Brida did chuckle as they stood side by side, staring out on the moonlit view. They descended into silence, taking in the wonder of this night, before she broke the silence.

'Beautiful, is it not?' she murmured.

'As was the music you played, Brida,' he said softly into the night. 'I had no notion that you had such hidden talents.'

It had been exhilarating that she had risen to the challenge of playing the lute—an instrument that had once meant so much to her and had once been something that she had shared with her formidable and powerful father—Diarmuid MacConaill, Lord of Clarmallagh or

Clár Maí Locha—who had taught her everything that he had known about how to feel the music with the emotions she felt as she played the instrument.

It was why she had abandoned the instrument after he had been mercilessly killed—hanged in front of her, along with the rest of her kinsmen. And try as she might, she could never erase that horrific day from her memory. She could never forget any of them, least of all the stricken look of her young brother before he was dragged up the scaffold and that horrible, horrible rope placed around his neck… God, it had been truly awful and the incessant screaming of her mother, or mayhap her own, would live with her until her dying day.

In the aftermath of that dreadful time, every time she had attempted to pick up the one item that reminded her of her late father, his beautiful lute made from the oak from their lands, Brida felt an icy coldness sweep through her, making her fingers unable to play or engage with the music. That was, until this night.

She was still perplexed and surprised that she had done it, feeling every emotion that she had kept contained flowing through her fingers, losing herself in the melody she knew well. A melody that reminded her of home in Upper Osraighe in Éireann and all whom she had once loved.

It brought an ache in her chest that she had not felt in an age—a pain that she had kept enclosed in her heart, never wanting to experience it ever again. But as she closed her eyes and played the haunting music, she could see the faded, shadowy figures of her father and all her brothers around her again.

Somehow tonight, as she let go of her constraints and the need to manage her emotions closely, she had found a path—a link back to her past. And it brought her a semblance of peace that she had not felt for years. When she opened her eyes, they were all gone except Thomas Lovent, who now stood beside her and gazed at her with a shimmering brilliance in his eyes that made her pulse race.

'It has been a long time since I played and I must say I enjoyed it far more than I can say.'

Tom flicked his head behind towards the camp. 'Well, at least this rowdy lot were good at enticing you to play the lute again.' A ghost of a smile touched his lips. 'For I am still in shock, Brida O'Conaill.'

She did not correct him, but it was Tom in his inimitable way who had encouraged Brida to be more impulsive and live in the moment rather than the minstrels. She looked up at him from the corner of her eye and exhaled a shaky breath. How achingly handsome he was, with his tall, broad, muscular frame and his dark blond tousled hair that he was dragging back with his fingers. She itched to do it for him and had to clench her hands into fists at her side to stop herself from doing just that.

Mayhap she had drunk too much cider, but she could not seem to stop thinking about touching the poor man. It perplexed her the way he affected her senses. Tom tilted his head around and caught her staring at him. Oh, yes, he had just said something, had he not?

'And how have I shocked you?' she asked a little too breathlessly.

Oh, dear...

'In every way imaginable,' he drawled and dropped his gaze to her lips. 'That was the single most incredible performance I have ever had the privilege to see and hear. You are exceptionally talented.'

She watched him as he stood, his eyes fixed on her.

'Stop, or you will put me to the blush.' She did not know what else to say, but the intensity with which he studied her face was making her heart trip over itself.

'Truly, I will never forget it,' he murmured as he lifted her chin up with a single finger. 'And you are already blushing, Brida.'

Her skin felt hot and prickly as her pulse quickened. She wet her lips and lifted her eyes to his and what she saw almost made her swoon. Not that she was a woman prone to swooning. Yet the barely concealed intensity of longing she saw in those green and gold depths sent a jolt through her. He slowly dipped his head towards her.

'What are you doing?' she whispered, pulling her head back. Her feet, however, were still rooted to the ground.

'Oh, Brida.' His lips stopped, hovering so closely to hers that she felt the warmth of his breath on her skin. 'You really do speak at the most inopportune times, sweetheart.'

One hand circled around her neck and jaw, while the other cradled the back of her neck. Desire bloomed in his eyes as his fingers caressed her skin softly, making the pulse at her throat throb uncontrollably beneath his touch. It stole her breath and sent a shiver of anticipation through her.

He kissed the corner of her lips. 'And you know what I am doing.'

'I do?'

'Yes.' He pressed his lips to the other corner and kissed a trail across her jaw and down the column of her neck. The hand cradling her head tilted it back so that he could gain better access to the tender spot behind her ear. He kissed and nipped her skin as she gasped.

Oh, Lord... All thought scattered as she moved slowly into him.

'I am being a persistent gnat on a cat, remember.'

'My mistake, I thought you were about to kiss me,' she whispered breathlessly.

'Oh, yes.' His eyes danced in the moonlight as he gave her a slow wicked smile. 'That too.'

The pad of his thumb brushed across her lower lip before Tom dipped his head and caught her mouth with his. Her lashes fluttered closed as he covered her lips softly, shaping them with a mixture of warmth and need. She melted into him as his hand moved from the base of her neck to flexing around her waist, the tips of his fingers pressing on the small of her back.

He moved closer until his body pressed shockingly close to hers and she could feel the hard wall of his chest. A desperate ache burned low in her stomach as an unexpected heat licked through her veins. His arms wrapped around her as Brida's hands moved to his wide shoulders and then snaked around to the back of his nape, pulling him, oh, so close.

His mouth moved unbearably slowly and gently over hers, learning the shape of her. This kiss, unlike the first one they had shared long ago, somehow chased the memory away with its exquisite tenderness. A soft moan escaped her lips when he licked her bottom lip, nipping the corner. He did it again, catching her lips with his teeth. The shock of it drew a gasp from her, lips parting and allowing him to slide his tongue inside her mouth, deepening the kiss.

Everything changed. Suddenly the passion between them became wild, demanding and desperate as he licked into her mouth, tasting her. She touched his tongue with hers and heard him growl. A powerful rush of need, hunger and a frenzied desire merged as the kiss became heady and more sensual.

She knew somewhere in the recess of her mind that she should put a stop to this madness, but, unlike that first kiss that had shocked and surprised her, she wanted more. For just one night she wanted to forget everything she could never have and surrender to the pleasures that she yearned, *with him*—with Tom Lovent, God help her.

The kiss became more and more carnal. He tasted of everything she could not have, but needed all the same. And she wanted it to go on and on and never end. But in the end, it was Tom who gentled the kiss, ending it by pressing a few tender kisses on her lips, her cheeks and each eyebrow. He pressed his forehead against her, catching his rasping breath.

'Oh, God, Brida.' A sharp hiss escaped his lips. 'What have you done to me?'

She found that, for once, she could not speak. She could not utter a word as she tried to slow her hammering heart. She wondered how long time had stood still as everything irrevocably shifted and changed.

'*What have I done to you*?' She wasn't sure whether she actually said the words, but knew that this kiss had altered the nature of their friendship. It altered everything between them. She could not put into words or express how she felt just then. Only that she had never encountered anything like the exquisite splendour that she had experienced in his kiss.

His hands moved to either side of her shoulders as he gently pushed her away from his embrace. 'You are far too much a temptation for me, Brida O'Conaill. Did you know that?' His words were muttered softly and altogether a little detached.

It had all been far too fleeting. The magic that pulled them together had dissipated too quickly. Their splendour had to fade in the end as she knew it would and mayhap Tom had not felt the same as she had.

How utterly embarrassing.

Brida felt a wave of shame, confusion and remorse wash over her as she realised how close she had come to losing herself to this man. She had been ready to give herself in the most wanton way imaginable—but thank God that Tom had come to his senses before she had.

'You must know that I am not a man who can form an attachment with anyone, Brida. My work and my circumstances are such that it prevents me from ever doing so.'

She lifted her head as she put back together the crumbling walls surrounding her heart. 'You mistake, Tom, as I am not looking for any such attachment.'

'I realise that, but I just thought that…'

'I believe you think far too much about it. It was only a kiss after all,' she said as she stiffened her spine. 'A pleasant interlude on this auspicious night but, I assure you, it was nothing more.'

'Well, I am glad we clarified that.'

'As am I, Tom. Now, if there nothing more I bid you goodnight.' She turned on her heel and walked away, only to hear Tom mutter an oath from behind her.

Chapter Twelve

They began the last day of their journey to Carreghofa Castle at dawn and followed the wagons of the troupe of minstrels who continued in their good spirits the following day. Thank God that this would be the last day of their travels and hopefully, without any misadventure, they would reach the castle by dusk.

Brida would then be reunited with Gwen and Ralph, Lord Kinnerton, and no longer have to suffer Thomas Lovent's company again. Not that it was a true sufferance, but they had both found it increasingly difficult to say more than a few words to each other all day. It was surely for the best. They could resume a cordial yet distant acquaintance as though none of the last week had ever happened.

She snatched a quick glance in Tom's direction and noticed the dark smudges beneath his usually friendly green eyes as he rode further along, indicating that he had probably had very little sleep. Just the same as Brida, who had tossed and turned all night, only to be roused early and bleary eyed to embark on this journey.

Even as they had broken their fast earlier and then

stopped later for a light repast, they had been friendly, but altogether distant and remote. The need to discover more about one another and their strange rapport that had pulled them closer was seemingly at an end. As it should be, Brida thought to herself, even though it had made her feel a little confused and hurt. It was for the best, she reminded herself.

Yet despite all this, Brida could not help but think about everything Tom had said as the events of the previous night whirled around her head. He had encouraged her to believe in other possibilities, to use her better judgement and be more impulsive and to somehow embrace the past, however painful.

'If you believe it might bring you comfort, if it can in some way reconcile you to whatever this instrument represents and that it might ease your distress, then do it.'

How had he known about what the lute signified? Mayhap he had not, but had seen the anguish on her face and realised something about her aversion to it. Either way she had been glad that she had played the instrument again. In made her feel liberated and connected her to the past in a more visceral way than she could ever have believed possible.

Yet it had been evident that Tom had not taken his own advice regarding his own difficult past that he had described. That was what had been the most surprising aspect from the night before. Tom had stripped away his usual façade and had reflected on how he held himself culpable for the downfall of his family and a fire that claimed their lives. Though why he felt the responsibility of that tragedy, Brida had yet to learn—and might never discover.

Either way, Thomas Lovent was a far more complicated and multi-faceted man than the one he presented to the world at large. Despite herself, Brida's heart ached for the adversity he'd had to face and the loss of so many whom he'd loved…*much like her.* And he had spoken about his sister Joan, whom he clearly loved, cherished and protected, whose spirited manner somehow reminded him of her.

Oh, Lord, it was no wonder that after the amount of cider they had imbibed, loosening their tongues, they ended up baring their past to one another. And no wonder that they found themselves moved to kiss one another in such an all-consuming manner.

Yes, it would be for the best that they ceased this growing friendship and attraction between them. It would serve neither of them well. There could be nothing beyond the end of this journey for the two of them. Nothing beyond their closeness, their comradery or even the pull of attraction. No matter how many scorching kisses they shared, it would be of little consequence since they could never have a future together. Parting, before she'd invested more of her heart and even more of herself in Tom, would be a welcome relief. In fact, it could not come soon enough.

Tom dragged his hand across his forehead. They had thankfully managed to cross the border into Wales without much ado, but there was a strong possibility that Tom was still a wanted man, so accomplishing getting inside the castle would not be so easily done without alerting the attentions of officials who might be searching for him. The closer their entourage got to Carreg-hofa Castle, the more he would have to attend to the pressing matter of gaining access inside the castle walls. He could not risk either Brida's safety or his own and had to contemplate what awaited them once they approached the Welsh castle, so close to the English border. And then he could act accordingly.

Notwithstanding this imminent precarious situation as they gained closer to their destination, he couldn't help his pensive musings regarding the previous night with Brida. God, but what a damnable fool he had been to have given in to his base desire for her, when he had nothing to offer the woman. He was not a man who could afford any serious attachments with anyone. Certainly not with the important work that he did for the Crown—that is, if he somehow managed to prove his innocence of the crimes he had been accused of. Not that Brida had sought anything from him, anyway.

Yet, regardless, Brida O'Conaill had stormed into his ordered and purposeful life and wreaked havoc on his senses. Or rather Tom had stormed into *hers,* but it was the same difference in the end. He felt torn with wanting her desperately, yet keeping her as far away from his person as possible. Which was the reason he had resigned himself to conversing with her only when necessary and only about vague mundane matters. However, it would not do. His conscience would not allow him to disavow their tentative friendship and to part as indifferent acquaintances as they once had.

He brought his horse around to ride next to Brida's. 'We will be reaching the castle soon.'

She rode on without meeting his eyes. 'I am glad of

it. This journey has grown a little exhausting, if truth be told.'

'At least it has been uneventful.' He caught the confusion in her glance and knew that he must clarify his meaning. 'In that we have not had anyone follow us on our trail.'

'True—do you anticipate any difficulties once we reach Carreghofa Castle?'

'That I cannot answer, which is why we must remain cautious and assess the situation once we arrive there.'

She nodded as they resumed riding in silence beside the wagons for a long time, both lost in their own musings.

Tom took a deep breath before looking in Brida's direction. 'I wanted to say that I hope I did not cause you any insult last night.'

God's blood, but he sounded so damn formal. In truth, he had never spoken to anyone, least of all Brida, in this manner, but he could hardly resort to treating the matter with his usual flippant levity again. He needed to make amends and not exasperate their relations even further. Especially if he had offended her.

'No, you may be assured that no insult has been made and certainly none was taken by anything that transpired last night. In fact, it was a perfectly amiable and enlightening evening.'

'I am glad to hear it, Brida. However, I would also like to convey that—'

'True, we shared much about our pasts, which I believe was the reason that led to that acceptable kiss. I'll concede that it was rather nice and altogether satisfactory.'

'Acceptable? Nice?' He scowled. *'Satisfactory?'*

She shook her head. 'I cannot think of it being any more than that. In fact, we can call it an early farewell kiss.'

Tom's jaw dropped. He was in two minds whether he should kiss her again just to show her how 'nice' and 'satisfactory' his kisses could be. Yet she was still talking in an incessant manner.

'However, it's possible that it dragged on a little too long, but mayhap we had consumed too much cider.'

He should just leave this alone and move away. He had apologised, in a rather indirect manner, and the woman had assured him there had been no offence taken. That should be that.

'You think that the kiss was acceptably nice and fairly satisfactory, do you?'

No, it seemed that he could not leave it well alone. He knew she was goading him or trying to diminish what had happened between them, but, damn, it was his masculine pride at stake here.

'Indeed.' She pasted a bland smile on her face. 'It was enjoyable and quite passable.'

He returned her smile. 'I shall endeavour to do better next time.'

She snapped her head around and frowned. 'Next time?'

'Oh, yes. You cannot issue a provocation like that to a man who enjoys nothing better than a challenge and not expect that there will be a next time.'

'And when might this happy event take place?'

'I believe it might be best if I employ an element of surprise, do you not agree?'

'No, sadly we are not of the same mind.'

'I am sorry to hear that. But I shall not be deterred.'

Tom smiled inwardly, feeling relieved that a little of their spark and comradery had somehow been restored with the usual flippant sparring between them.

Not that he would mind kissing Brida O'Conaill senseless again. Even though he had vowed to himself that he could not be caught in another fraught and risky situation with this woman. It would be tempting fate again. But, by God, he had desired and wanted her so desperately last night that it had taken every drop of will and resolve that he possessed to pull away from her when their kiss had caught and blazed frantically.

He had sensed from her response that she had lost herself to it as well, which meant that they would either both lose control of the situation together or that he would have to be the one to gain some semblance of order by bringing about an end to their desperate and intimate kiss. God only knew what they might have tumbled into had he not stopped it when he had. And here he was, promising to do it all again. All because it might somehow ease the mood, accord and cordiality between them, as it once was earlier on this journey.

'We shall have to see, then.' Brida sunk her teeth into her lip, evidently trying to suppress her laughter, as he watched on.

'We shall, indeed.' He winked at her. 'But I warn you that I shall enjoy surprising you at my convenience, when I enlighten you with my skilful, accomplished and, may I add, ardent kisses.'

This time she did laugh—a low throaty chuckle that made him grin. 'You jest?'

'I take the art of kissing very seriously, Brida, and cannot allow your assessment of last night's acceptably nice and fairly satisfactory kiss to stand. I have standards to uphold after all.'

She threw her head back and laughed before wiping her eye. 'In that case, I cannot wait.'

'Good,' he drawled softly, all the previous humour dissipated. 'Because when I kiss you again, I want you breathless, boneless and desperate for more, Brida O'Conaill.'

Her laughter slowly ceased as she turned to stare at him, blinking several times, before blushing. God, he had seemingly done it again and taken this uncontrollable longing too far, when he had meant to make light of her provocation and tease her. What in heaven's name was the matter with him? He seemed unable to rein in his desperate need for her but, by God, he had to. Tom had to damp down this growing desire he had for the woman and abandon these feelings once he left her in the care of his friend, Ralph de Kinnerton. And that moment needed to arrive far more expediently than he had considered before.

'We approach the castle. It's over that hill, yonder,' Baldwin the Tame bellowed, as he twisted his head around.

The relief that Tom felt with this statement was palpable. It seemed that his prayer had been answered. Yet the closer they rode to the castle and its surrounding area, the more apprehensive he felt. Something was not as it should be here, yet he could not quite put his finger on why he felt so agitated. His hackles were raised by the difficulty in which they were gaining admittance. The area was as crowded as he knew it would be, but then it was also heavily guarded. Tom could see from afar that the security in the whole vicinity around the castle was exceptionally tight. Yet he felt it in his bones—it was as though they were riding to their downfall.

He cantered towards Brida, riding beside her. 'Something is amiss here.'

She tilted her head to meet his worried gaze and frowned. 'What makes you believe that?'

'I anticipated that there would be many guards and soldiers here, but never this many. We have not even reached the village and the castle curtain.' He dragged the hood of his cloak over his head. 'It is likely that the news of the murder in Westminster Abbey has reached the king and Hubert de Burgh to account for this much extra security.'

She took a deep shaky breath. 'Dare I ask what that would mean?'

'It could mean trouble or rather the high possibility of it, because if the news of the murder has reached here, then so has the name of the man accused of the crime as well as the made-up charge of plotting against the Crown—namely *me*.'

'Oh, Tom, what are we to do?'

He looked around as they approached the busy village square. 'Nothing…for now. But soon, I will want you to do exactly as I say when the moment is nigh. Do you think you can do that?' he asked in a gentle yet serious voice.

'Yes,' she whispered.

'Good,' he muttered before addressing Baldwin, the leader of the minstrels. 'You carry on ahead there and we shall catch yer up later on.'

The time to part ways with the troupe had arrived, especially as it might cause unforeseen problems if they were stopped and asked questions. Best to minimise any possible damage that they might cause, now.

The man scratched his head. 'Why might that be, friend?'

'We need to stop as my wife needs the privy, if you understand my meanin'.'

He chuckled. 'Very well and yer can catch us up ahead, otherwise I am pretty sure our paths shall cross some more, Thomas the Simple.'

Tom inclined his head. 'I am sure we shall, Baldwin the Tame. Until later.'

The man doffed his hat before turning back and trudging along with his convoy of wagons.

Tom pulled the reins of his horse and dismounted before turning around to grab the reins of Brida's young horse. 'The castle is surrounded and I must think of a different way to get you to Ralph.'

Brida looked exceedingly apprehensive as she nodded.

'Do not worry. It's me they're after, not you.' He strode around to her horse and helped her dismount. 'But even so, I want you to know that your safety is of the utmost importance to me.'

'I know,' she muttered.

They led the horses down a narrow path off the main route to the gatehouse.

'And because of that I cannot take you inside the castle myself. I would bring danger to you as well as myself. You understand what I am saying?' He looked around in both directions, making sure that they had not drawn any sort of attention. They hadn't, thank God.

'I think so. You want me to go in by myself.'

'Not quite. I cannot leave you alone and unprotected

in an unknown place like this. We shall find a couple of young lads in the village whom I shall offer coin to in return for giving you escort.' He exhaled through his teeth. 'I am sorry, but it is the best I can do.'

'Never mind about that, I shall be fine. What about you?'

'The least you know about my movements, the better.'

She shook her head. 'But I have to know—'

'Listen to me, Brida. We have not got the time for this,' Tom interrupted as he placed his hands on either side of her waist to turn her around to face him. 'I need you to do something for me. I want you to tell Ralph everything once you get the chance to and ask him to meet me in the woodland demesne at the rear of the castle wall tonight at dusk after vespers. Do you think you can do that?'

'Yes, of course.'

'Good, now we must make haste.' He bent his head and inhaled the cool air into his lungs before lifting his head 'It's time to resurrect the guise of the knight and his oaf squire, I think.'

She worried her bottom lip. 'Tom, you will take care?'

He gave her a quick smile. 'As always, Brida. As always.'

Chapter Thirteen

The royal lodgings were made up of the large solar chambers in the keep of Carreghofa Castle, while the rest of the two courts had erected pavilions and tents in the large baileys inside the fortified stone curtain wall. The English court had been given use of the outer bailey and it was here that Brida was finally reunited with her friend, Gwenllian de Kinnerton, and her husband, Ralph, inside their spacious gold and green pavilion. And, after Brida delivered Tom's message, the women could do nothing but wait in a state of apprehension.

Brida had been pacing inside with Gwen, who was bouncing her young infant son, Roger, on her lap, feeling agitated as they waited for Ralph's return.

'And you travelled here alone with Tom Lovent on account of his being a wanted man?'

'Yes, I had unwittingly brought trouble to my own door when I tended to his wounds myself.'

'Very commendable, Brida. But it seems that you took a great deal of risk in giving him the aid you did.'

'I had to, Gwen. He had dropped unconscious with fever at my door, or rather inside my door.' And on her bed… Brida grimaced, knowing what her friend had said was true. She had taken a huge risk and not just what people might have perceived. 'Besides, everyone in Kinnerton mistook him for my *husband.*'

'Oh, Lord, say they did not.' Gwen covered her mouth with her hand, trying to hide her amusement.

Brida did not know whether to groan or join in with Gwen's mirth. The scheme that she had devised and Tom had gone along with had been nothing short of preposterous. 'But they did think it. And I did nothing to dissuade them. If anything, I encouraged that belief since it suited my purpose.'

Gwen tilted her head, studying her friend for a long moment. 'I always thought that you did not care for Tom.'

'I do not… I mean, as in I care, but merely as a friend or an acquaintance would.'

'When I kiss you again, I want you breathless, boneless and desperate for more, Brida.' Tom's words from earlier did indeed make her a little breathless just thinking about it.

'I see.'

Brida hoped with all her heart that her friend did not *see* anything beyond what she had said. It really would not do to garner any speculation regarding herself and Thomas Lovent. And it did not help matters that Gwen was looking at her so curiously. Thank God Ralph, Lord Kinnerton, arrived just when he had and for more important reasons than *this.*

Brida looked up at him as the man strode inside the tent. Without saying a thing, he poured each of them a mug of ale and took a sip before he finally spoke.

'Dare we ask what has been decided between you and Tom?' Gwen asked her husband.

'Nothing,' he said before addressing Brida. 'He was not in the woods you mentioned.'

What? 'There must be some oversight, my lord.'

The man shook his head before pinching the bridge of his nose. 'There is none, I am afraid. I went with a couple of my men and scoured the area, but Tom was nowhere in sight.'

She felt as though the blood had drained from her veins. 'I don't understand. Do you believe some misfortune has befallen him?'

'I cannot answer that, Brida.' Ralph replied gently. 'But knowing Tom as I do, I am sure there is a perfectly good reason why he was unable to meet me at the assignation he arranged. And if something was awry, he would have changed his plans. After all, he would not risk the exposure.'

She flicked her eyes to Ralph briefly. 'I assume that you know the nature of his work, my lord?'

A slow smile spread on his lips. 'Indeed, I have always known. But what I find interesting is that Tom has obviously told you.'

She caught the look that passed between husband and wife and flushed further. 'I suppose Tom… Sir Thomas realised that he had little choice other than to inform me from the moment I heedlessly became involved.'

'I see.' Now it seemed that Ralph de Kinnerton was also observing far more in this situation than he should. Never mind. They could both think what they liked. It mattered not.

'But where would he have gone?' she muttered more to herself then anyone.

Ralph shrugged. 'My guess would be that he is in hiding.'

She took a shaky breath. What could have become of Thomas Lovent?

'Come, Brida dear.' Gwen stepped in. 'There is no need to distress yourself. I am sure Tom is perfectly safe, otherwise we might have heard of some disturbance or other by now.'

Ralph met his wife's eyes and smiled. 'Exactly. Best get some rest before the evening banquet. We can only hope that Tom makes contact soon. I, for one, believe it to be sooner than we think.'

Later that evening, Brida was sat in the busy great hall of Carreghofa Castle with Ralph and Gwen de Kinnerton, attempting to eat morsels of the delicious food that had been prepared in honour of the distinguished guests. There was Welsh spring lamb cooked in myriad spices with vegetables, pheasant stuffed with sweetmeats and rabbit in plum sauce, all accompanied with warm wheaten bread, nuts and local cheese. The ale and rich Burgundian wine that complemented the food was consumed a little too readily, but heightened the night's revelry.

Yet Brida could not find her appetite to enjoy the occasion at all. She was increasingly worried about where Thomas Lovent had got to and where he might be at that very moment. Ralph de Kinnerton had been right that something must have occurred for Tom to have altered his plans as much as he had, but that knowledge provided little comfort.

Gwen reached over and gave her hand a reassuring squeeze, yet Brida still felt the darts of unease run-

ning through her. She tried to smile and even that felt
far too difficult a task. But this would not do. It was
imperative that she had faith that the man was somewhere hidden safely. And would eventually find a way
back to them—*back to her*—once the time was right.
Not that she wanted to examine her feelings beyond
wanting Tom to return unharmed and well. That was
all that mattered. In the meantime, Brida would put all
her efforts into finding out more, where she could—if
she could—to help him.

Her eyes scanned the large imposing hall which was
thrumming with the clattering noise of servants bringing in trenchers of hot food as well as the noise of chatter, laughter and merriment. On the raised dais at the
end of the hall were the royal courts of England and
Wales. The Welsh party consisted of the host, the enig-
matic Llewelyn of Wales, Prince of Gwynedd, the most
influential and powerful man in all of Wales, who sat
with his men and his young wife Joan—half-sister to
the young King Henry of England. He was with his
aides—the powerful Marcher Earls of Hereford and
Chester as well as the Bishop of Hereford. But there beside the King himself was arguably the most powerful
man in England: Hubert de Burgh. And the man that
Tom needed to find an audience with once he managed
to gain entrance inside the castle.

'Are you unwell, Brida? You have hardly touched
your food,' Gwen whispered from the corner of her
mouth.

'No, I thank you. I am perfectly well, just a little
tired.'

'We shall retire soon enough. In fact, I am eager to

get to Roger before he sleeps for the night. I won't stay too long beyond the entertainment.'

'The entertainment?' Brida groaned. 'With all the concern regarding Tom I forgot about them.'

'What do you mean?' her friend hissed.

'We travelled the last leg of the journey here with a troupe of minstrels who believed Tom and I to be performers—married performers.'

'It seems you have been quite busy convincing many of your marital state.'

'This is no jesting matter, Gwen. I cannot have them see me here, among the esteemed guests without Tom. It will make them suspicious about who we really are and alert the authorities.'

'They will not do so, Brida, I promise. I can see that your nerves are a jangled mess tonight, so at the first opportunity we shall slip away back to our pavilion.'

'That would be most welcome.'

'In the meantime, please calm yourself.' Gwen poured a splash of the deep red nectar into her mug. 'Here, have some wine. It will fortify you and take the edge off your current agitation.'

'Thank you.'

Brida sat back a little, taking small sips from her mug as she continued to survey the room. Gwen was quite right, she was worrying unnecessarily. And to prove the point, it was at that moment the troupe whom they had travelled with came into the middle of the hall and began their ribald, bawdy performance, which was indeed a bit of this and a bit of that as they had explained the night before. They were so absorbed in providing their entertainment that, as predicted, they did not notice her sat with the guests. Gradually Brida began to feel a little more relieved and even managed to enjoy the silly performance, until, halfway through their performance, something caught her off guard. Something that she had difficulty comprehending. Mayhap with all the uneasiness that she had felt this was just a figment of her imagination.

But, no, it had to be.

She recalled two days previously, when Tom had shown her the contents of the leather purse and had mentioned the man's name in passing, that she had tried to remember where she had seen the gold ring with the strange emblem.

Now she could. And when Hugh Foliot, Bishop of Hereford, agreed to be part of the minstrels' routine to rapturous cheers, Brida remembered and understood the possible implication of what she was suddenly so wary of. She had seen that strange serpent emblem on the gold ring given to Tom by the murdered man in London. She had seen it when the Bishop of Hereford and his clergy had visited Kinnerton Castle.

That night she tossed and turned, unable to sleep on the uncomfortable pallet that she had been allotted. But it was not because the bedding had been lumpy which made sleep evade her. It was more that she could not shake off the unsettling feeling regarding Tom Lovent. Every time she closed her eyes, she imagined him lying on a dirt track with a broken neck or alive but beaten and tortured before being thrown in the pits of the donjon. No, this incessant concern over the man's well-being would not do—it was not as though she were actually his wife...never *that*. But that did not mean that she wished him to be exposed or, worse, harmed in anyway.

Brida opened her eyes and sighed in exasperation. She needed to do something. Mayhap she could do something to assist Tom in this interim and gain some snippet of knowledge and understanding that might help. Anything other than this needless anxiety.

The bells of the church rang out, signalling the time for the matin prayers. She pulled the coverlet away and got to her feet, padding to the wooden coffer and drumming her fingers against it for a moment. With the decision made about her next course of action, Brida quickly dressed in the clothing she had previously worn when dissembling as a squire. She pulled on a hooded cloak and left the tent that had been provided for her use and slowly made her way out of the Kinnerton pavilion, after making some excuse to the perplexed hearth knight standing guard. Blowing her warm breath into her cold hands clasped together, she made her way through the stone gateway and into the inner bailey. Having ascertained where the kitchens were during the banquet, she made her way through the herb garden and the kitchen garden before entering the large, busy chamber which was already preparing the many meals for the day. Cartloads of firewood were being carried in, to fuel the hearth that already had huge metal cauldrons balanced over the fire with the previous night's foods blended and mixed together for potage. Warm bread was being made in one area reserved for baking, while young scullions were mopping and scrubbing the surfaces in another part of the kitchen ready for the day's butchery.

Brida walked through the main kitchen which opened up to the long, cobbled passageway with her heart beating furiously in her chest. Thankfully no one questioned her reasons for being there believing she was one of the many young lads working there. Looking in both directions, she noticed a couple of young serving maids walking up to the arched doorway, carrying wooden trays laden with jugs.

She waited until they walked away before she descended the stairs down to the buttery. She took a deep breath before filling a jug from the casket of ale and assembled this, along with a couple of pewter mugs, on a tray before walking through the buttery to the second stairwell at the back of the small chamber.

If she wasn't mistaken, this would take her to the hall and from there she would step outside again before attempting to find the Bishop of Hereford's chambers. Brida knew that he would be likely to be at matin prayers already, so this was a good opportunity.

She had no notion what she might find there, but she needed to search the man's rooms in case she might find evidence that might aid Tom later. There was always a possibility. And this was certainly preferable to lying on her pallet and counting the many lumps she had to contend with.

Brida took a deep breath of the cold night air as she burst through the great hall, pulling her hood over her head.

'What might be the quickest way to the Bishop of Hereford's chambers?' she muttered in a voice she hoped would convince the knight standing guard at the entrance to the tall stone keep, belonged to a young squire. 'Only I lost me barin' after going through a different pass.'

The man's eyes narrowed. 'I don't believe I saw you earlier.'

'And nor would you 'ave, since I've only just come on duty. Come now, this tray is heavy and his Excellency the Bishop shall want his morning ale.' Brida surprised herself at how impassive she managed to sound despite feeling jittery.

Thank God, however, that the guard seemed to believe her as he nodded and pointed her to the entrance. 'Follow that, you'll come by the entrance of the tower around the back. The rest will be familiar to you.'

'It will be unless my lord Bishop has changed chambers as he threatened to from where he was to the second floor.'

'Not to repeat what I say, but the man likes to complain. And he's already on the second floor.'

'True, but at the rear of the tower.' Brida gambled. 'As he doesn't like the view around the back there.'

'Well, there just isn't enough room to change anything.'

She pulled a sympathetic face. 'I will be sure to mention that to his Excellency.'

Brida stepped inside the stone stairwell that was thankfully lit by flickering torches held on ornate, metal wall sconces and climbed up the cold dank steps, reaching the second floor. She held her breath as another scullion rushed past her, and ambled through the arched hallway towards the rear of the building, glancing back and forth, making sure that she was not being followed. Thank goodness she was alone in the darkness just as dawn was breaking outside.

Pushing open the creaky wooden door, she went inside and laid the tray down on the coffer table and began looking around the antechamber. A few clergymen passed through before leaving the room while she lowered her hood and pretended to toil away at a few menial tasks. As soon as they left the antechamber, she quickly retrieved the tray and moved from every chamber that stemmed from this until she finally came to the one in which she was certain Hugh Foliot, Bishop of Hereford, was staying. She hoped it was, especially since a few parchments that had been absently left on the trestle table had been addressed to the man.

She exhaled impatiently, rubbing her brow, wondering where else she should look. The truth was that Brida did not even know what she was looking for, only something that might give an indication or a link with the gold ring left in the dead man's leather purse. Something that might also have the strange, almost serpentine emblem on it. She looked under the pallet, inside the saddle bags and even the leather-bound books left on a stool beside the pallet bed. She even drew the heavy curtains in the narrow-arched doorway in the corner of the chamber which housed a few wooden shelves, but was otherwise empty. Indeed, there was nothing more to see in the sparse chamber.

She was about to leave, when Brida was suddenly alerted to noises—footsteps advancing in the antechamber and getting closer. Oh, Lord! Her gaze darted around the room and fixed on the curtained archway. It was the only place to hide behind since her path back the way she had come might now be blocked. Unless she grabbed the tray, dropped her head low and scurried past whoever happened to be approaching. No, her nerves would not hold out.

Brida scampered behind the curtain, taking small steps backwards in the darkened space until her back pressed against the wall, and steadied her rampant heartbeat. She heard it then—the clicking sound of the door on the other side of the curtain creaking open as someone walked into the chamber. At that exact moment, what she had believed to be a stone wall against her back also made a small clicking noise and opened out.

Before she could turn around, something reached out and grasped her from behind and a hand clamped around her nose and mouth. She was lifted off her feet and dragged out into a different space altogether—a passageway hidden behind the main chambers…a secret passageway. She opened her mouth to say something, anything that might get her out of the trouble she had found herself in, when it was covered in a kiss—a kiss that was demanding, possessive and utterly delicious.

'I told you that the next time I kissed you, I would leave you breathless,' Tom Lovent growled in her ear before covering her mouth with his again in a searing kiss unlike anything Brida O'Conaill had ever experienced.

Chapter Fourteen

Tom was furious with the woman he had just snatched from the small closet in the Bishop of Hereford's chamber. He was so mad with her that he did not know whether to embrace her, rage at her, or scold her as she was inclined to do with him. Instead, he settled on kissing her with such ravenous craving, such hunger, that it felt as though his life depended on it. He deepened the kiss, tasting her and letting all his fury melt into her.

No, this was certainly not a *nice* or even just an *acceptable* kiss. It licked a flame so bright it blazed through his whole damn body, and convened down in his groin. He pulled Brida closer, his body pressed to her glorious soft curves, and wrapped his arms around her. Running his fingers up and down her spine, Tom settled on cupping her round pert bottom, giving it a squeeze. God, but how he wanted this impetuous woman.

He groaned into her mouth as a surge of desire, anger and even relief swept through him. Relief since she was safe, unharmed and in his arms. And anger because it had been a close thing and she had heedlessly put herself in a precarious situation in the first place.

God's blood.

What the hell had she been about, intruding in the Bishop's bedchamber at this time of the morning anyway? As far as Tom was concerned, he had kept to his end of things by depositing the maddening woman safely in the care of Ralph de Kinnerton and his wife, so that he could get on with what he needed to do and get to Hubert de Burgh—not that he had had much success so far. The man was difficult to get to, heavily guarded as he was. But Tom would find a way. What he did not need was the distraction from Brida O'Conaill, however comely and delicious she was.

He tore his lips from hers and placed his finger to her lips, shaking his head. He noted the look of shock on her face, her lips red and swollen from his kisses and the gentle curve of her breasts with her chest rising and falling as she caught her breath. Oh, yes, he wanted her. Not that he really should.

'Not here. We can talk when we get away from this place,' he whispered as he dipped his head and pressed his lips, open mouthed, on the throbbing pulse at the column of her neck.

He lifted his head and nodded towards the direction he intended for them to go. Grabbing her hand, he began to walk along the dark passageway that ran along in between the main chambers of the keep, linking them by the interconnecting secret passageway that brought them down a very narrow and slippery spiral staircase, winding itself around to the rear of the building. They made their way down, taking care not to fall or slip along the uneven flagstone steps before they crawled out of the small arched doorframe that brought them outside the building. He turned around to face her, pulling her hood low over her head.

'Now.' He glared at her. 'Would you like to explain what the hell you are doing, Brida?'

'I would like to ask the same?' She glared back.

Tom admired her fortitude, he truly did, but she had shaken him beyond all measure. And she claimed that she was never impulsive. Mayhap he was not a good example to her after all. What would she have done if someone happened upon her in the Bishop of Hereford's bedchamber?

'This is serious, Brida, we are no longer in Kinnerton, pretending to be married for the sake of appearances.'

She flinched as though he had hit her before recovering herself. 'I am fully aware and would remind you that I hardly went looking for trouble.'

'Then what, in the name of all that is holy, were you doing there?'

'Trying to help you. You great oaf!' She prodded his chest with a finger. 'Because I have been excessively worried about you.' She prodded again. 'Since you had failed to turn up at the rendezvous—' another prod '—that you made me set up with Ralph de Kinnerton.'

He grabbed her finger before she prodded his chest further, trying to hang on to his composure. 'I expressly set up that rendezvous as a way to ensure *your* safety, you infuriating woman.'

'Me?' she gasped in outrage. 'I am the one considered infuriating here? And what exactly do you mean setting up meetings as a way to ensure *my* safety?'

He raked his fingers through his hair in exasperation.

'By Ralph arriving at the exact place I told him to meet me after you gave him my message, I could assume that you were safely ensconced with both Ralph and Gwen.'

She frowned. 'Are you telling me that you never intended to meet him in the woods after all?'

'Not quite. It all depended on whether the circumstances were conducive for the rendezvous. They were not. And Ralph would have known this, once he realised that I had failed to turn up. He would have known that I could not have risked meeting him at that time or place. More importantly, I knew that he had got my message through you and that you were safe.'

He exhaled through his clenched teeth. 'But then rather than staying put and resting in their pavilion as a sensible woman should, you undermined all that effort by traipsing all over this castle *alone* and into the Bishop of Hereford's chambers, of all places, at the break of dawn. Now I admit that I encouraged you to be impulsive and even a little unpredictable, Brida, but not to this extent.'

She raised a brow and pasted a bland smile on her face. 'Well, I am indeed sorry that I was so concerned about your well-being. And, I repeat, I was trying to help, you ungrateful ox, after I remembered that I had seen the emblem on a gold ring somehow connected to the Bishop of Hereford. Not that it excuses your manhandling my person and taking liberties.'

'I did not manhandle you, Brida, I kissed you as I promised I would after you issued the challenge of sort… Wait.' He lifted his head. 'What did you just say about the Bishop and the gold ring?'

'The emblem on it seemed familiar to me, as you might remember me saying to you. And when I saw the Bishop at the banquet last night, I recalled when and where I had seen it.'

He narrowed his eyes. 'Go one.'

'It was when the Bishop and his clergy visited Kinnerton recently. I was struck by the strange two-headed serpent pattern of the emblem—I suppose that is why it was imprinted on my memory.'

The Bishop of Hereford...involved in conspiracy? Involved in a plot against the Crown? He could hardly believe it.

'Are you sure about this? You saw the emblem of the ring on the Bishop himself?'

She shook her head. 'That I cannot recall, Tom, although... Although it was definitely when he, along with his clergy, visited, because I remember reflecting how odd it was to see such a strange serpent pattern linked to such persons as the clergy and men of God. It seemed so incongruous.'

The significance of this and the huge political implications were not lost on Tom. However, he needed hard evidence. He needed to learn and comprehend more. As if reading his mind, Brida continued to explain.

'And although I found nothing in his chamber that could support that claim, I do remember it quite clearly now.' She pulled the edges of her cloak, smoothing the creases in the woollen material, the gesture so conflicting with her attire of a squire. 'Incidentally, I never challenged you to...to kiss me in that manner.'

The corner of his lips twitched. 'Then in future, I advise that you refrain from stating that a man's kiss is just nice or merely acceptable. That is nothing short of provocation.'

'You really are quite insufferable, Thomas Lovent.'

'I do try.' She gave him the kind of look that made Tom want to take her into his arms once again and wipe it off her face with another searing kiss. But not now. He had far more important matters to address. He looked in every direction before grabbing her hand. 'Time to get you away from here and back to Ralph and his retinue.'

This time, it was easier getting back to the Kinnerton pavilion since they were already inside the castle walls. Nevertheless, Tom was still extremely cautious, changing the way he walked and even the way he held himself, making sure that his spine was bent, his shoulders were rounded and that his arms hung out in front. It was not the best guise in which he had ever concealed himself, but it would do. Especially as only a few, apart from servants scurrying around and a small group of the clergy, were up at this time in the morning.

They proceeded to amble back to the Kinnerton pavilion in silence. And once there, Brida managed to smuggle him in without much of an issue. Tom made a note to inform Ralph of the laxity in his security, which really needed to be strengthened. After all, he could have been anyone accompanying Brida. But it was not long before they stumbled into the main tent to witness the most domestic scene he could ever have imagined. Gwenllian was sat on a stool, beaming at her husband who was holding their gurgling baby son in his arms. Something about the scene pulled tightly in his chest and before he knew what he was doing his eyes flicked to Brida, who was also staring wistfully at the happy family picture. Tom dismissed his reaction and coughed in an attempt to gain their attention.

'I see that you have managed to locate our missing

friend, Brida.' Ralph was clearly diverted by the two of them arriving in the manner they had.

'Indeed, my lord,' she muttered, greeting Gwen and taking the baby from Ralph.

Tom refrained from watching Brida interact with their baby son and smiled impassively instead. 'Apologies from leading you on, Ralph. I had meant to meet you, but things arose that made it impossible to do so.'

'I realised it would be something like that. Good to see you in one piece, my friend. From what I hear it has been a close thing.'

'A very close thing.' They clasped each other's arm in greeting.

Gwen moved forward with outstretched hands. 'It is lovely to see you in good health, Tom.'

'And you, my lady.' He smiled, pressing a kiss on her hand. 'And I see that young Roger has grown from the last time you brought him to court.'

'Indeed, he is growing to be a fine, strapping boy.' Ralph looked at his son with immense pride before he turned his attention back to Tom, his countenance suddenly far more serious. 'Although I know you have not travelled here to discuss Roger's progress and development.'

'No. And I assume that Mistress Brida has enlightened you on everything that has happened?'

'Indeed.' Ralph pinned him with his gaze, making Tom look away uncomfortably. Damn, he hoped she had not divulged *everything* that had happened between them.

'We shall leave you to your discussions.' Gwen smiled.

But before the women could leave the tent, a Kinnerton hearth knight entered the tent and spoke with some urgency. 'My lord, you are needed in the castle right away.'

'Do we know the reason for this summon, Le Ruisseu?

'Yes, my lord.' The man spoke grimly. 'The Earl of Kent, Hubert de Burgh has taken ill, with the suspicion being that he has been poisoned! The court is in an uproar.'

Tom had turned his back to the young knight, but with this announcement he had come close to turning around and demanding more information from the man.

God's blood!

De Burgh poisoned? How the hell had this happened? The situation was becoming untenable and far more dangerous than Tom could ever have predicted.

'You bring extremely grave news, Le Ruisseu. And I shall come presently,' his friend said to the young knight.

'My lord.' The man inclined his head before leaving the tent.

Ralph quickly turned to Tom, frowning. 'This changes things and does not bode well, Tom. It looks even more dire for you now, my friend.'

Tom swore an oath under his breath. 'There is much to do, Ralph. We need to formulate a plan and rally around the young King as he will now be vulnerable. With de Burgh weak and incapacitated presently, there is a good chance that this might be a plot for more treachery. And I know you owe your loyalty to the Earl of Chester, Ralph, but both the Marcher Earls can use this situation to their own advantage.'

'That might be so, my friend but we must tread with

great care here as this is fast becoming a political disaster.'

Tom nodded at Brida. 'Ah, there is more unless you already know. Have you told them what you have discovered about the Bishop of Hereford and his clergy?'

'Not yet.'

Brida explained everything she had divulged to Tom earlier. He in turn revealed the gold ring with the strange emblem with its connection with the Bishop of Hereford. But she omitted the part where she trespassed into the Bishop's chambers earlier. Nevertheless, Tom knew that Ralph comprehended the difficulties ahead.

'God's breath! It's an understatement that this might present potentially explosive implications.'

'And herein lies the problem as there needs to be more evidence to back up a possible plot against the Crown from one of the most powerful men in the land.'

'What do you suggest?'

'Well, if I could hide here, Ralph, with your agreement, I would then be able to begin to investigate into these claims.'

'No, my friend. You cannot stay here. Not now. There will be even more of a reason to believe that you had a hand in this, especially if you are found hiding in the castle.'

Tom scowled. 'How on earth can I possibly seek any answers if I'm not here?'

Ralph sighed deeply before answering. 'We shall investigate and be your eyes for you.'

'What? No, I cannot agree to that.'

'Hear me out, my friend,' Ralph muttered holding out his hand. 'If you remain within the castle, there is a far greater chance you will be discovered and then what?

The person who is implicating you for these crimes will deal with you swiftly by incriminating you and more, with or without de Burgh's consent, believe me.'

'Lord Kinnerton is right, Tom,' Brida said softly. 'You cannot stay here. Not until we can be certain of Hubert de Burgh's condition.'

Tom tilted his head back in frustration. This was not how he wanted this predicament to be resolved—by proxy. But he knew they had a point.

'It does not sit well with me that I shall be essentially running away from this situation and leaving you all to be "my eyes", as you say.'

'I know more than anyone how you feel, Tom. But there are times when evading a situation is the best strategy and far more prudent. It allows you to live to fight another day.'

True. Ralph had done exactly what he proposed Tom should do when he had left Kinnerton after it had effectively been besieged by his upstart cousin and not returned until three years ago. Tom, however, did not have that long. This matter needed to be resolved soon.

'Very well,' Tom said reluctantly. He was not happy about this, but could think of no other alternative. At least he could use the time to ponder on everything he had learnt so far.

'And I shall do everything I can to help you.' Ralph rubbed the scarred part of his face, as he always did when he was feeling agitated. 'I will confer directly with Hugh de Villiers and Will Geraint—Lords Tallany and de Clancey—who should have arrived here by now.'

'My thanks to you all. Although I cannot think what can be done. I need to parley with Hubert de Burgh as soon as may be, but obviously that is not possible presently.'

'We shall think of something.'

'And this conference which was supposed to broker peace between the two Crowns is looking more precarious.'

'Mayhap that is the outcome whoever is behind this wants.'

'That is precisely what I have been thinking. But whether it is someone from the English or the Welsh Crown who is behind this remains to be seen.' Tom rubbed his jaw. 'For now, however, I must leave this castle as soon as possible, as you all decree, as I am seemingly the main culprit for all these crimes,' he added wryly.

'But where would you go?' Brida stepped towards him, losing all the pretence of the insouciant manner she had adopted ever since she had stepped into the tent.

'Does it matter?' Tom said softly as he walked the remainder of the way and took her hands in his. 'With de Burgh debilitated—possibly mortally so, God forbid—I must wait until my lord's situation is resolved. I cannot hope to get to the bottom of this dangerous predicament or clear my name until then.'

'Oh, Tom, this all seems so impossible.'

He could not help but smile faintly at her. 'Come now, I do not consider "impossible" to be in the lexicon of words that I can ever advocate.'

'What now, then?'

'Now I must wait, preferably somewhere I can hide discreetly and not have the trouble of being hunted down by the King's men.'

'And there I believe I can help you, Tom.' Gwen nodded at her husband before facing him again. 'Deep in the woods near the village outside the castle is a small woodsman's abode by the stream which stands empty presently.'

'And how do you know it's empty?'

'Because it belongs to my Welsh kinsman and, since the woodsman is visiting Clwyd, we know for certain that no one would be there.'

'I see.' His lips curled upwards. 'It seems that woodsmen and their cottages are to come to my aid once more.'

Chapter Fifteen

It was dusk by the time they set off from the Kinnerton pavilion. Brida's heart thumped wildly in her chest as she strode through the bailey beside Tom. It had been decided that she was to be the one to accompany him to the woodman's cottage for him to hide out until it was safe for him to return back to Carreghofa Castle. Although much of that decision had been at her insistence.

'I find it fitting that that I'm to provide you escort to the cottage in the woods in lieu of the escort you provided me here.' Brida tried to lighten the tension as they moved closer to the castle gatehouse.

'That may well be, dearest Brida, with your wonderful ideas, but this attire is not in the least bit *fitting*.'

'Stop grumbling. No one will recognise you in what you are wearing.'

'God, I hope not!' He shuddered.

'And you look very…' she looked him up and down '…pretty.'

She was still surprised that Tom had eventually agreed to escape from the castle undetected by this mad scheme of dissembling as a *woman*. He wore the clothing of Brunhilde, Lady Eleanor Tallany's maid, whose large and voluptuous physique was the only one that could accommodate Tom's wide shoulders and sculpted chest. Of course, with his great stature and height, Brunhilde's kirtle came only to his knees and the women all had helped, tearing old linen towels and stitching a layer at the hem in the hope that it would make it longer.

Over his head, they had fashioned a long veil that covered his head, neck and shoulders and topped it with a plain circlet. And beneath Tom's disguise they tried to change his shape by adding padding so that he might in turn resemble a frumpy matron.

'Pretty, eh? I'm so glad I am providing you with such amusement.'

She shrugged. 'I'm merely assisting you and trying to boost your confidence.

'Of course you are, Brida.'

'Indeed,' she retorted, trying hard not to chuckle. She threaded her arm through his, huddling closer and giving an impression of two maids walking together. Thank goodness that darkness had almost descended.

'It seems you take great joy in the humiliation that I must endure. First you want me to play the role of your love-torn husband, then it was Thomas the knave and now this—your matronly aunt.'

'Not a knave, but just *simple,* if you recall.'

'Quite. And now I look like a…' His eyes widened. 'Damn.'

'What is it?'

'One of my bosoms has just come undone,' he hissed through clenched teeth.

This was not a problem they needed and especially as they were about to pass the guards. If it were not so ridiculous, she would burst out laughing at the absurdity of the whole situation. And why Brida had been the one woman who readily volunteered for this task she would never know. Especially since Tom had taken great pains to get her to Carreghofa Castle and into Ralph and Gwen's care. Yet here she was, actively courting more trouble.

But she *did* know why she had insisted—it was because, for better or worse, she cared deeply about Thomas Lovent and was concerned about his situation. She was behaving recklessly in every way possible—especially with her position in the Kinnerton household. Yet it seemed immaterial at present. Indeed, very reckless and ill advised, but everything she had done from the moment Tom had re-entered her life had been so.

In truth, she wanted to spend more time with him. The man made her feel things that she had no right feeling. And, Lord above, when he had kissed her earlier she had felt just as breathless—boneless, as Tom had asserted—her heart soaring with wild abandon. Just contemplating that unbelievable kiss and the way it made her feel sent a warm frisson through her. However hard she tried to resist him, she could not help being drawn to him.

'Brida? What do you propose I do?'

'Just lift your "bosom" with your free elbow,' she muttered from the corner of her mouth.

'I feel so exposed,' he muttered quietly from the side of his mouth as he complied with her suggestion bolstering up his 'bosom'. 'And I doubt I can convince this group of guards that I am a *woman*.'

'You shall do well enough, if you incline your head, slump your shoulders and stoop with a bent back. Yes, just like that. In fact, you look like a rather charming, if not exceedingly tall, dowdy lady.'

'How wonderful. I had always hoped for being mistaken for one of those.'

'We're almost upon them,' Brida whispered, knowing that she had to act as guide for Tom since his head was stooped low. She put on a friendly smile and nodded pleasantly at the guards who let them pass through the gatehouse without much bother.

Tom played his part admirably as Brida knew he would. And in return she became more confident just having him by her side. Yet there was no real need for her to accompany him. Not really—but she had suggested that it would be more authentic if a woman was not walking outside the castle on her own and even Tom had reluctantly agreed to that.

They continued to meander away through the stone gateway as Brida felt the apprehension rise with every step, so she pulled her mind to think of the rest of the scheme. They would continue to the woodman's cottage and she would leave him there once a Kinnerton hearth knight arrived to escort her back.

Just then one of the guards began jeering and calling after them behind their backs, making lewd insinuations, as his friends laughed.

'How dare he?' A muscle flicked in Tom's jaw. 'I have a mind to walk back and smash the bastard's face in.'

'Take no heed of what he is saying.' She pulled his arm, walking more briskly in an attempt to get him away from the situation as quickly as possible.

'I will not allow them to talk in that disrespectful way to you.'

'It's nothing that I have not heard before. I am an unmarried woman, if you recall. Come, let us be away.'

'Very well, but know this, Brida—you should never endure that kind of behaviour. No woman should and especially not you.'

'What is so special about me?' She shook her head. 'I am no different to anyone else.'

'You are to me.' He clasped her by the elbow, turning her around so she faced him. 'And God, Brida, do you really need me to answer that? Because I can kiss you again, if you are really unsure?'

She snapped her head up to gaze up into those unfathomable green eyes and her breath hitched. Kiss her again? Every part of her longed for that. Every breath she owned yearned for that...*for him.*

You are special to me, too, Tom. She wanted to say it to him, but smoothed the creased fabric of the veil and smiled, muttering instead, 'Best not. If those guards catch a charming dowdy woman in an embrace with me, Lord knows what they might think, especially one who is pretending to be my aunt.'

The intensity of his gaze was suddenly replaced by mild amusement. 'I know exactly what they might think. Come, let us be away.'

They eventually managed to find the woodsman's cottage tucked away in the deepest part of the woods. Thank goodness, as it was growing late. It was propitious that Gwen had given them clear directions, otherwise they would doubtless not have found the place, since it was so well hidden. But it was a well-appointed dwelling with a pitched thatched roof, set near a small stream. The interior was sparse yet clean with a large pallet in one corner, a hearth in the central area and a tall wooden trestle table with some pots and other utensils stacked on top. And the woodsman's tools of his trade hung from the wooden beams from the ceiling. A long wooden coffer, that could also double as a seating area, was set against another wall.

'Well, this is a presentable abode, do you not think?' She opened the lid of the coffer, finding clean bedding and a coverlet which she brought out and shook out. In truth, she felt like giving her head a big shake as well. Every time she caught Tom's eyes she felt as though she might actually melt just from the intensity of his gaze.

'Indeed. I am sure I shall be quite content here for a day or two,' he drawled.

'I dare say you shall.' She watched as he removed the circlet and veil from his head and shoulders. 'Let me help you with that.'

She ambled towards him and helped him remove the headdress and paused, her eyes meeting his as their fingers accidentally touched. She exhaled a shaky breath before dragging her eyes away and quickly moved her fingers to deftly untie the laces on the front of Brunhilde's kirtle.

'I never thought I would be helping you out of a kirtle.' She smiled, hoping to dispel the simmering tension.

'Neither did I,' he murmured, playing with a loose tendril of her hair. 'Damn, but that was tightly pulled. I could barely breathe.'

'Ah, welcome to my world.' She chuckled.

'Really, now...' he looked her up and down '... I cannot see how you would need anything to pull you in anywhere. You are quite perfect as you are.'

She flushed, unable to think of anything to say for a

moment, so she decided to ignore his comment. 'Well, there's no need to worry, Tom, you shall be back to being your charming male self soon enough.'

'Oh, I am not worried about that.' He grinned. 'In fact, my charming maleness can survive the ignominy of being pushed, pulled and padded to become a dowdy old baggage.'

'Baggage indeed.' She shook her head as he moved closer. 'I cannot have such terrible aspersions cast on my aunt. Frumpy? Well, yes. But baggage? Certainly not.'

She untied the last lace and the kirtle fell to the ground.

'Thank you. Now the belt if you please.' He patted the tightly wrapped material around his waist that had the padding stitched on to it. 'And I am indeed lucky to have you as my champion, trussed up in Brunhilde's old clothes.'

Brida helped untie the belt that had been tied around his waist several times, allowing the many layers to fall to the wooden floor. 'Brunhilde has impeccable taste and I believe we agreed that you were a charming frump.'

'You are benevolence itself in maintaining that my appearance was not that bad.'

'Indeed. Not bad at all.' She chuckled.

'Ah, but seemingly bad enough.' He grinned. 'And there I was taken in, when you uttered something about looking charming and you know how I like that epithet.'

Brida carefully took off the padding around his stomach and chest before Tom removed his tunic, exhaling in relief. And it was then she found herself staring at a very hard, muscle-bound chest and huge powerful shoulders—and very naked down to his narrow hips, holding up his hose loosely.

He was magnificent…even with so many new and old scars from past wounds scattered on his arms, shoulders and chest. They confirmed his credentials that not only was he a knight, but an experienced warrior. Apart from this, his skin was smooth, sleek and covering hard bone and whipcord muscle. A smattering of hair on his chest ran all the way down in a thin line before disappearing under his hose that clung to his hips. Not that she should be noticing such things. Nor should she notice that his fresh, clean male scent had wrapped around her senses, making her want to touch him. She dragged her gaze away, her mouth suddenly dry.

'It worked, nevertheless, as those guards were certainly taken in. But in truth you are too tall, too wide and far too male to ever pass for a woman, Tom,' she muttered far more breathlessly than she ought to.

'Is that so?'

'Oh, yes.' She swallowed, catching her lip between her teeth to stop herself from stating any further embarrassing revelations.

'Brida, Brida, Brida.' He raised a brow and glanced down at her. 'You are not flirting with me are you?'

'No,' she said affronted. 'Why?'

'A man likes to know such things.' He wrapped a dark tendril that had escaped from her sheer cream veil around his finger. 'And I am glad that you have informed me of my failings after we've successfully managed to get out of the castle. But note, I am to use the same disguise when I need to re-enter it, in a day or so, God willing.'

'And you shall prevail once more.' She lifted her head and smiled at him as Tom stared at her for a moment before returning her smile.

'Have I told you how much I enjoy, nay, love your willingness to enter into the spirit of puerile banter with me?'

'It must be because I have been in your company and under your influence for too long.' She chuckled. 'But I admit I enjoy sparring with you, too. I believe you have corrupted me.'

He gave her such a heated look, his smile so indecent that it made her think he wanted to corrupt her far more.

Instead, he pressed his forehead against hers as she closed her eyes, inhaling the intoxicating male scent of him. At some point he had wrapped his hands around her waist, standing close to her. So close that she could hear the beating of his heart. The very air around them hummed with a strange tension filled with longing and desire. Too close.

'You will take care, won't you?' she whispered. 'When you return to the castle?'

'To satisfy you, Brida, I shall endeavour to do so.'

Tom dipped his head, making her pull away a little and look up at him. 'Are you going to kiss me? Again?'

'Yes,' he said drawing her closer in his arms. 'Why?'

'Only because a woman does like to know such things.'

'You're adorable, Brida O'Conaill.' He chuckled. 'But then I have always thought so.'

Tom bent his head slowly, giving her the chance to pull away from him at any time, but she did not. She wanted him to kiss her and so he did. He caught her lips with his, covering her mouth so sweetly, so tenderly, that Brida felt she might swoon. He pulled her even closer so that her chest was against his as those huge arms of his closed around her, his hands resting on the back of her spine.

She tentatively touched the bare skin of his chest, her palms resting on his solid frame, feeling the pounding of his heart. And that's when she heard a growl at the back of his throat. He deepened the kiss, tasting her deeply, licking into her mouth, making her blood sing. His lips moved from hers as he grazed behind her ear, along her jaw, the curve of her neck and down to her collarbone.

Dear God...

What was happening to her? She felt as though she had no control over how her body was responding to him. The truth was that she—a woman who was always restrained, always so cautious of forming any attachments—now desperately longed for Thomas Lovent. She seemed certainly willing to enter into the spirit of something more with Tom, even when there could be nothing more between them.

Was she going mad? Apparently so, because in truth she wanted him to *corrupt* her. She wanted to touch him as he was touching her. Oh, she wanted so much more. Her tongue slid against his tentatively, which sparked something a little wilder and sensual between them.

Just then there was a thump against the wooden door. Tom tore himself from their kiss and was there in a flash by the door with his dagger unsheathed. For such a tall, broad man, he was exceedingly quick and agile. Always prepared.

'Mistress Brida. It is Le Ruisseu, sent from my Lord de Kinnerton and I have come to provide escort back to Carreghofa Castle.'

Tom leant back and exhaled as Brida adjusted her kirtle as she tried to settle her rampant breathing.

'Thank you. I shall join you presently after I bid farewell to…my charming aunt.' She lifted her head and hoped that she sounded far more composed than she felt.

'Very good, mistress' the voice muttered from the other side of the door. 'I shall with your permission fill my flagon with water from the stream.'

'Yes, by all means, Messere.'

She glanced up and met Tom's eyes glittering with an unfettered fervour that he seemed to have some difficulty dampening down. As did she.

'That was a timely interruption,' he muttered, dragging his fingers through his hair.

'I know.' She smoothed back her veil, which had somehow come askew on her head, and sighed. 'I had better leave.'

'Or you could…stay.' He moved towards her and took her hands in his as he pinned her to his gaze. They stood there like that for a moment before he swore an oath under his breath and shook his head, releasing her hands. 'Hell, what am I even saying to you? Believe me, I meant no insult.'

'I know that,' she murmured. 'I felt *this,* what happened between us as well.'

'Either way I should not dishonour you by asking for things that cannot be.'

'Dishonour me? How could that be when I even teased you about kissing me?'

'Nothing between you and me has ever been as simple as that.'

'I doubt a kiss would be ever described as such.'

'Certainly not one between us, as it always makes me

long for more. Much more than I should.' He dropped his arms by his side, his hands clenched tightly. 'I cannot help but constantly misstep around you.'

'And what if I feel the same? What then?'

Brida watched as a flash of emotion flared in his eyes.

'Go. Now,' he muttered, closing his eyes. 'Please.'

She nodded, unable to say more, and went up on her toes, pressing a kiss on his cheek. 'Very well. Look after yourself, Tom and take care,' she said softly before she closed the door behind her.

Brida left the stone cottage and took a deep breath before meeting the Kinnerton hearth knight who was providing escort back to the castle. They walked away through the woods and across a shallow stream in silence. Yet all she could think about was Tom and the dejected way he had looked as he'd tried to regain his composure. How had it descended into that sheer incredible madness, so quickly?

Yet if she were honest with herself, Brida knew her foolish attraction to Thomas Lovent had been something she had been trying to resist ever since she had found him unconscious in her home in Kinnerton village. She had never, until now, understood her reaction to the man and why she had always been drawn to him. And it was not just because Brida knew she could never risk forming any attachment, but that she could not risk anything with *him*. She was cursed never to marry. But it was of no consequence now. He made her body sing—in truth, he made her heart sing, even if they could never be together.

Oh, Lord, what was she to do? Brida knew what she yearned for and what her heart whispered, was so very ill advised and altogether reckless. She knew it was a risk to everything she held dear—her heart, her soul, her reputation—not to mention being a terrible sin that could result in catastrophe. She knew all of this, but for once it did not matter. This enticing pull was far too strong to resist.

Tom could quite literally kick himself for getting so carried away with this passionate desire for Brida O'Conaill. Damn, but the way he had behaved was no better than those disgraceful guards at the castle gatehouse shouting lewd obscenities at them.

He wanted the woman so much that it was bordering on being considered improper. He had almost compromised her completely, which would have been unacceptable—not that the lady had in any way objected to his kisses or his ardour. In fact, she had seemingly *felt the same.*

He needed to take care not to be caught alone with her again because God knew that he was not safe around the woman. He needed to make sure that he would see her only as a friend. Firstly, he needed to stop kissing Brida at every opportunity. He needed to behave with courtly manners and nothing more. He needed to…

'I hope you don't mind that I returned. I felt I should come back and attend to my charming, yet frumpy aunt.'

Tom snapped his head around and found Brida standing in the doorway, so utterly beautiful, so enticing and still breathless with swollen lips from his kisses. God, she was so damn tempting.

'You see, I am very fond of her,' she murmured.

He took a few long strides towards her before he

was standing in front of her, his own breath uneven, his pulse skipping a beat.

'Are you indeed? Your charming, frumpy aunt gives her thanks.'

She smiled slowly. 'She is all benevolence.'

'Quite.' He frowned. 'But why did you return, Brida? What of Ralph and Gwen? What will they think once they realise that you did not return with the escort they sent for you?'

'They will receive the message through the afore-mentioned escort that I twisted my ankle when cross-ing a stream and so was forced to return to this cottage and stay overnight with my aunt.'

'This is not the time to jest, Brida. They know "her" as she truly is.'

'I am not jesting and I am sure they do.' She sighed and pressed her hand on his chest. 'And I am not a child, Tom but a grown woman.'

'Brida...' He groaned softly as he cupped her cheek, his thumb caressing her smooth, creamy skin. 'You can-not stay here, sweetheart.'

'Besides, they must also be aware that I spent a cou-ple of days and nights in your company during my jour-ney to this part of the kingdom. This is no different.' She reached out and touched his face. He covered her hands with his.

'You must know that is not true,' he said softly.

'Either way, at this moment I do not think about them.'

'Then what are you thinking about?' he whispered.

'You, me. This. Tonight.'

His breath hitched in his throat as he stilled, taking in what she had just said. He knew he should not accede, but it was impossible to deny this flare of attraction and desire any longer. So, he didn't. He did what he had longed to do and gave into the irresistible temptation.

He dipped his head and pressed his mouth to her and kissed her deeply, devouring her as before. Brida's hands were around his neck as he swooped her into his arms and carried her to the pallet bed hidden behind a curtain in the corner of the one-room chamber. No more words were needed.

This, tonight...

Chapter Sixteen

Tom stared at the enticing woman he had laid down on the pallet, his breathing heavy and rasping. She reached out for him and he went to her. Slowly, very slowly, he divested her of every item of clothing she wore, peeling off her kirtle and tunic, removing her linen veil and unpinning her braided hair, watching in awe as the dark, silky strands tumbled down to her waist. She was all but naked apart from the sheer linen chemise that adorned her glorious curves. Her breathing was just as laboured as his, rising and falling rapidly.

God, but she was so exquisite, so utterly beautiful. It made his chest ache just looking at her. Brida looked so alluring with her glorious raven hair spilling around her. Her midnight-blue eyes glittered and glazed under the low hazy light of the flickering candle. He traced his fingers along her arched eyebrows, the sharp line of her cheekbone and across her enticing, plump lips. He wanted to commit everything—every little detail about her—to memory.

She parted her lips, licking his fingers with her tongue, and smiled wantonly, making him groan. Well now, if she was going to torment him a little, then mayhap so should he.

Keeping his eyes fixed on hers, he lifted her leg and kissed the instep of her foot. Working his way up, he began to press open-mouthed kisses, his tongue sliding across her skin, licking and nipping, oh, so slowly from her ankle, to her knee and up her leg. He heard her gasp as his fingers grazed and caressed, climbing higher until he reached the inside of her thigh. She trembled as he licked and nipped the inside of her thigh near the apex of her femininity, teasing her. So close, yet he ventured no further. Not this time.

Tom almost pulled away at that and wondered whether there would ever be a next time and why he had even thought of it at all. Annoyed with the direction of these reflections, he pushed these musings away and started anew on the other leg, before moving to the flare of her hips.

Brida let out a shaky breath, as he moved higher up her body, kissing and caressing her stomach, swirling his tongue around her navel. His hands cupped her breasts as he pressed kisses on the underside of each one. He then flicked his tongue over one of her dark rose-coloured nipples before taking it in his mouth, sucking it gently as she arched her back. She tasted delicious.

Her hands in turn moved all over his chest, around his shoulders, drawing him closer, her fingernails digging sharply into his back. Oh, yes, pleasure and pain. Joy and sorrow. Hope and despair. These were the emotions that constantly rippled through him whenever he was near Brida O'Conaill. And far more besides. She made his heart break into a thousand little pieces before coming back together again as one.

Tom hurriedly took off the remainder of his clothing. He lifted himself and moved above her, his body over hers as he shifted his weight on to his elbows, his legs tangling with hers. He gave her a wicked smile before continuing his onslaught of pleasure. He slanted his lips over hers and kissed her so softly, so tenderly. But even this was too much, too potent, and it wasn't long before he deepened the kiss and wanted more. Always wanting so much more.

His hands roamed all over her, learning every sweeping rise and curve of her glorious body. God, but he had never felt like this before in his life. He was reduced to being a man driven to madness by this woman in his arms. He swept his lips and tongue over her body making his way along her collarbone, the curve of her neck, behind her ear. God, but her scent was so sweet, so tempting.

'You should not have come back,' he whispered in her ear.

'I know,' she gasped again as he caught her earlobe between his teeth.

Even if it killed him, he had to give her a moment to reconsider. A moment to remind her of what was about to happen between them. Remind her that there was no turning back after this. It would change matters irrevocably between them, hurling them both into the unknown. And this was something he knew implicitly about her—that she would not be so careless as to abandon her fiercely guarded convictions and beliefs on a mere whim. It had been because fate had thrown them together. And after just a few days and nights in each other's company, they found that spark of attraction still existed between them even after three years of being apart. But now it was blazing out of control.

'I...we should not be doing this,' he said again.

'I know that as well. Would you rather I leave?' she said breathlessly.

'Oh, God, what are you doing to me, Brida O'Conaill.'

Her brows furrowed in the middle. 'What am *I* doing to you?'

'Yes.' He kissed her neck, his finger grazing her smooth skin. Her sweet floral scent mixed with her essence was making his head spin with desire. How he still managed to speak, he did not know. 'Do you not understand that this will complicate everything between us?'

'I know that, too, Tom.' She moaned. 'But please do not stop. I want you...this desperately.'

Hell's teeth.

Desperately, indeed.

His blood roared as he entered her then, pushing in one long thrust. He stilled as he tore his lips from hers, watching her with concern as a soft gasp escaped from her lips.

'Are you well, sweetheart? Did I hurt you?'

She shook her head and reached out to stroke his jaw. He turned his head into her palm and kissed it. 'I am perfectly well.'

'Ah, good.' A slow smile spread on his face. 'Because there is more. An awful lot more.'

Reason and rationale had dissipated from Brida's mind as she had given in to temptation and desire so extraordinary, so potent, that she had not been able to contain herself. He had reduced her to this. And she had desperately hungered for every touch, every kiss, every surge of heat that coursed through her. And if she were not careful, she would not only give her body, but surrender her heart and her soul to Thomas Lovent as well. Mayhap she already had.

She could feel him inside her, stretching her far more than she could ever have imagined after that initial burst of pain subsided, and welcomed him in the most ardent of ways. And then he started to move deeper and further as she gripped his shoulders for support. He kissed her again as he quickened his speed. He built such unfettered sensations as the heat in her veins blazed and gathered like a wildfire, licking through every part of her body. More and more until she felt as though she might burst with something she had no experience of.

Brida had never felt so alive, never so enthralled and vital, so heightened on the brink of a precipice. And then it happened, she reached the cusp, the very edge before she shattered into tiny little shards. Tom continued for a moment more before he, too, found his release and shuddered, falling beside her. He gently gathered her into his arms as they both brought their ragged breathing back to something akin to normality. Even though nothing about what had come to pass between them had been remotely normal or usual.

At that very moment Brida did not care, not when she had just experienced unbridled joy rippling through her. Had she ever felt anything close to this? Never. But then her life had been one of restraint and loneliness— which it would soon go back to being…as before.

But for just one night she had wanted to know what she had been missing and to give in to what her heart wanted. And it had wanted Thomas Lovent—a man she not only trusted and desired, but cared for deeply. Far more deeply than she cared to examine.

'Wait there.' He got up and walked to the coffer and wrung the linen towel in the big washing bowl of cool water and returned back. 'Allow me?'

'Thank you, but I think I shall take that.' She flushed as she administered the cool towel briskly over her sore body. Tom handed her a mug of ale from the supplies he had brought and sat up beside her.

His smile made her pulse trip over itself. He had looked so dishevelled, so virile, so very wonderfully handsome. It made her chest ache just watching him. But she did—she drank her fill of him, wanting to remember everything about him. The way he prowled so effortlessly around the room, that gorgeous mole by his right eye which disappeared into the crinkles when he smiled. The sound of his laughter, his scent. Everything. Oh, yes, tonight she would allow herself to remain content and happy. To feel this giddy joy. She would not think about what she had done or feel the inevitable shame and guilt. Those would come soon enough. But not *this...tonight.*

'Hold me, Tom.'

'Gladly,' Tom whispered as he turned to her and kissed her forehead. 'Sleep sweetheart.'

The hazy glimmer of dawn had come far too soon for Brida, who had blinked a few times before stirring from a deep, dreamy slumber. She opened her eyes and yawned, stretching her arms, before suddenly recalling where she was and who she was lying with. A huge, taut arm had been casually draped around her waist and her legs were tangled with a pair of hard, muscly, male ones.

No, it had not been a dream, but something close to one. She carefully peeled the arm away and turned her head, watching the sleeping knight beside her with a faint smile on her lips. She itched to run her fingers along the angular plane of his jaw line, but she did not want to wake him. If only this had not been bound to the one night they had shared. If only they could have more time. But it was a fool's dream. It could never be more than it had been between them. That was the promissory oath she had made with herself—that it would be just this one night. One night of pleasure in exchange for loneliness and heartache for the rest.

She sighed and slowly pulled the coverlet away, getting up from the pallet. She ambled to the coffer and used the linen towel and cool water to quickly wash before beginning to dress, feeling her body ache in areas she could never have conceived. She pulled on her tunic and stepped into her green woollen kirtle, sliding the bodice up and over her shoulders.

'Making your escape already?' a voice drawled from behind.

Brida spun around on her heel to find Tom sat up in the bed *dishabille*. He looked so gorgeous with his chiselled jaw, a day's worth of stubble, that wide expanse of naked male chest and his mop of dark golden hair over one eye. He dragged it back as he arched an eyebrow, waiting for her reply as she had naturally been staring at him.

She blinked, dropping her gaze. 'I must go,' she said, turning her back and continuing to dress. 'The Kinnerton knight from yesterday will be back to provide escort to the castle. And I find my *ankle* has been well rested.' God, but that had been the flimsiest of excuses for her to have returned to Tom. Her behaviour had been bewildering at best, wanton at worst. But Brida had not pondered on any of the misgivings she had felt—in fact, she had purposely pushed them all away. And although she had acted without due care or consideration, she would not feel any remorse about it.

'Well, that is a blessing.'

She sat down on a stool and pulled her woollen stockings over her feet and legs, tying them to the ribbons of her chemise as the silence grew between them. As did the awkwardness. She stood and walked away from the pallet, attempting to tie the laces of her kirtle at the back. Her fingers fumbled, making far more work of it than they should. But before she knew it, Tom had quickly dressed and was there behind her.

'Allow me.'

She could feel his breath teasing the skin on the back of her neck, making her shiver. 'Thank you,' she muttered, as he began lacing up her kirtle from behind. Brida could feel his nimble fingers graze her back, through the sheer layer of chemise she was wearing beneath it. She swallowed uncomfortably. 'It is extremely difficult to tie the laces on this dress without help. It's one of Gwen's old ones,' she added inanely, filling in the silence.

'There. I believe the deed is done, in that your laces are fastened as you had them before…last night.'

'Yes. I thank you again.' She turned around and gave him a what she hoped was a friendly smile. God, but she could hardly meet his eyes, her stomach knotting itself into a nervous coil. She smoothed down the non-existent creases on her kirtle and took a step back and then another. 'I had better leave.'

'Wait, would you care for a mug of ale before you go? Or mayhap break your fast? I have brought enough provisions.' He sighed and continued in a low voice, 'Don't leave like this, Brida.'

'Very well, a mug of ale would be most welcome.' She watched as he padded to the coffer where he splashed ale into two mugs.

'I must say that I have a new-found respect for women with all the restrictive clothing you have to wear.' He walked back and pressed a mug into her hands.

'Thank you,' she said, taking a sip. 'That is nothing compared to what women face on a daily basis. Especially if they are on their own.'

He stared at her for a moment before he wrapped a dark tendril behind her ear.

'But you don't have to be alone, Brida,' he said so softly that she felt a lump form in her throat.

She turned her back and walked to the coffer, placing her mug on top of it and absently pouring a little more ale, taking a big gulp in the vain hope that the lump might dissipate. It didn't.

'Unfortunately, I do. I have to be,' she mumbled, looking up to find him watching her, leaning back against the wall with one hand crossed across his chest and the other holding his mug.

'Ah, but I forgot that you have forsaken your own happiness.' His voice was laced with a measure of bitterness. 'And for what? The undying love for your late betrothed? Your devotion may be admirable and I admit to being a little jealous, but I am sure your deceased betrothed would prefer that you lived your life, Brida, rather than pledge yourself to his memory, in perpetuity.'

'You do not comprehend any of it, Tom.'

'Do I not? A thousand pardons. Why do you not enlighten me then?'

'I do not choose to be alone as you presume and certainly not for those reasons… But it is only that I have to be alone.' She exhaled in exasperation.

He narrowed his eyes. 'What precisely does that mean?'

She ignored his question and asked one of her own instead, realising the enormity of what he had uttered: *'You don't have to be alone, Brida.'*

'And what are you saying, in any case, Tom? That I should be with you, to redress my loneliness?'

She could see from the look on his face that he had not realised the implication of what he had said on the spur of the moment. He nodded. 'Indeed, we can be together, Brida. If we will it to be. After what happened last night, there might even be the possibility of a child.'

She felt the blood drain from her face. That could not be. The implication would otherwise be disastrous—for all of them. Besides, it was not as though he truly wanted such an attachment. It was proposed in haste without due thought or consideration.

'It's not as though you wish to take a wife, Tom. You have maintained many times that a man like you, working for the Crown, cannot have such obligations.' She sighed in frustration. 'That is what I believe you are alluding to—marriage, a family? All this because we shared a night of intimacy. It's preposterous.'

'Apologies, you believe *that* to be preposterous, but not denying yourself the chance of happiness?' he muttered in an irritated tone. 'And you did not answer me before, Brida. What exactly do I not comprehend about your past?'

'The truth is that I did not know him—the man I was betrothed to.'

'I do not understand.' He frowned. 'Why then have you forsaken the future you could have had all these years?'

Brida considered telling him something entirely different to the truth, but in the end, she wanted him to understand everything about her past. She owed Tom Lovent that much at least.

'It is rather a sad and sordid tale, I am afraid. But you shall hear it, even though no one else ever has. Not even Gwen knows the whole sorry tale.' She sighed sitting on a stool. 'My real name is Brighid Ni Diarmuid. I am the eldest daughter of Diarmuid MacConaill, Lord of Clarmallagh, o' Eireann—Ireland.'

Tom's eyes widened in surprise. 'Even I have heard of your father. He was a formidable warrior lord with an impressive reputation.' His brow shot up. 'And that in turn makes you a noblewoman, Brida.'

'It would if I still claimed my family name,' she muttered sadly. 'My father lost everything he had ever built, Tom, and in doing so I also lost my name and with it severed all family connection, as well as leaving my homeland for good. Not that it makes any difference now anyway, as I am the sole survivor of my kin.'

'What happened?'

'Years ago, a powerful seer declared a prophecy stating that a tragedy would befall all the children of Diarmuid MacConaill and that his line would end with him because of the sins of his past. No one took heed of this warning until our castle and land were besieged on the eve of my betrothal banquet by my father's enemies. My father, my betrothed and even my young brothers...were...they were brutally murdered in front of a huge crowd.'

'Oh, God, Brida, I am so sorry.' Tom sat on the stool beside her and covered her hand with his own. 'That's truly shocking.'

'Yes, and my mother and I were spared and given clemency as long as we left, never to return, and agreed to enter a convent. Which is what my mother did, but not before telling me that our downfall was my doing since I was to be a wife and mother. She said that one could never escape one's destiny and ours had already been determined.'

'How in heaven's name could she blame *you* for anything?'

'Easily, Tom. She told me that I was cursed. Needless to say I was devastated and believed everything she said and I've carried that terrible guilt with me all these years. But I vowed to her that I would lead a life of celibacy for penance of what happened and would always remember the prophecy and heed the warning.'

He swore an oath under his breath. 'But you did not take the veil?'

'No.' She smiled bleakly. 'Rather than enter a holy order I joined the household of William Marshal and Lady Isabel de Clare. The Countess had known my father through her family in Ireland and took pity on me. So I joined her ladies and met and befriended Gwenllian ferch Hywel, now Lady de Kinnerton, as you know, and came with her to Kinnerton once she married.'

'I would never have imagined any of this.' He

dragged his fingers through his hair. 'And you have held on to this…this guilt for all of this time?'

'Yes.'

'With this being the reason you have never married?

'Yes,' she repeated. 'And never intend to. On my oath.'

'Oh, Brida…' He shut his eyes for a moment. 'Again, I must wonder how any of it could be considered to have been the fault of a young, innocent maiden as you must have been back then. Your mother was wrong to have blamed you.'

She stood. 'Either way, I hope this explains the reasons why I have remained unwed and alone. And will continue to do so.'

'Yet I must wonder why someone as intelligent and enlightened as you would believe in curses and prophecies.'

'Because my mother made me swear never to forget it. After all, I saw the horrific events unfold before my very eyes. I saw the devastation it left in its wake, Tom.'

'But consider that this kind of brutality, although gruesome and harrowing, Brida, especially when it involves your kin, occurs far more than you know.' He stood and took her hand in his. 'I, too, have witnessed horrors on bloodied battlefields and the destruction that it leaves, as you say. But the outcome of any combat is far more to do with chance and luck than it has with any prophecies of doom, as was the case with what happened in Ireland.'

She gaped at him, unable to speak for a moment. There could be no wisdom to what he had said, could there? The situations were not the same.

'That was different to the victors and losers of any combat, Tom.'

'How so?' His brows furrowed in the middle. 'The situations may not be the same—but both were just as unpredictable and uncertain as each other and equally impossible to determine.'

'Yet you forget that what happened to my family, Tom, had already been decided long before it had even occurred.'

'By a prophecy? Given by whom? Who was this seer? And to whom had this person given allegiance— loyalty? You forget that as an agent of the Crown I gather information, knowledge and detail, examine every fact before I can penetrate the truth. I have seen how men use any weakness they find and twist facts to crush their enemies and that is before they've even ventured on to any bloodied battlefields.'

'Are you suggesting that what happened to my father, my brothers and the man I was meant to marry was… was planned and arranged beforehand?'

'I cannot say, Brida. But I do know how such words can seep into minds, taking hold slowly, spreading poison insidiously to garner the desired effect—the belief that an event was wholly out of one's control. As if destiny had a hand in determining the future. Do you not see, nothing in life is that certain?'

She screwed her eyes shut, rubbing her forehead. 'For so long I have believed that I was to blame for all of it. And left here on this earth to face the penance for what happened.'

'And now?'

Now, she was wrestling with his perspective on what

had happened to her family. 'I simply cannot take it in. In truth, I do not know.'

'Indeed this is something for your conscience to resolve. And although I would never tell you what to believe, I would ask you to apply sense and reason, Brida.' He gave her a brief glance before continuing. 'Remember that your mother was grieving—as were you—for the terrible loss of your kinsmen in that horrific manner. It is understandable that you clung to a prophecy as a means to explain it all. There is no shame in that.'

'You make it sound so very comprehensible and yet it is far from that.'

No, it could not all be so easily explained, much as Brida longed for it to be. This was something that she had lived with for such a long time, that she did not know how to accept another explanation for the terrible events that unfolded all those years ago. For so long she had held these beliefs. She could not possibly have been wrong all this time. Could she?

He sighed. 'I do understand, Brida, far more than you realise about carrying a huge burden of guilt.'

She snapped her head around. 'In what way?'

'I told you about my family's demise by the devastating fires that claimed the lives of all members of my family, and all our dependants. And like you, I believed that the blame lay with me. I had been a selfish reprobate at the time and the fault of what had happened was something that many believed to be mine. I was a terrible son, brother and friend, and devoid of any of the usual responsibility that I should have had for my family.'

'I cannot readily believe that.'

'Can you not?' He looked away. 'Had I been a better man, then the fires might even have been avoidable, Brida,' he added bitterly.

'I do not understand.' She frowned. 'How can any of it have been your fault?

'Just as easily as your belief in yours, Brida.'

'But you must have been a boy—or a young man at best?' she said, ignoring the voice in her head reminding that she, too, had been exceptionally young when her family had perished.

He shook his head. 'I was old enough to know that my father had a sickness of the mind, which was progressively getting worse. Rather than take heed to my mother's pleading missives begging me to come back home for support and help, do you know what I did instead? I continued with furthering my own selfish ambitions as a knight. I knew where my duty lay, but chose to ignore it.'

'But how could any of what happened, the fire and its aftermath, be anything to do with you, Tom? You were not even there.'

'That is precisely the point. I was not there when my family needed me, Brida, they *needed* me. And instead of doing my duty and returning, I turned the other way and ignored their summons. Then one fateful night my father, who was not well in his mind by then, set a fire in the manor house in order to purge it from evil, or some such nonsense.' He spat. 'But all he did was devastate the whole area with the raging fires from hell itself, claiming the manor, the land, all the livestock and, more importantly, all the inhabitants including my family. All except Joan, my poor frightened sister.'

'I am so sorry, Tom.'

He shrugged. 'It happened a long time ago. But in

time—a very long time—I eventually learned to live with my past, accept it, even though it was—still is exceptionally hard to do. I threw myself into work, made it my mission to do my duty by my liege lord and more importantly by Joan.'

'How did you manage it?' she whispered.

Tom did not answer, but closed his eyes for a moment as if remembering.

'By forgiving myself.' He opened his eyes and gave her a faint smile. 'It is something that William Geraint recommended I do, having experienced similar difficulties himself.'

'I see.' But, no, she did not see. There was so much to take in.

'I, too, felt the guilt of surviving. But until you can accept the past and forgive yourself for being left behind, you cannot move forward with your life.'

'It was not your fault, Tom.'

'And neither were the murders of your betrothed, your father and your kin the fault of you or some curse.'

Brida took an uncertain step back, staring at him. For a long moment they stood in silence, lost in reflections of their past marred with their personal tragedy, misfortune, heartache and anguish.

'I should go.'

'Tell me something before you leave, Brida,' he said softly. 'What did your estimable father do that garnered such retribution—such a heavy price on his kin?'

'He took what did not belong to him.'

Chapter Seventeen

'Fool,' Tom reproached himself in a harsh whisper. 'Idiot.'

'Did you say something?' Ralph de Kinnerton threw a sideways glance at him.

'No. I am just muttering to myself.'

'Dear me, I had not believed that we had left you *that* long in the woodsman's cottage.' William Geraint, Lord de Clancey, snorted, shaking his head.

Ralph smirked. 'Indeed, not long enough for madness to set in.'

It had been longer than Tom had expected until he'd received a message that Hubert de Burgh had not only lived, but was feeling in better health—thank God. By nightfall, his friends had come to provide escort back to the castle.

This happened just a couple of days after Brida had scrambled out of the cottage in haste—although, in truth, it might as well have been a hundred. Two long days and nights that Tom was forced to spend alone in that damn cottage, with the lingering memory of their night together, made him turn everything that had occurred, and all that they had said, over and over in his head. From trying in vain to resist their desire to tumbling into that night of passionate intimacies, to the shocking revelations of their past—so strikingly similar in many ways. Then he'd opened his foolish mouth and intimated that they should be together. That he could somehow save her from the pitiful loneliness that she had inflicted on herself.

He had intimated this—*intimated*. There had been no words for how she filled his lonely heart, or how she made him smile, made him laugh with her witticisms when she joined in with his nonsensical jests. Or that Tom ached for her in ways he could barely comprehend, or that when she was close by, his whole world somehow made sense. There had been no words of *love*…

Damn, but he had made a mess of it. And the timing of his asinine offer could not have been more dire. The morning after the night of pleasure—and not before he had taken exception to her beliefs about her family's demise. Tom had more or less questioned the validity of those beliefs in a prophecy that had obviously caused Brida a huge amount of pain.

Yet, he had to give her time to consider all her options. He had no choice but to let her go, fool that he was. And he had spent the last couple of days lost in his own contemplation, hoping that she would somehow want him as much as he wanted her. Not that he was in a position to offer Brida O'Conaill much anyway. He was a knight, an agent of the Crown, and as such there was no room in his life for anyone. Even now, when he should be turning his mind to the dangerous predicament he faced and all the preparation that he needed to make for a meeting with Hubert de Burgh, his thoughts were flooded with her—*with Brida.*

Madness indeed...

'Is everything well?' Ralph muttered as they crossed a burbling stream that washed over craggy rocks and stones, winding its way through the woods.

Tom's eyes fell to the clear water pooling around the stepping stones and blinked. He wished his head was as clear as the water. 'Of course. Why do you ask?'

'You do not seem like yourself, my friend.'

Tom tried to defuse his friend's perceptiveness with his usual humour. 'You wonder at that when I am forced to once again don the dress of a frumpy, yet exceedingly tall woman.'

'You look splendid as a frump, Tom, but I was not commenting on your appearance, as you well know.'

'Is that so?'

'I might also add that Brida is just as out of sorts as you,' Ralph said in a low quiet voice before continuing, 'I hope there is no need for me to have a conversation about why that might be or insist on an explanation regarding what occurred here when she stayed with you in that cottage.'

'You may ask what you like, but it would be none of your damn concern.'

'That is where you are wrong. It is most certainly my concern, Tom. Brida is Gwen's dearest friend—she is like a sister to her and in turn like a sister to *me.* I will not have anyone upset or trouble her.'

'Neither would I,' Tom retorted through clenched teeth. 'I care for her a great deal, Ralph. But whatever has or has not happened is between Brida and myself, without reference to anyone.'

His friend beside him must have heard something in his voice that made him soften his. 'I understand well, Tom. You know my own uphill difficulties convincing Gwen that we should be together.'

Tom knew how exceptionally hard Ralph had found persuading his now wife that they could have a happy future. But then Ralph and Gwen had always been destined to be together, whereas Tom was still trying to ascertain what his future was and Brida felt her destiny lay in a life spent in lonely solitude. And all because her mother had ingrained in her that that was all she was worthy of and conveniently wrapped some absurd prophecy around it.

'You misunderstand, Ralph, it is not the same situation.'

'Either way, take care, Tom. From what I understand, Brida wishes to remain an unwed maiden. And I will not have her harassed…by anyone. Not even you, my friend.'

'If you do not mind, I prefer to talk of more pressing matters,' Tom said coolly, dragging his mind back to the situation that needed his attention. 'Tell me more about the Bishop of Hereford and whether anything has been uncovered regarding the damn emblem on the ring.'

'Very well.' Ralph watched him from the corner of his eyes. 'De Burgh is, as you know, recovered from his malaise. And the peace treaty with Llywelyn of Cymru is going ahead as previously arranged, but not before a grand banquet to mark the occasion, which shall take place in two nights from now.'

'And what news of the Bishop of Hereford?'

'Unfortunately, there is nothing to report there. The

man is a beacon of piety as well as being an intellectual stalwart.'

Will sidled up to them. 'We searched everything from Foliot's alb and his hooded cape to his episcopal robes and vestments. This as well as the possessions he has brought: a wooden box where he keeps his bishop's ring and other trifles. Every parchment, missive—everything. All cleaner than a nun's habit.'

Tom frowned. 'There must be some connection.'

'Unless Mistress Brida is somehow mistaken?' Will gave him a wry glance. 'Not that I doubt the strength of her convictions.'

'Of course not.' Tom did not meet his friend and one-time mentor's curious gaze. 'If Brida believes that there is a connection here with that damn ring the murdered man purposely left in his leather purse, then there must be one. We just need to sniff it out.'

'That's just it, Tom. I haven't been able to find anything that ties the Bishop to this case. Nothing. And although my days as an agent have long been over, I have not totally lost my keen sense of observation or the knack for investigation. I have personally followed him day and night. But I tell you that Foliot is not your man, Tom.' Will pressed his lips into a thin line.

Tom muttered an oath under his breath before looking back up. 'Then the only thing we can do is to somehow lure the culprit out.'

'If they are here, that is.'

'How can they not be? If this is an attempt to discredit the treaty between the two Crowns, they will almost certainly be at the castle. Waiting and plotting.'

'We shall have to wait and see, but time is running

out as the treaty will be signed anon by Llewelyn and King Henry. In fact, after the banquet,' Ralph added.

'If that is the case, I believe that the best opportunity for this culprit to carry out whatever nefarious scheme they have planned is at the banquet itself.'

'Yes, I believe you might be right, Tom.'

'But what of the attempt on de Burgh's life? What of the young King?'

'The security arrangement at court has naturally been strengthened, which of course will make granting an audience with the man even more difficult.'

'Never fear, I can dissemble in any given guise, as you can well see.'

'Oh, yes.' Will looked him up and down, smirking. 'And a most fetching, if not hefty woman you make, too.'

Tom ignored the remark. 'Either way, I shall somehow wheedle my way to de Burgh's chambers. The man cannot elude me again. I must have some satisfaction this time.'

'As long as you do not get yourself arrested on the many counts of treason. There's a tidy ransom on your hide, Tom.'

'And we, along with Hugh de Villiers, can help shield you and give you all the aid you might need.'

Tom knew he was lucky to have the support and friendship of these powerful and influential men. But this was his mission to complete, his honour at stake. 'You have my sincere thanks. All of you,' he said on a choke.

'However, I had better warn you before you find out for yourself, Tom. Brida has already taken it upon herself to assist you, even before your arrival back at the castle.'

What?

Tom stopped walking abruptly and went very still. 'In what way, exactly?'

'She managed to inveigle her way into de Burgh's chambers by insisting that she can provide comfort to the Earl at this, and I quote, "trying time".'

A muscle ticked in Tom's jaw. 'God's blood, Ralph, could you not have prevented this?'

Will gave him an amused glance before shrugging. 'Not only did Ralph refrain from preventing Mistress Brida from this folly, but she was encouraged by his own fair wife as well.'

'Only because they were adamant about it, fuelled, I might add, by Isabel, your own equally fair wife's encouragement that this was a good course of action.'

'True, when Isabel gets something in her head, it's very difficult to dissuade her. And I am not the man to do it, especially when she is quite right, as she is in this instance.'

'This is serious, for God's sake,' Tom hissed. 'A man was murdered and I have been hunted from London to Kinnerton, and all the way here, with trumped-up charges. Yet you both believe that Brida and your women should be involved?'

'You know, Tom. I have really missed you.' Will grinned, slapping his back. 'But, alas, in this case I leave it all to you to make those interfering women see sense.'

'You understand that they wanted to help,' Ralph muttered apologetically.

'Lord have mercy.' Tom exhaled through clenched

teeth. 'And exactly how has Brida seen to de Burgh's damn *comfort*?'

'By plucking at a lute. And marvellous she is, too.'

'In truth, the Earl is delighted by the beautiful music Brida plays. It soothes his nerves and helps him think.'

'I don't care how much it soothes the blasted man, I do not want her involved.' Tom screwed his eyes shut for a moment. 'It is far too dangerous.'

'Calm yourself, Tom. Mistress Brida and Lady Gwenllian are both quite safe.'

'Indeed. Not only has Brida been privy to the many parleys in de Burgh's chambers, but she has managed to be all eyes and ears in there.'

Tom wondered whether his friends had all but lost their rationale and reason. He gave Ralph a disgusted look, feeling quite frustrated with the whole situation. It was all getting out of his grasp. Especially as Brida had been doing this all the while he had been hiding in the woodsman's cottage. And the thought that she had willingly put herself into harm's way made him want to punch something. Hard. He did not want her anywhere near de Burgh or any other of the powerful men at Court. He would have thought that Ralph might have felt the same about his woman. Not that Brida was in anyway his. Yet Tom could not help feeling protective of her.

'Either way. I do not like it.' He grimaced. 'I do not like it at all.'

Tom, dressed as a woman, with the two powerful lords at his side, had managed to slip back inside Carreghofa Castle with relative ease. It was another matter attempting to gain an audience with Hubert de Burgh, but the following morning, he had finally been granted an audience in his makeshift privy chamber, dressed once again in female attire.

When he entered his lord's chamber, he was glad that there were only a handful of people, apart from the prerequisite guards both outside the door and a few inside as well. His eyes flicked briefly to where Brida was sat with Gwen in the corner, a Kinnerton hearth knight standing beside them. He had not seen her since their night at the cottage and she had plainly avoided him since his return to the castle.

She was wrapped in the soft, lyrical melody that she was creating and made no outward sign that she had registered his entrance, dressed as an old biddy, wearing Brunhilde's clothes once again. An ache throbbed in his chest at the sight of her. She looked tired, with dark smudges beneath her closed eyes and a pinched look to her face, as she wrestled with the emotion of the music. But to him, Brida had never looked so lovely.

Tom hobbled in with his spine bent, and head stooped low, escorted by Lord Tallany, Hugh de Villiers. Very few were aware that Tom had more than a passing acquaintance with Hugh, so it made perfect sense for him to be the one who escorted Tom. They made their way slowly to the end of the chamber, close to the hearth where his liege sat with a couple of fur blankets thrown over his legs to keep warm, while another couple of guards stood on either side of him.

Despite his ordeal Hubert de Burgh seemed just as hale as when Tom had last seen him. No one would know by looking at him that the man had almost succumbed to a deadly poison.

'My lord Earl,' Hugh de Villiers addressed de Burgh.

'May I introduce my elderly Lady Aunt who wishes to pass on her good wishes to you in person?'

'Come forth, my Lord Tallany, and bring this *lady* to me.' De Burgh clicked his fingers to his guards, muttering something that made the two men initially look a little perplexed before bowing their heads and retreating to the furthest stone wall, seemingly dismissed. 'Come, my dear, sit beside me here and rest your weary legs,' he muttered, tapping the stool beside him on the dais.

Tom walked up the steps and sat gingerly on the stool, arranging the skirt of the kirtle around him. De Burgh inclined his head before finally speaking.

'Plague take you, Lovent, you took your time in getting here,' de Burgh muttered quietly, while keeping a placid smile fixed on to his face. 'And this, I suppose, is one of your better disguises.'

How typical of de Burgh to be one step ahead of everyone here.

Without batting an eye, Tom responded, 'Apologies, my lord, but I have been waylaid and had a most arduous time in getting here.'

'So I gather,' de Burgh hissed. 'You have made a catalogue of errors on this mission. As well as getting yourself embroiled into the centre of what could become a political nightmare.'

'Yes, my lord.'

'Firstly, you bungled meeting an informant at Westminster Abbey.'

'Indeed,' Tom muttered through gritted teeth.

'And then you had half of the Bishop of London's blasted men on the hunt for you all over the kingdom.'

'Yes, my liege,' Tom muttered, allowing the man to expel all his pent-up spleen and fury.

'Not to mention putting my whole supposedly secret organisation in jeopardy by allowing your friends to provide aid. Damn it, man, you have exposed yourself quite inexcusably.'

Tom bit back an oath he would happily have uttered. 'Without wishing to contradict, only the Lords Tallany, de Clancey and de Kinnerton are aware of the true nature of my work, my lord. And they are men of unimpeachable character whose loyalty I am fortunate to have. They would never betray me.'

'You are lucky to have such powerful friends, Lovent,' he sneered. 'But what of the woman? What say you about her?'

Hell's teeth! How had de Burgh known about Brida? This situation was fast unfolding, becoming more and more of a disaster. Tom had wanted to shield her, but it seemed that there was little his liege lord was not aware of. His eyes flew to Brida at the other end of the chamber and took in her loveliness as she tilted her head, swaying from side to side in time to the music she made. God, but how he wished he could march up to her and take her away from all of this. And he would once this was all over—*if,* he corrected himself, *if* she would have him. Her eyes fluttered open and caught his for a moment before she looked away and said something to her friend.

'I can only surmise from your silence that you had not anticipated that I would be aware of Mistress Brida O'Conaill—or I should rather say Brighid Ni Diarmuid?'

Tom's jaw dropped at how the man could have knowledge of this. But then again Brida had been one of the Countess of Pembroke's ladies and lived in the household of William Marshal, Lord Protector of England, just before the great man's death.

De Burgh gave him a sly look. 'Why in heaven's name would you suppose that I had the woman in this damn confining chamber making that clatter, otherwise? Although, in truth, she does play rather well, as her father did on the one occasion I had the pleasure of hearing that old war horse play.'

Tom took a deep breath. 'There was little I could do when Mistress Brida all but guessed the true nature of my work, my lord. Especially when the Bishop of London's damn men, who trailed me from London, burst into her cottage in Kinnerton.'

'Yes, but you allowed this woman into the inner sanctum of our operation. I would wager that there is very little she is not aware of regarding this mission. That puts her in a very precarious position, Lovent.'

Tom bent his head low to stop himself from glancing at Brida again. Exhaling, he swore an oath. 'There was no choice, my lord, especially as I was badly injured near Kinnerton and needed a place to convalesce.' He leant forward a little to the man. 'After all, we cannot always know of an assailant wishing to harm us, as you yourself are too aware.'

'Impudent pup. Tell me, how the devil can you be assured of her secrecy, anyway?' he hissed. 'God's blood, man, what were you thinking?'

That was just the point. Tom had not been thinking at all—not properly since he had collapsed in Brida's cottage, delirious with fever. He knew that everything Hubert de Burgh had said was true, even though it was painful having to hear it from his liege's lips. Tom had erred and made many, many mistakes, but not where she was concerned. Brida was and never would be a mistake. Not to him. And he'd be damned if he regretted the time he had had with her.

'Mistress Brida is not only exemplary, but irreproachable, my lord. On my honour I would vouch for her character. She would, without hesitation, keep my confidence.'

'Formed an attachment, have you eh?' He shook his head. 'It never ends well, Lovent. Never. Mark my words.'

Chapter Eighteen

Hanging on to his temper by a thread, Tom merely inclined his head before needing to drag this discourse away from Brida. And quickly. 'Indeed, my Lord de Burgh. But there is another matter of huge importance that I have wished to bring to your notice. The murdered informant did manage to pass to me this before his demise.' Tom dragged his hand from under the folds of the kirtle's skirt, holding the leather purse.'

'I was not aware of this.' The older man scratched his beard absently.

This was the first time during the whole meeting that Tom could see that Hubert de Burgh was far more discomposed than he let on. 'What in heaven's name is in the blasted thing, Lovent?'

Tom moved his legs wider, allowing the material of his kirtle to drape. He pulled out the contents of the purse, one by one, and laid them out inside the folds. With their heads bent together, an unsuspecting observer would think that Hubert de Burgh was having an intimate conversation with his fancy old paramour. Heaven help him.

'It is an artless array of predictable items put together by a novice in such a ham-handed clumsy manner. Every item here looks like it could be part of a jest.'

'I would have to agree.' De Burgh nodded.

'Only it wasn't. What is most astonishing is that a man was killed because he intended for me to have this purse.' Tom scowled. 'And the only item I had initially believed to be of some value was the parchment with codices I cannot decipher.'

'That is because you are not meant to, Lovent. I have purposely made it my business that the agents working for me are not privy to every single method of ciphering that I implement. That way I can administer and direct our organisation effectively.'

And keep everything tightly under his control, Tom thought wryly.

Hubert de Burgh clicked his fingers. 'Pass me the parchment, if you will. I would like to take a look at it.'

Tom obliged as he continued his reasoning. 'But as I said, my lord, that was what I initially believed. With Mistress Brida's assistance I have since realised that the item of real value here is actually the gold ring emblazoned with a strange serpent marking. Have you ever seen the like?'

'No, never.' The older man frowned. 'And how has Mistress Brida helped you realise the importance of this ring?'

'Because she recognised the emblem. She saw it when the Bishop of Hereford and his clergy stayed at Kinnerton Castle, not so long ago.'

Tom resisted glancing at Brida as the older man inhaled sharply through his teeth, muttering under his breath. 'God's breath, Lovent! The Bishop of Hereford?

The man is practically a saint. How can you be sure of Mistress Brida's word?'

This time Tom did look up and caught her gaze from the other side of the chamber. A faint smile touched his lips as he saw a blush spread and tint her face. 'Easily, my lord. Brida is one of the most perceptive and intelligent women I have ever met. If she believes she has seen the emblem, then most assuredly she has.'

Hubert de Burgh looked from him to Brida before letting out a frustrated sigh. 'One thing is for certain. This parchment is also a work of contrivance.'

Tom snapped his head around, frowning. 'How so?'

'It all but implicates you, Lovent—and any other agent who would otherwise have undertaken this mission. Not that I understand the reasons why, but either way, the contents here are designed as a way to incriminate you and, through you, *me*.'

This time it was Tom's turn to swear an oath.

'My sentiments exactly. I have many, many enemies, Thomas, as evident from my recent affliction.' He rubbed his forehead and for the first time during this interview, Tom could see the man was weary and even a little dispirited. 'There are dark forces at play, but we must do everything to counter it.'

'Yes, my lord. But the only item here that does not implicate you, but rather points in a different direction altogether, is the gold ring.' Tom lifted his head. 'I believe that the informant must have found out about this plot and the one proof he had found he dropped inside the purse, in the hope you might realise the significance of it. And he got silenced for his troubles.'

'That is just the issue here, Thomas. I do not comprehend the significance of this. Not one bit.'

'Then I suggest that we devise a way to entrap him then, by making him desperate. This would be in the hope that then he might make a mistake and expose himself.'

'The banquet tomorrow.'

'Precisely, my lord.' Tom smiled.

'We must protect the ones that are precious to us, Thomas. Never forget that.'

With those ominous words Tom's eyes flicked to Brida briefly. He could not agree more.

Brida got the message through Gwen that Tom would be waiting by the entrance they had come out of days ago, when she was dressed as a squire. He would wait for her in that obscure secret passage at the rear of the keep, from the moment the chapel bells tolled for compline prayers until the end of mass, when their rendezvous might be chanced upon. He would be there, whether she came or not. But in all honesty, Brida was unsure whether it would be prudent for her to meet with him anyway. Not that she did not feel safe with Tom, more that she could not trust herself whenever he was near.

She had spent the past few days since her arrival back at the castle in a frustrated heap, swinging hopelessly from one emotional inclination to another, with all that Tom had said perpetually swimming around her head. In truth, everything he had said was both rational and convincing. But try as she might, Brida could not muster the same sense and reason that he had implored her to use. She wanted to be brave enough and reach for him and the promise of everything he offered. But she was too scared. And this made her feel more frustrated and irritable with herself than she had ever been in her life.

So, instead Brida channelled her pent-up frustrations elsewhere. She put her mind to helping Tom in any way she could with the more pressing and dangerous situation that he was in. She put all of her feelings into the music she played, trying in vain to see, hear and understand more while she was in Hubert de Burgh's chambers.

And when today she watched Tom amble into de Burgh's chambers with Lord Tallany she almost sagged with relief. And it was with this that she threw away her astute caution and strode to the assigned rendezvous with a poor hearth knight in tow whom she summarily dismissed, barely suppressing her exhilaration. God, this would not do. She had to damp down these feelings. Especially as she was still bewildered and unsure about everything that had happened with Tom.

She reached the appointed meeting place, checking that she had not been followed and frowned. She could not see Tom anywhere. She looked all around, with her veil flapping around in the breeze wondering where he might have got to. She waited for a while and then some more. Mayhap he had not been able to come after all. Just when she decided it might be best to head back to the Kinnerton pavilion, someone grabbed her and lifted her from behind, with their hand clamped around her mouth. Oh, God, not this again. In a blink of an eye, she was carried inside the narrow entrance of the secret passage running behind the stone cavity of the walls of the keep.

She swung around to face Tom still dressed in Brunhilde's clothing. 'Must you do that every time we meet in this fashion?'

'Apologies, but I do not recall the last time in the Bishop of Hereford's chambers being quite the same as an agreed assignation such as this.'

'Is that what this is?' she hissed. 'A clarification of sorts?'

'No, I haven't even kissed you yet, which I will most certainly rectify,' he said drily. 'And note that, once again, I am giving you fair warning.'

'You most certainly will not,' Brida mumbled, convincing no one. She would welcome his lips on hers as the blasted man knew full well. She dragged her mind away, back to the reasons why she was there in the first place. 'What was the urgency for this rendezvous, Tom?'

His eyes softened as he cupped her cheek. 'Do you think it would need some urgency for me to want to see you?' he drawled in a low voice that sent a shiver through her.

'I could not say.' She tried to keep her voice even, as her heart hammered in her chest. 'But why now?'

'For the simple reason that I needed a moment alone in private with you, without being under the speculative gaze of so many.'

It was true that ever since she had arrived back from the woodsman's cottage a few nights ago, Brida had raised more than a few eyebrows. And yet, neither Gwen or even Lord Ralph, nor anyone else, had uttered a word, but she had felt mortified anyway, by those, as Tom put it, speculative gazes. It had felt uncomfortable and stifling, but that did not mean that Brida should have leapt at the chance to meet with Tom when her head was still in such a muddle. How had he managed so effortlessly to break through her defences? When it came to Thomas Lovent, she was vulnerable and powerless.

She pushed this thought to the far reaches of her mind and attempted to make light of this encounter. 'But here, again? With you still bent on wearing Brunhilde's attire?'

'Ah, but last time we met here, you were wearing male clothing, so I thought to repay the compliment in kind. Besides, you always believed me to be charming in this attire—unless you were only boosting my male ego.'

She chuckled softly. 'I am sure you have not lured me to talk of your male ego, which certainly does not need boosting any further than it already has been.'

'You wound me.' He smirked. 'But, no, my attire has more to do with Hubert de Burgh's assertion that it would be imprudent for me to come out of hiding, which I have to agree with. After all, we do not want the assailant alerted to the fact that I have successfully breached the castle walls and have met with de Burgh and passed on the murdered man's leather purse.'

She nodded. 'That sounds reasonable.'

'What I don't appreciate, however, is your involvement in this, my mission, Brida. What were you thinking?'

'That I could be of some help to you.'

Her breath caught on a gasp as she glanced down in surprise. When had his hands come around her waist? And when had it felt this natural for someone to simply hold her?

'I am not going to pretend that I like this, Brida. I would much rather you were not involved.'

'There is really no need to worry.'

'There is every need. A situation like this can be unpredictable and I would never live with myself if anything happened to you.'

'I shall be careful, I promise.'

He frowned. 'I would much rather hide you somewhere no one could possibly find you and hurt you, ever again.'

She lifted her head up to find his eyes filled with so much tenderness that it made her heart ache.

'Thank you, but I shall be perfectly well. I am more concerned for *your* safety, Tom.'

'Concerned for me?' He shook his head, with a mixture of mortification and amusement glinting in his eyes. 'Come now, there is no need.'

'Of course there is, Tom. You are involved in a dangerous assignment, when nothing is actually known about your foe. And all the while, you're still being pursued as a wanted man—hence your disguise.' She motioned with her hand. 'Tell me, have I missed anything?'

'No.'

He kissed her then softly, gently and, oh, so tenderly. He nipped and pressed his lips to the corners of hers as he cupped her face. 'And thank you for the summary, sweetheart, but I have been in just as many perilous situations as this. You need not waste your concern on me,' he whispered before slanting his lips over hers.

'That does not allay my uneasiness or my apprehension,' she mumbled far more breathlessly than she had wanted to. 'And do not for one moment think that I am not aware of what you are about.'

He gently pulled her veil away, nipping her behind her ear. 'Oh, and what is that?'

'You are purposely distracting me.'

'True. I am.' His smile was so wickedly lazy that it sent a wave of delicious warmth through her. 'I find that I cannot stop kissing you even if I actually wanted to, Brida. And, believe me, I don't. You have very kissable cheeks.'

'Cheeks?'

'Brows,' he said softly, pressing his lips to her eyebrows.

'Ah, my brows?'

'But above all, your lips. They're quite delectable and taste so very sweet.' He kissed her long and hard, devouring her mouth. 'So sweet,' he whispered against her lips.

'That would be...' she murmured, drunk on his kisses. 'That would be because I ate some honey bread.'

'Ah, that must be.'

'You need to stop, Tom.'

'I do?'

'Yes. How can I think properly when you're kissing me like this? And, trust me, I have a lot to think about.'

'Mayhap that is my real intention, sweetheart. I want you to stop thinking so diligently and tell me how you feel instead.' He buried his head in her neck, kissing her from her jaw down to her shoulder.

'Scared, terrified, confused.' She pulled away a little. 'Not at all like myself and I do not like it.'

'I feel much the same, especially since you have yet to find out my preferred colour or even my favourite food. For shame, Brida. For shame.' He gazed into her eyes and shook his head.

Her brows furrowed in the middle. 'I am afraid that

there may never be a chance for me to discover those important aspects to you, Tom.'

'I shall enlighten you. Green—the same shade as my eyes—and a hearty potage. I am a man of simple tastes.' He shrugged. 'There, it was not so difficult after all.'

She shut her eyes and sighed. 'Tom...' she whispered as an appeal.

The amusement in his eyes was replaced by something far more serious and determined. 'You may not like it, but know this, Brida, I am determined to fight for you. And I never give up.'

'You do not understand.' She gave her head a shake. 'Our fate cannot be changed, Tom, it is not something that is within our control.'

'Oh, I understand perfectly well. I feel your dread, your fear and uneasiness and for someone who has only had a sister to look out for and no one else, I must confess that I feel just as terrified as you. And I am not ashamed to admit it. But I will not allow it to cower and overwhelm me.' His fingers grazed her cheek softly. 'We all have the key to our own destinies, Brida. Never forget that.'

That was not precisely what she had meant. This was infatuation and nothing more. Wasn't it? Her heart whispered that there was more, far more that she felt for Thomas Lovent if only she allowed herself to embrace it. These feelings for him were like no other.

'Look at me, Brida.' He tipped her chin up gently with his fingers and looked into her eyes intently. 'You need to trust your heart, however difficult or fearful it makes you.'

'As you have?'

'As I have.'

She stared him for a long moment in the moonlight before breaking the silence.

'Blue. I have always loved the colour blue.' She smiled, her eyes filling with tears. 'And since I have a sweet tooth—it would be the same honeyed bread that I enjoyed earlier.'

'Just so.' Tom chuckled, pulling her into his arms and kissing her on top of her head. 'It could be nothing other than that.'

Brida knew in her heart that everything Tom had said was true and right. Yet after all these years of believing that her fate was immovable, it was extremely arduous and difficult to attempt to reconcile that with Tom's reasonings. But she desperately wanted to. Brida wanted to grasp a different future to the one that had been foisted on her. She wanted to be brave and fearless enough to reach for what she wanted. Even so, she could not help shake off the ominous feelings that ran down her spine.

She went up on her toes and pressed her lips to his, hoping to dispel them.

Chapter Nineteen

The following eventide's banquet was the most lavish that had been put on at the great hall of Carreghofa Castle during the peace treaty negotiation. Rows and rows of long trestle tables had been erected, covered in crisp, clean linen and decorated with flower garlands with the colours and cut vines that were symbolic of England and Wales.

Ornate silver trenchers groaned with an abundance of seasonal foods—succulent lamb cooked on the spit and infused with herbs and spices. Thick pastry pies with small coronets that looked like crowns gilded in silver and filled with rich offal stew. Thin slices of venison and wild boar that had been caught on the royal hunt that day doused in caraway seeds and mustard, as well as pheasant and grouse, all dressed in delicious velvety sauces. Sweetmeats, fat soft bread rolls, rounds of cheese and stewed fruits embellished the table and it was all washed down with huge vats of ale and wine.

At the very top dais sat the most important men of the two kingdoms, the young King Henry and beside him the formidable Llewelyn of Wales, Prince of

Gwynedd, with his wife Joan. Dotted around them were their advisors and men at the very heart of Court. The Marcher Earls of Chester and Hereford, the Earl of Kent, Hubert de Burgh, and beside him, Tom noticed, sat Hugh Foliot, the Bishop of Hereford.

For tonight, Tom had discarded his female attire thank the heavens, and was now in the guise of a kitchen server from Hubert de Burgh's household, no less. He had donned the ubiquitous grey woollen tunic and a belted short cape, over a pair of brown hose tied to a pair of equally unattractive braes. And in an attempt to avoid recognition, Tom wore a specially made contraption over his own teeth, enabling him to change his whole facial appearance. From a vantage point of constantly moving around among the distinguished guests, Tom could examine closely, observe, listen and wait. He was primed and ready to act.

Yet, for all the boisterous, noisy hum in the hall, the eventide had been relatively mundane and uneventful— for now. Tom carried large pewter jugs of wine and went from one table to the next, filling up mugs and other smaller vessels while keeping his ear and eyes alert to anything that might rouse his suspicions. If only he had more of an idea what this unknown assailant was intending. And it was this unknown that was making him feel more and more apprehensive. Thank goodness his guise at least had not given him away. That was one less problem.

He meandered to the long table where the Kinnerton party sat and poured wine into Ralph's mug, deferentially as he acted the lowly server.

'Where's Brida? I assumed she would be in attendance this evening,' he whispered from behind.

'She will be here anon,' Ralph muttered quietly over the rim of his mug. 'I believe she is readying herself to perform after your awful minstrel friends here finish their dreadful exhibition. Really, I forget how young our King is at times, but he seems to be enjoying their round of fart jokes immensely.'

'What the hell do you mean, readying herself to perform?' Tom hissed.

'I would prefer it if you do not overreact, my friend, but it was de Burgh's request that Brida play her beautiful music—to which she acquiesced.'

Tom had filled up the mugs of the other guests along the table before returning to stand behind his friend, whom, at this particular moment, Tom would happily throttle.

'And you permitted her to do this?' he muttered through gritted teeth.

'I had little choice, Tom. De Burgh made his requests and Brida agreed to it.'

'For what gain other than putting her in a precarious position and, in the process, making me exceedingly agitated?'

'I don't doubt it. But she is a remarkably resourceful woman and mayhap de Burgh wanted another pair of eyes in the middle of the hall for the short duration of her performance. I must say she has made quite an impression on the old goat.'

'He can keep his blasted impressions to himself. Hell's teeth, Ralph, I don't know how I am supposed to be doing my job tonight while worrying about Brida.'

'Then stop worrying and catch the bastard. Here and now.'

His friend had a point. The quicker he could complete this damn mission the better. 'Yes. Let's.'

Suddenly he felt her presence as the hairs on the back of his hand rose. Without even looking up Tom knew that Brida O'Conaill had entered the great hall. She ambled along, resplendent in a long-sleeved tunic with a long midnight-blue kirtle dress over the top and a long floaty veil with a simple silver circlet on her head. Her spine was straight and she looked ahead with her head tilted up.

God, but she was lovely. And looked every bit the Irish noblewoman that she was. His heart lurched as he watched her sit down on the stool, smooth down the skirts of her dress, take a deep breath before playing the lute that she had borrowed from de Burgh. Just as that night in the woods where Brida had played to him for the very first time, the haunting evocative melody flowed from her instrument and wrapped around him. The music wove around the busy, noisy hall and gradually lulled the guests into a hushed silence, as they listened to the mesmerising music. It was so exquisite, so tender and heartfelt that it made Tom's chest ache.

Brida's eyes were shut, her face full of expression as she lost herself to the emotions of the melodious music—the rise and the swooping descent of the music as though a songbird was singing. She opened her eyes suddenly and locked them with his. His blood stirred, his mouth went dry and his heart thumped against his chest, rousing a different primal chant in response to her. It was as if she had known all along where he would be standing, so far in the shadows at the back. But it mattered not. In that brief moment it was as though no one else existed in this time and space save them. It was then that he became in tune with the wordless melody she was playing—an expression of love that she was bestowing on *him*.

He wanted to march up to her and declare himself as well. He wanted to tell her everything that he felt for her in his heart, his soul… Here and now. Words of love. Yet it was Brida who was showing him in the most ardent manner, what she felt for him…through the music she played. It was the most singular moment of his life. And it was perfect.

But he wished they had been together alone. He wished this was a different time where he could give her proper attention, rather than having to drag his eyes, his heart and his mind away from her and focus on the task in hand. To find an assailant who might be present even in this perfect moment.

Reluctantly he broke away from her gaze and directed his attention to where it needed to be instead. Tom watched the hall for anything that might be deemed to be suspicious as he moved in the shadows. He glanced at the top table on the dais, studying every single person, especially the Bishop of Hereford sat next to Hubert de Burgh. And yet, nothing. He behaved in exactly the manner anyone here would expect him to.

Tom moved his gaze to every other table, to the servers milling around quietly, and again came away with nothing. There was no sign of anything unusual or out of the ordinary. But then he saw it. What he had been patiently waiting for. A flame flickered, dancing softly from the merest of draughts near the long table at the side. Tom's jaw clenched as he realised what he had seen. He crept nearer.

* * *

Brida had been excessively nervous about this evening, but had agreed to play the beautiful instrument that Hubert de Burgh had presented her with. All in the hope that she might, somehow, be of help to Tom. Yet the moment her fingers danced deftly across the strings, gliding and plucking the instrument, she had been lost to the music. She poured everything she felt for Tom into her music, wanting him to know all that she retained in her heart. It was quite the most absurd time to make such a declaration, but it had come from deep inside her and could never have been held back. Not even if she had wanted to. Yet Brida knew that there was far more at stake here than just the two of them. So, she continued to play on and on, creating music that was purposely slow and soporific. A balm to whatever might come next.

Brida watched as Tom looked away and noticed as he moved stealthily between the shadows, casting off his servant's guise as he went, and prowled to the left-hand side of the hall to where the Bishop of Hereford sat at the corner. Something was about to happen, but she was unsure what it might be. With her heart pounding furiously, she caught the movement in the periphery of her vision, just as she brought the heightened emotional melody to its climactic end. It was then that many of the guests got to their feet to applaud her efforts.

Brida stood as well and darted her gaze around the chamber, unable to locate Tom. The sound of cheering and clapping merged and became a low buzzing noise in her ear, as she snapped her head around in the hope of finding him. That was when everything suddenly happened quickly. A scream pierced through the din as a table was thrown over, the clatter of food, cutlery and the trenchers hitting the floor. There was a sound of a scuffle as guests moved out of the way. Tom pushed through the huddled group, holding a large man by the scruff of the neck and throwing him to the middle of the hall, as a noise of a woman's shriek reverberated around the chamber. Guards pushed through and stood around the main table on the dais, protecting the heads of the Crowns of England and Wales.

'Stand down!' Llewelyn of Wales bellowed as many of his knights rallied around him, pointing their swords at Tom and the man he had flung to the centre of the chamber.

'What is the meaning of this, Sir Thomas?' Hubert de Burgh stood up as did the men along the table, their stools scraping the wooden floor as they all stood in unison.

'This is the man we have been searching for, my liege.' Tom held the man from behind.

'I think you must be mistaken, sir, for that is Father Peter of Salisbury,' the Bishop of Hereford ground out. 'He is a priest and a man of God.'

'I am afraid there is no mistake, my lord.' Tom pulled up the sleeve of the man's cloak and there on his sword arm was a leather armband, emblazoned with the same two-headed serpent emblem that had been on the gold ring left in the leather purse.

Brida gasped as she suddenly recognised the man the Bishop had called Father Peter as the same one she had seen in Kinnerton. It was this man she had associated the emblem with and it was this man who had been travelling with the Bishop himself. Yet on this night, he was wearing a surcoat with Llewelyn's coat of arms on it. It seemed that the man's objective was to implicate the Welsh, regardless of who his intended victim was to be.

The man snarled as he unsheathed a dagger from the leather armband, catching Tom unawares. He caught Tom's right arm so unexpectedly that Tom loosened his grip, allowing the man to pull away. He swung around and faced Tom, as a deadly silence enveloped the chamber. Tom also unsheathed a dagger and moved around the man, lunging forward in attack. The priest was unexpectedly skilled in the art of combat as he dived forward, circling Tom.

'Give yourself up, man. You are surrounded.'

But the priest continued to fight as though his life depended on it. The metal daggers clanged furiously as they engaged in striking at different angles again and again and with such quick motion that it was difficult to see. For a tall, broad man Tom was light and nimble on his feet as he lunged with deadly strikes that the other man had to continually deflect. Brida caught the glint of ruthless determination in Tom's eyes as he circled the other man in an attempt to overpower him. He pushed forward, making the man lose his footing, but before Tom could disarm him, the man took a jump out of reach and looked around the chamber and shook his head.

He then uttered some strange and ominous words before then plunging the dagger into his own heart.

'Et non abscondam ab inferno possit, si anima tua sit liberaremur. Mutatis mutandis.'

The hall erupted into chaos as guards surrounded the standing man lowering his weapon and glancing at the one fallen to the floor. The priest had taken his own life, knowing it was forfeited anyway. Noise and mayhem ensued, but Brida could only think about the strangeness of the man's dying words.

'You can never hide from hell, if your soul is to be cleansed. Mutatis mutandis.'

Yes, it was excessively odd and made little sense, but it mattered not. It was all over, thank God.

The celebratory atmosphere continued in the Kinnerton pavilion long into the night. There had been a huge sense of relief that the evening had not ended in disaster and calamity, with a culprit who had finally been caught. Which had been the sole intention for many here—to catch an assailant bent on treachery and treason. All things considered, it had been a resounding success.

Tom had been held up in a private discourse with his liege lord, the Constable of the castle, the Marcher Earls, Ralph de Kinnerton as well as the Bishop of Hereford. Before long, the two men returned, sauntering into the private tent to an unexpected round of applause.

Hugh de Villiers passed them both a goblet, pouring wine into each one.

'I believe this might be a prudent time for a toast,' he said with a lopsided smile. 'To you, my friends, especially Tom, who managed to overcome an assailant who would otherwise have caused much havoc and destruction to these important peace negotiations.'

Everyone gathered together to toast Tom on this fortuitous night and drank the rich, fruity wine from the Tallany vineyards.

'And that was the priest's intention—to cause mayhem that would somehow prevent the treaty being signed?' Will Geraint asked over the rim of his goblet.

'It would seem so.' Tom nodded. 'However, without a proper confession it is hard to say for certain. But we have had a full interview with the Bishop and gone through the priest's belongings and there is enough seditious material to come to that conclusion. The Bishop naturally did not know any of the plot brewing under his very nose.'

'And is his word to be trusted?'

'For now. De Burgh has already invited him to court in London to discuss various legal ecclesiastical changes but I believe it is a ruse to keep a close eye on Foliot, for a while.'

The men nodded.

'Well, I would like to also add my thanks for all you have done, Tom.' Gwen held up her goblet. 'I believe we can all sleep easier in our beds tonight.'

'Thank you, my lady,' Tom muttered, inclining his head. 'I was only doing my duty.'

'You weren't hurt in the scuffle with the priest, were you?' Brida blurted out before she could stop herself.

'If so, I could certainly patch you up, Tom. I have a most potent unguent that might help,' Isabel de Clancey added.

'No, I thank you. It was nothing, nary a scratch.'

'Tom?' Young William Tallany pulled his gambeson. 'Will you now marry Brida?' the little imp asked with a mischievous look in his eyes.

The whole party fell silent before Eleanor Tallany took in a frustrated breath and spoke to her young son. 'Now, William, what have I said about talking before thinking? I must ask you to apologise for your impertinence.'

'But that's exactly what you asked, Papa. You said that it would lovely if...' His mother must have given him an admonishing glare as the young boy quickly collected himself and turned to Tom. 'I apologise, Tom. Of course, it would be marvellous if you did marry Brida, especially as you both keep looking at one another when you think no one is watching. But I shan't mention it again.'

'No harm done, William. I must say, that is the most heartfelt apology I believe I have ever heard.' Tom grinned before glancing Brida's way and giving her a wink.

Brida felt her cheeks flush. Oh, Lord, if she could only but vanish into thin air at that very moment. How very embarrassing to think that the two of them had garnered so much speculation, as Tom had observed only last night.

However, instead of either of them having to remove themselves from the situation, the assembled group quickly dispersed. Gwen and Ralph suddenly needed a moment alone and the two ladies of Tallany and de Clancey had to also have a private word. It was not long before Brida found herself facing Tom, separated from the others who had gathered in the tent.

'I also wish to congratulate you on your endeavours, Tom.'

He waved his arms about absently. 'Oh, cease, Brida, or you shall make me blush.'

'Better that it's you than me.' She chuckled. 'I cannot help think that I am being constantly observed here. It is most disconcerting.'

'That, it certainly is. Come.' He guided her by the elbow, drawing her outside the main tent. 'We might be able to have a more private conversation here.'

They moved outside the Kinnerton pavilion and into the bailey, now quiet and still in the night.

She wrapped her arms around herself.

'Are you cold, Brida?'

'No, I am perfectly fine. Although the changeable weather is decidedly vexing at the moment, do you not think?' Brida knew that she was prattling in an attempt to disguise her sudden nervousness at being alone with Tom.

He was watching her before sighing and shaking his head.

'Here, take this. It should keep you warm.' He pulled his cloak over his head and handed it to her.

'My thanks,' she muttered, knowing that despite shuddering, she did not actually have a problem with *'keeping warm'*. If anything, she was becoming exceedingly too warm. But the moment she pulled the cloak over her head she felt cocooned by Tom's residual warmth and enticing scent.

'You must be glad that it is all resolved.'

'Yes.' He frowned. 'Yes, naturally.'

She touched his sleeve. 'What troubles you?'

He stared at her hand on his gambeson. 'Nothing. I just cannot help that I have missed something.'

She dropped her hand to her side. 'Mayhap it is just relief from finally having your name cleared and uncovering a plot against the Crown.'

'It must be that. Although the priest's final words were perplexing.'

'Yes, but considering he was a man who was about

take his own life, they were the words he had obviously wanted to part with, strange as they were. How did you manage to catch on to him, anyway?'

'I caught a glimpse of the emblem on his armband and recognised it to be the same one as on the ring.'

'Ah, the two-headed serpent.'

'Exactly.' Tom stepped closer, brushing away a lock of her hair that had escaped from under her veil. His fingers grazed her skin and made her take a short breath. 'But let us not talk of such matters any more. At this moment, all of that seems so inconsequential.'

Her pulse quickened. 'Compared to what?'

'Everything that has also happened between you and me.'

She looked in his eyes then and saw so much heated longing that she almost swayed into him. 'I suppose a great deal has happened.'

'Tell me, Brida, are you to leave with Ralph and Gwen on the morrow?'

'Why?'

'Because I need to ascertain how long I have to woo you.'

Brida swallowed, feeling a little breathless, her pulse fluttering wildly. 'You flatter me, but then you were always exceptional at that.'

'Ah, but if only that was true. Although I have been called an unscrupulous charmer, now and then.'

'Unscrupulous rogue charmer, don't forget.' She chuckled. 'Tell me, what will you do now, Tom? What are your plans?'

He shrugged. 'Hubert de Burgh needs to confer with me again in the morn and then…then I would like the opportunity to talk with *you,* Brida. If you'll honour me.'

She nodded. 'Of course.'

'Good, because there is a particular question that I wish to ask you.'

'And you cannot do that now, beneath the stars and the moon?'

'No,' he whispered. 'What I have to say or, rather, ask you needs to be done on a new day and a new dawn. One that is not shared with everything that happened in the hall on this night.'

She lifted her head and locked eyes with Tom. For a long moment they stared at one another, unable to move or even breathe. Dare she hope to consider what he would need to ask her? Something that needed to be done on a new dawn? Could she risk fate and be brave enough to trust in her heart—trust him? Her heart whispered *Yes* again and again, while her head remained unconfident and hesitant.

Tom broke the silence. 'I have been meaning to tell you that the music you played in the hall was utterly enchanting, Brida.'

'I… I expressed everything in the music that I was unable to with words.'

'Is that so?' he said softly, curling his hands around her waist. 'Well, I, too, have something that expresses exactly how I feel.'

He pulled up the sleeve of his tunic and revealed a ribbon made of vivid blue hues tied around his wrist.

'Where did you get that from?'

'I believe that you wove this with Gwen some time ago and once I saw the shades of blue, from opal to crocus and even woad, I had to have it. It reminds me somewhat of the colour of your own mercurial eyes.

But see here, this is my message to you.' He took it off and passed it to her.

On the ribbon, she could just about see a message embroidered in green thread—his favourite colour: *Gan tú níl aon gháire ann.*

'I want to gift it to you.'

She felt a little chocked as he tied it around her wrist. 'Thank you. I love it. It is the most precious thing anyone has given me. And I love the message: *Without you there is no laughter.*'

The foolish man had written his message in Irish, making her feel like sobbing.

'What? No. It says, "Without you there is no *love*".'

'You are mistaken. If you had wished to say "there is no love" it would be *"ghrá ann"*. It is quite similar.'

'For shame, Brida.' He raised a brow. 'Are you going to give me Irish lessons when I am professing my most ardent declaration of love for you?'

'No…no, of course not. It is truly wonderful and I love the sentiment.'

'And I have to say that I always had an inkling that your sentiments towards me were far more ardent—after all, you pretended that we were married in Kinnerton.'

She pulled away, feeling a little outraged. 'You know perfectly well why I had to pretend…'

'Brida. I am only jesting with you.'

She blinked. 'Can you never stop jesting?'

'No, I am afraid I can never stop jesting, I can never stop vexing you or being a misbegotten fool, I can never stop uttering ridiculous nonsense, or teasing you. And I certainly will never stop loving you.'

'Oh, Tom,' Brida said on a slight gasp, feeling as

though she might burst with the unadulterated joy that was bubbling up inside her. She went on her toes and wrapped her arms around his neck, just as he bent his head to close the distance between them. Just as they were about to seal their affirmation with a kiss beneath the stars and the moon, William Tallany came out of the tent and called out to Tom.

He smiled against her lips and gave her a quick kiss on her forehead. 'Until tomorrow, Brida. And then I do not give a damn who walks in while we happen to be kissing.'

'Is that what you believe we might be doing?' she asked, trying not to laugh.

'Indeed.' He winked at her, grinning. 'And as always I give you fair warning.'

Chapter Twenty

Tom had a fretful, unsettled night of sleep later. His dreams were dark and terrifying where hideous two-headed serpent monsters breathed fire and brimstone and could never be defeated however many times he tried to use his sword to conquer the beast. It would never submit to him. Instead, it would grow more malefic heads, slowly twisting and choking out the air with its noxious fumes. It became larger, disfigured, more sinister and destructive, spitting out wrathful blazes of a burning inferno, devouring everything in its wake.

His dream moved and spun to his family manor on that fateful night where fires destroyed everything. Tom ran faster and faster, his breathing loudly pulsating through the nightmare. But he could not get there in time. The fire was at its most virulent, ferociously claiming the lives of his mother, father, sisters and young brother. He held out his hands, but they were always out of reach. And soon their charred faces crumbled away and were replaced once again by the monster.

Through its mouth the strange eerie words that the

priest uttered before taking his last breath were then said over and over again.

'*Et non abscondam ab inferno possit, si anima tua sit liberaremur. Mutatis mutandis.*'

It made just as little sense as it did before. Tom thrashed his head from side to side and then all of a sudden, he opened his eyes, fully alert, bolting upright in a cold sweat. Those ominous words fell into place, making far more sense now.

Tom jumped up from the pallet that he had been sleeping on and quickly got dressed, waking the Kinnerton men up as he went along. He dashed outside, darting his head around in every direction, taking in the horror of it. A raging fire was consuming the castle. He rushed over to the tent he knew Brida and the other ladies were sleeping in as they streamed out of it, along with Ralph and Gwen.

'Are you well, Brida?' He took her hands in his as she nodded. Over her head he saw Ralph coming out of his large tent along with his lady, carrying their baby son. 'Good. I want you to go with Gwen and the other women and children. Go outside the castle, now, Brida. To safety.'

'What about you? Where are you going?' she muttered over the noise and commotion outside.

'I have to help get everyone from inside the castle to safety.'

Brida crossed herself several time. 'Dear Lord, no! Please, Tom, do not go. It is far too dangerous.'

'I must,' he muttered. 'It's my duty, sweetheart, and I am honour bound to fulfil it, especially when the King and my lord could still be in there.' He let go of her hands. 'Go. I cannot talk now.'

'Please, Tom, be safe.'

He grimaced as he gave her a single nod of the head before spinning on his feet and joined Ralph, Hugh and Will.

'King Henry, Hubert de Burgh along with Llewelyn and the many of the English and Welsh Crowns are not accounted for.'

Hugh muttered an oath under his breath. 'How the hell did this happen?'

Tom snapped his head around. 'There were two of them.'

'Two of whom?'

'Two-headed serpents. And we only got one of the bastards. The other is the one who no doubt started this blazing *inferno.*'

'Hell's teeth!'

The outer walls of the castle as well as the curtain wall might be constructed from hard stone and other impenetrable material, but the floors and many of the internal walls, not to mention tapestries and many personal items, were highly flammable.

The dead man's words were even more prophetic, as these looked precisely like the fires that had been wrought from hell. And solely for the purpose of cleansing the sins of others. Tom now realised why he had not wanted to register those words from the madman in the hall—why he was quick to forget and had not taken heed. They had reminded him of another mad fool who had no doubt started a similar fire to cleanse and absolve the sins of everyone close to him—*his father.*

However, now was not the time to feel that familiar guilt that he had lived with for so many years. It was not the time to dwell on any of that. Tom had to assert and redeem himself from past mistakes. He needed to be more than he had ever been. He pushed forward with purpose, alongside his friends, as the men began to separate and direct small groups of the rescue operation.

'I am going inside the keep to give aid where I can,' Tom exclaimed to his friends.

'I am coming with you,' Ralph bellowed. 'I cannot have you take all the glory.'

They rushed in as the flames of fire spread throughout the castle keep and pockets of the inner bailey.

Tom was relieved to find that the cluster of men in two huddled groups, walking through the great hall, were the principal nobles from the two Courts, including King Henry, Hubert de Burgh, the Marcher Earls and behind them Llewelyn and his nobles. He rushed to help escort the group out. The chamber became filled with smoke and on the far side of the room, the wooden roof looked more and more precarious. It suddenly gave out and collapsed.

'Hurry, sire, my lords! We have to get you all to safety.'

Covering their mouths with their hands, they all rushed out of the hall and wove their way out of the inner bailey and eventually out of the gatehouse. By this point Tom had managed to gather more knights to protect the King and the nobles. But he still felt uneasy and unsettled. Someone who might still be in the castle had meant to exact a great deal of destruction. And they still might not be done.

He helped guide the group of nobles to a quieter area outside the castle walls flanked by the Kinnerton and the de Clancey retinue and took a deep breath of clean air into his chest, coughing out the bad humours. More and more knights and villagers poured back inside with vats of water in an attempt to contain and douse the flames which were beginning to smoulder and smoke.

Tom caught sight of Brida, who looked ashen with the tension palpable on her beautiful face. She instantly sagged with relief when she saw him, advancing in his direction as she wove her way through groups of people to reach him.

'Oh, Tom, I am so happy that you are seemingly unharmed. I was so worried.'

'There's really no need to be.' He shook off her concern. 'Are you well? Did everyone get away safely?'

'Yes,' she whispered.

'Good. I shall be with you anon.'

Just then in the periphery of his vision he saw a movement that was not quite as it should be. A stranger who should not be where he was—by King Henry. And it was the sheer look of malicious intent etched on the man's face that made Tom bolt back to his sovereign. He glimpsed the glint of silver metal as the man unsheathed a dagger and drew his arm out to attack. Just as he was about to, Tom threw himself out in front, shielding the young King. He kicked the man, winding him, and punched him square in the face as the man waved the blade about. One more punch and Tom disarmed him, kicking the man to the ground. This time, thank God, it was over.

'Guards, take this man away.' He turned to de Burgh, who was giving him an approving look. 'I would wager that he was behind the fire, my lord,' he said a little too breathlessly. Mayhap he'd inhaled too many of the fumes earlier as his vision was becoming blurry.

'I am sure you are right, Thomas. You have proven yourself beyond measure once again with your valiant efforts.' His smile faded only to be replaced by concern. 'But you do not look as you should, sir. Is everything well?'

No, it was not. He felt dizzy and completely off-balance. He touched a sticky damp patch on his chest, with his hands coming away with blood—*his blood*. In the distance he heard someone scream before he rounded the night off nicely by collapsing to the ground.

Brida paced outside the small tent provided by Hubert de Burgh, where Tom had been brought to convalesce after he'd been caught by the assailant's dagger. She took a deep breath before venturing inside to find him sat upright on a pallet surrounded by comfortable bolsters and cushions.

'I am glad to see that you're recovering, Tom.' She gave him a small smile and approached his side. 'It seems that you must once again have time to recover after what happened.' He held out his hand and she took it.

'Ah, but that is because I have this knack for getting in the way of daggers and other sharp weaponry.' He shrugged.

'Well, you would engage in heroics.'

'Only the valiant kind.' He smiled. 'I'm glad to see you, sweetheart, especially after the countless meetings I have had with de Burgh among others.'

'At least the peace treaty with Wales has finally been resolved.'

'Yes, I just pray it endures.'

'Do you know who the assailant was?'

He frowned, shaking his head. 'No, and just like the priest earlier, the second man took his own life before he could be interrogated. Those damned inept guards had not looked properly on his person otherwise they might have seen that he carried another blade.'

'Two blades. Two men. And a two-headed serpent.'

'And with both men dead, we have no real way of establishing who was involved with this. In fact, there is a strong possibility that there are more embroiled in treason than just those dead traitors. But for now, that is for de Burgh and other agents to uncover.'

She raised a brow. 'Does that mean that you intend to cease working for him?'

'Not quite. We have yet to negotiate the finer details on other roles he has in mind for me. I should also say that King Henry has made an annuity to me for services rendered. I am to gain enough silver to be able to rebuild the manor in my family seat near Coddington.'

She smiled. 'That is such marvellous news, Tom. I am very pleased for you.'

He squeezed her hand, kissing the back of it as he kept his eyes on her.

'I would be far more pleased, gratified even, if we could go back to the conversation we were having before the nightmare started last night.'

She shook her head sadly. 'I am afraid we cannot go back to those conversations.'

'I see.' He blew out a frustrated breath. 'You have changed your mind.'

She gave him a stricken look. 'Of course not. I love you desperately and want nothing more than to spend the rest of my days with you.'

'It seems that you are going to spoil the question I had fervently wished to ask you. Why the change of heart?'

She cupped his jaw. 'For one beautiful moment I dared to dream, Tom, but it can never be. A husband, children—these are not for me.'

'Because you were once told that you were unworthy of having a life more than you should? Because you were told you were cursed? Or that some prophecy declared your life to be thus? Or mayhap because your mother made you believe it all—that every terrible thing that happened to your family was somehow your fault?'

'Yes,' She whispered in a choked voice.

'But none of that is true. I love you, Brida. I want to marry you. I want to make you happy. Do you not believe that you are worthy of that?'

'I wish I could believe in everything you say, everything you have already said, but don't you see? It is impossible.'

'Why?'

How could she make him comprehend that for that one moment when he had fallen to the ground after being struck by the blade of a madman, an icy shudder had trickled down her spine. It resembled the same sickening moment when her brothers, her father and the man she was betrothed to were murdered as she watched. And the terrible aftermath when she was forced to listen to her mother's vitriol and poison—the blame, the condemnation leading to a perpetual shame that Brida constantly had to contend with.

'Do you not see that everything that happened last night was immediately after the promises we made to one another. I watched in horror as you stormed the castle to help rescue people still trapped inside and I was scared that you would not come back. Yet you did and so I thought, for one fleeting moment I believed, that mayhap you had been right—that I should trust in my heart and let go of the past, just as you seemed to have done. But before I could even reach you, you were hurt.' She drew in a sharp breath. 'Sadly, a new dawn never arrived. And I do not believe that it ever will. Not for us.'

'What can I say to that?' He grimaced. 'Other than I never thought you would be afraid to live the life you wanted.'

'I wish it could be different.'

'But it could be if you allow it.' He exhaled through his teeth. 'Do you not believe that I, too, am scared of an uncertain future? Do you not think that I have not known the pain of losing those whom I love?' He slid his hand down the length of her arm, grasping her hand. 'I have felt that loss, too, and it was and still is painful. But to honour those I have lost I must go on and live a whole life—as should you, Brida.'

'I wish I could.'

'You can. My sister Joan had the shame of believing that she was cursed, as I once explained—all because of her near blindness and that she was the only one to survive in the fire that claimed our family. But I didn't want that to destroy her chance of happiness. Tell me, Brida, am I to stand by and let another spurious, false curse threaten someone I love? Are you going to allow this to take such a hold on your life, or are you going to take a chance on the life you could have?'

She could not trust those words, could she? They were like a balm to her troubled soul, making her want to believe in possibilities that were unattainable. But it could never end well for them if they pursued this dream of being together. In truth, it would be best for both of them if she removed herself from his presence altogether. The temptation would then not be so forthcoming or so difficult to resist.

She carefully removed his hand and stood, shaking her head. 'I am sorry, Tom, but this is futile.'

A mop of his hair fell over his eye as he dragged it back. 'I see that I cannot convince you.'

'No...' she muttered more to herself than him. 'No, I am afraid you cannot.'

'But I shall.'

She lifted her head. 'Please do not make our parting more difficult than it needs to be.'

'Is that what you believe?'

She nodded and took a step back and then another. 'I must go, Tom. We're leaving presently for Kinnerton.'

He did not say anything and just watched her for a long moment, pinning her with his gaze. A storm raged in his eyes before he finally spoke.

'Then I trust you have a safe journey. Godspeed.'

Tom sat staring at the empty space after Brida had left the tent in a state of shock. She had left him. She was rushing back to Kinnerton. And she had refused to use sense and reason as he had urged her to do in the woodsman's cottage about a damned ridiculous curse.

Hell's teeth.

It was all nonsense. Yet, had Brida been resolute in her convictions, then he would have no choice but to let her go. But she hadn't. He had seen the uncertainty and doubt in her eyes when he'd asked her to trust in their love. Tom knew for certain that the woman was terrified of a future that stepped anywhere outside the boundaries that rigidly held her tied to a lie—some absurd prophecy. One that she believed in. He just had to convince her otherwise—he had to. Tom had to think of a way to make her take a chance on a future with him. But how? He had to come up with something expediently.

This was not over. He was not going to give up Brida O'Conaill without a fight.

Chapter Twenty-One

It had been seven long days and nights since Brida had last seen Tom. In that time, she'd had time to reflect, pine and be sufficiently miserable. God, but she missed the man. She missed every little thing about him—his slow, knowing smile, his teasing, witty manner, his kindness and his huge heart. Try as she might, Brida could not push Tom out of her mind, even though the whole purpose of removing herself from his company had been a vain attempt to achieve just that. But it had not worked.

She could barely eat, she could barely think and she had had barely slept since she had last seen Tom. Brida looked down at the food set out on great big trenchers in the hall at Kinnerton castle and her stomach roiled. Her eyes darted around the busy, noisy chamber and suddenly she recalled that it had been three summers since she had been here under this beamed roof and had eventually acquiesced to dance with Thomas Lovent at Ralph and Gwen's wedding banquet. And it was later that same night under the moonlight, that she had pressed her lips to his for the first time, taking them both by surprise.

Everything had changed when once again he had burst into her life. Now nothing seemed to be the same. She could not bear to look at anyone in the eyes—from the villagers who had hosted a feast in honour of the return of her 'husband' some weeks ago and who now gave her pitying looks, to Gwen who tried to distract her with as many things as she could. Yet it was of little use. Brida ached for him and looked for him everywhere in Kinnerton, the memory of him so potent and real.

Mayhap she should leave altogether and make a life elsewhere for herself. But even that would never work. Wherever she went, it could never be home, without that blasted man in it. And whatever she did, Tom Lovent would still be there, plaguing her all the time—even in her dreams.

Her eyes fell on the blue ribbon that he had given her, tied around her wrist, and smiled. She recalled how he had mistakenly embroidered the word *laughter* instead of *love* in Irish because the two words were quite similar.

But in Thomas Lovent's case it might have been the same, for he had given her much laughter as well as offering his love. And she had refused it all. God, had she made a horrendous mistake?

'Brida,' Gwen muttered from beside her. 'You have not eaten. Can I get you anything? The lamb is particularly delicious.'

'No, I thank you.' She took a small sip of ale. 'But tell me, what possessed you to employ the same minstrels from Carreghofa Castle?' They were there in the hall, presently in the middle of their dreadful performance and this time with huge props that made farts every time they stumbled over them. God, but she was not in the humour for any of this.

'It was to express our gratitude to them since they ensured your safety into the castle, as you recall.'

'Indeed.'

Yet it reminded her of that first time Brida had played the lute after Tom's encouragement, then shared their past with one another later, before sealing the night with a scorching kiss.

'Is everything well?' Gwen asked softly.

No. Nothing was well. Not until she could see Tom again—this she suddenly understood with clarity. She *had* made a huge mistake. She knew now that she wanted to risk her heart. She wanted to put her faith in love…and in *him*. In truth, a life without Tom wasn't one worth living at all.

'Forgive me, Gwen, but I believe I need a little air.'

Standing abruptly, Brida pushed back her stool, and turned on her heel.

Ralph de Kinnerton also stood. 'Where are you going, mistress?'

'It is a little warm in here, my lord. I shall return shortly.'

He held out his hands. 'Can I be of any service, Brida?'

She shook her head. 'No, I thank you.'

'Very well, but why not wait until afterwards?'

'There is no need to worry. I shan't be long.' She inclined her head and moved away.

She could not spend another moment here surrounded by everything that reminded her of Tom—the hall, the minstrels, even his friends. She glanced down the hall, noticing for the first time, that not one, but all of Tom's friends and mentors, including William Geraint and Hugh de Villiers along with their wives Isabel and Eleanor and their children, had stayed on at Kinnerton.

Will Geraint smiled at her as she passed. 'Why not stay for this one performance, Brida?'

She raised a brow 'Is there a reason I should, my lord?'

'Why, yes, mistress.' Hugh de Villiers clamped a hand on his friend's shoulder. 'You might come to enjoy it.'

As much as having her tooth pulled out, but she remained silent and gave the two men a gracious curtsy before continuing to the back of the hall.

Just as she reached the large doors to the hall, she heard from somewhere behind a lute strumming and the first few lines of the music she had played that night in Carreghofa Castle echoed throughout the hall. *It cannot be...*

And then an accompanied voice she had not expected to hear began to sing. *Tom?*

She spun around and found that Thomas Lovent was indeed advancing slowly towards her with one of the minstrels—Baldwin the Tame, or mayhap it was Ulric the Fool—playing the lute as Tom sang. His voice was melodious, not that Brida cared. She wanted to throw herself in his arms, but instead stood still, unable to take any of this in.

'Since the moment, you my dearest one, began to simper and scold,

*I was in trouble for thine is the fairest of eyes,
deepest blue,
And never, my Irish dove, has such an affection
thus been told,
Yet, it is the greatest love a man hath known, so
tender and true.'*

Tom had reached her at the end of the hall and she could barely contain herself.

'Were you going somewhere?' He smiled slowly, making her knees feel as though they might buckle beneath her. God, she had missed him.

'You came back.'

'Brida, Brida, Brida… Did you think I would give you up so easily?'

'I am so glad that you didn't.'

'As am I. Especially as I believed I would have to woo, beg and plead with you to think more favourably about my suit.'

'I do, even without the begging or pleading.'

He reached out and caressed her cheek. 'I had wanted to surprise you, but mayhap I should have kept my declaration far simpler and more unequivocal.'

'You already have, Tom.'

'There are another six verses of this. Need I go on? Or I could burst into a new rendition of "A Dalliance with a Flower". Ulric has managed to add a line about the gnat on a cat.'

Brida giggled as she closed the distance and looked up into his green eyes glittering with so much pent-up emotion. 'I do not think so.'

'In that case, all that remains is for me to say, is I love you—*is breá liom tú, Brighid Ni Diarmuid.*'

'*Is breá liom tú, Thomas Lovent.*' Tears filled her eyes.' You might vex me with your incessant flippery and teasing manner, just as I am sure I vex you with my sharp scolding tongue, as your ode all but suggested… but I love you so very dearly.'

'You, my love? Vex me? Perish the thought.' He grinned.

'Cease talking and kiss me, Tom.'

'In front of all of these ladies and their notorious lords? You surprise me.'

'Ah, but I have been keeping tallies, sir, and you promised me a kiss.'

'Well I would never wish to disappoint a lady.' He cupped her cheeks. 'But I give you fair warning, that it will be neither nice nor merely acceptable.'

'I know,' she whispered as he dipped his head and kissed her passionately on the lips. Somewhere far away, she registered the sound of clapping and cheering.

Tom pulled away slightly. 'I must tell you that according to young William Tallany, you and I will have to marry now that we have kissed.'

She grinned. 'In that case, I believe we have a wedding celebration to prepare, once more.'

'We certainly do.'

And they did…

* * * * *

*If you enjoyed this book, be sure to read
the other books in Melissa Oliver's
Notorious Knights miniseries*

The Rebel Heiress and the Knight
Her Banished Knight's Redemption
The Return of Her Lost Night